PENGUIN BOOKS

# OTHER LIVES

Sarah Woodhouse is the author of *A Season of Mists*, *The Indian Widow*, *The Daughter of the Sea*, *The Peacock's Feather*, which won the Romantic Novelists' Association Boots' Romantic Novel of the Year Award in 1989, and *The Native Air*, all historical novels. *Enchanted Ground*, published by Penguin in 1994, was her first novel set in the twentieth century and was followed by *Meeting Lily*, also available in Penguin.

Sarah Woodhouse lives on a farm in Norfolk and has two children.

# OTHER LIVES

Sarah Woodhouse

PENGUIN BOOKS

## PENGUIN BOOKS

Published by the Penguin Group
Penguin Books Ltd, 27 Wrights Lane, London W8 5TZ, England
Penguin Books USA Inc., 375 Hudson Street, New York, New York 10014, USA
Penguin Books Australia Ltd, Ringwood, Victoria, Australia
Penguin Books Canada Ltd, 10 Alcorn Avenue, Toronto, Ontario, Canada M4V 3B2
Penguin Books (NZ) Ltd, 182–190 Wairau Road, Auckland 10, New Zealand

Penguin Books Ltd, Registered Offices: Harmondsworth, Middlesex, England

First published by Michael Joseph 1996
Published in Penguin Books 1997
1 3 5 7 9 10 8 6 4 2

Printed in England by Clays Ltd, St Ives plc

*For my family,
past and present.*

# I

$A$T sixty-three a woman is not supposed to cause a nuisance.

'Mother's in the paper,' Christopher told Bernadette with an indignation more suited to finding their parent naked in the hypermarket.

'What paper?'

'*The Times.*'

Bernadette naturally thought it must be something to do with Maurice. 'Widow of distinguished don at charity ball . . .' for instance. Only Lucy never went to balls. Or did she? And Maurice had been dead six years and had not, after all, been as distinguished as his children liked to pretend.

'Remember that rogue Lussom?'

'Rogue?' Bernadette found the word surprising. 'Oliver Lussom? But he was famous. I used to watch his programmes.' Her pig-tailed child self, she thought, transfixed by the man's charm, not by the ruins where he was leading her. Archeology seemed only toppled columns and ravaged friezes, even the treasures were vaguely disappointing. It was a living voice, a gesture, even the turn of his head that drew her. 'I was besotted,' she said to

Christopher. 'And he excavated Grandfather's city, didn't he? He took over when the old man died.' She extinguished the vision of her mother in an improbable ballgown to see instead a tall, severe figure in a panama against a background of jumbled masonry. She thought she remembered a moustache. But Lucy possessed astonishingly few photographs, most of them taken by a wobbling box Brownie and into the sun.

'He was always after women. And drunk,' remarked Christopher.

'Grandfather?'

'Lussom.'

'I didn't know. But he's dead, isn't he?'

'He died in 'ninety-two.' The date was in the newspaper article. He had his finger on it.

'Is this all to do with Mother in *The Times*?'

'He's left her his house.'

'He's what?' cried Bernadette.

'Left her his house in Greece.'

'How lovely!' It was an automatic reaction. A moment later: 'But Mother must have known. They would have told her when he died. Wouldn't they?' And so, slowly, groping among possibilities: 'Or *he* told her before he died.'

'How should I know?' Christopher had not imagined his mother capable of keeping momentous secrets. And why should she? He had not even known of an acquaintance between her and Lussom although it was true the man had taken over the site Harold Cavendish had barely scratched before he died, making half a lifetime's work of it between global excursions to lecture and play the fool with fashionable women. Still . . . Lucy had never shown the least interest in archeology or, to his knowledge, in any man but Maurice.

'What sort of house is it?' Bernadette was suddenly roused by new visions, confused but hopeful.

'There's a picture but it's rather small and blurred.'

Like Lucy's own, all small and blurred and put away for thirty years in the bottom drawer of the davenport.

'And is that all it says? That he's left it to Mother?'

'"Under terms of will . . ."' Christopher skipped hurriedly, a sense of alarm still making his hand a little unsteady. He lost his way for a moment. '". . . Mrs Lucy Flecker, daughter of the late Professor Harold Cavendish who first discovered and began to excavate . . . British School of Archeology . . . Greek minister said . . ." No, there's nothing. Look, Bernie, can you ring Mother? Find out what's been going on?'

'Well, why don't you?'

'I'd rather not. Laura's bound to have been pouring out the tale of my iniquities. I can't take a sermon.'

'Mother never gives sermons.'

'She might once she knows I've left Laura for good.'

Bernadette thought it unlikely. Lucy never encouraged histrionics. Besides, Laura would more probably be playing the abandoned wife to a circle of sympathetic friends from her aerobics class.

'I never thought you were a coward,' she said cheerfully. She enjoyed finding Christopher vulnerable. He had never seemed so when they were children.

'Just ring. Ring and ask about this house.' He was sure the explanation would be obvious and simple. How could Lucy be devious? Why should she want to be? He thought he knew everything there was to know about her. She was his mother after all. Only . . . 'I can't think why she didn't tell me,' he said. 'Since Father died she's taken my advice on money. She's always been so damn careless.'

'Mmm,' said Bernadette, and then, because this seemed inappropriate: 'I know you've done your best. I'm sure she appreciates it.'

After this, feeling a little ashamed, she sat looking at the telephone. Twice she raised the receiver. Then she decided to go out and buy *The Times*.

The picture was certainly no help to the curious. There

3

was a terrace, perhaps, stone pillars supporting vines. The rest was unfathomable shadow, distortion and mystery.

Lucy was appalled at how indifferent she felt.

'I see,' she said slowly at last. But could she see the situation from Laura's angle, through Laura's eyes?

Laura's eyes were still wet about the lashes like a small child's. They were big eyes, clear blue. In grief they were neither puffy nor ruined but simply appealing, demanding pitying attention.

'Oh, Lucy, you know how it is,' she cried, screwing and unscrewing the handkerchief in her hands. She was quite sure Lucy knew how it was. From the beginning she had been determined to make Lucy her ally for she had married the eldest son, the steady, capable, successful firstborn. If Lucy were not on her side she would surely be implacably against her. None the less she had always been aware of all the false notes she struck in trying to play in tune. Was she striking them now? For instance, the shedding of tears was considered unnecessarily dramatic in this house. She had only dared shed them once before, the night Christopher had been rushed off with appendicitis and she had scooped up the two children and fled here, white, choking with sobs, undignified. Then, as now, Lucy had been cheerfully brusque.

'I didn't know what else to do,' Laura said, just as she had done all those years ago when Lucy had opened the door to her, a Niobe on the front steps, with the baby in a sleepsuit, the small boy in a dressing-gown under his anorak. Her eyes still pleaded for understanding, for affection, for reassurance. But she also listened, as perhaps the piano tuner did when he came to tinker with Lucy's ancient grand, listened for the ring of true sound.

'Well, you're upset. You need a whisky,' said Lucy.

'Just to ring. Just to say something like he wasn't coming back. How could he behave like that? And I didn't even know,' Laura continued. Was she conscious of having said

4

all this before, maybe twice before, and on this same rising note, prelude to grief and hysteria? She began on several more clichés, all undoubtedly true. 'Aren't wives always the last to know? Why couldn't he talk to me? And he says it isn't another woman but I don't believe it . . .'

Repetition seemed inevitable in a crisis, thought Lucy, like cups of tea.

'I shouldn't do anything in a hurry,' she advised gently.

'I thought . . .' Laura's overnight bag was in the hall and earlier she had talked wildly of sending for Adam from school, as if there had been a death. As if Chris is dead, Lucy thought, instead of simply missing.

'You'd be silly to leave the house. He might ring again. And there are the children. Stomach upsets, broken arms . . . what if they need to get in touch?'

'I can give them this number. Adam . . .' Laura began but the tears started again, relentless, suffocating. Lucy passed over a tissue and watched it being dissolved.

'Darling, it's nearly the end of term. By the time they come home you'll be sorted out and can tell them what you and Chris have decided.'

'What *he's* decided. He's decided he wants a new life. He doesn't even have the decency to say sorry.'

Oh Lord, thought Lucy, why can't I feel any sympathy? I should do. I should. I ought to feel for both of them. He's made her as unhappy as she's made him.

'I was so sure you'd help,' came Laura's drowning cry.

'But Lolly dear, you don't really want to stay here. You're shocked and angry. Of course you are. But you need to be at home.' And Lucy supplied another tissue automatically and, as if Laura were a toddler, scooped the wet tufts of the last one from her palm. 'Have another drink and tell me about Ginny's hockey.'

'It's tennis now. Summer, remember? She says she'll make Wimbledon by the turn of the century.'

Laura was making an effort. I must try to appreciate it,

thought Lucy. 'What about that drink? Come on, Lolly. Then I'll drive you home.'

Laura sank back in her chair, comforted at last by this repetition of her pet name, the name her parents had used in the safe, so-distant past. She gazed gratefully at Lucy, always so calm, so sensible. And since Lucy's idea of a drink was invariably forty per cent proof it would be as well to be driven home, though it was fifteen miles and Lucy's car a small Citroën of great age.

'I'm spoiling your day,' she said. She had no real idea what Lucy's days were like, where she went, how she occupied herself. Sixty-three and a widow. I can't imagine what she does to pass the time, Laura thought. The Cambridge house always seemed unchanged – in need of decoration, Chris had always said – furnished sparsely with good antiques, Maurice's books lining the walls, flowers from the garden crammed into cheap pots and vases. There were a lot of pictures, a few photographs – Maurice, the children, Lucy's father in uniform for the Great War – no ornaments.

'Lolly, you're nodding off.'

'No. No, I'm not.' Laura sat a little more upright, sipping the drink as if it were medicine. She heard herself saying, as if from a very great distance, irrelevantly, quite foolishly: 'It was in the paper recently that they're thinking of getting drivers over the age of sixty to take another test.'

And would you be appalled if I passed? Lucy wondered.

'What a good idea,' she said mildly.


'Christ!' exclaimed Turk when told the news. 'Come to live with you? For how long? She's off her head.'

'Only temporarily. And where else has she to go?' Lucy was bundling flowers into a jug. She was as clumsy with flowers as with all things domestic, cobbling together, skimping, trying to achieve in ten minutes what should have taken an hour of concentrated effort.

'Well, I'll leave,' Turk announced, lighting a cigarette. Her hands, Lucy saw, trembled with passion. Anger or amusement? she wondered.

'What difference would it make to you? Your rooms are at the back.'

'She thinks I'm cat piss. What does she call me behind my back?'

'Apart from that? How would I know? If she calls you anything it's behind my back too.'

The woman at the desk bent over the paper in her hand. She read quickly, drawing on the cigarette. 'This is bloody,' she declared, and threw it down on to a small pile of similar discarded pages.

'Spare me the artistic temperament. Look at it later when you've finished being absurd over Laura. She's not staying, anyway. I drove her home.'

So how had they all come to call her Turk? Lucy wondered. She couldn't remember. Yes, she could. It was to do with one of the novels. Turk's first.

'Crazy how they all still come to you,' Turk said. She stubbed out the cigarette in a tin by Lucy's jug of flowers. A last thin thread of smoke rose and wreathed among the roses. 'Bernadette tries not to, of course. She'd rather grovel on her knees to all those priests.'

'You mean dear chubby Father Brace. If it makes her happy . . .' said Lucy gently.

'But it doesn't, does it?'

'You know, it's a function of motherhood. Being there. Listening. Giving advice no one really wants.' Lucy was plucking up fallen leaves and odd bits of stalk. 'They just want to hear the right noises. Motherly noises, I suppose.'

'You should know.'

It was possible Lucy had mothered Turk, in so far as anyone could take on such a responsibility. Turk had lived in the flat at the rear of the house for thirty years. When Maurice had objected, shying away from even the thought of a lodger, Lucy had not bothered to wear him down

7

with argument, she had simply bought a rent book and given the girl a key. 'She's a nice girl,' she had told her friend Nina. 'And the money's a godsend.' It was heartening how such a small amount made so much difference. 'You butter our bread,' Lucy said to Marianne – still Marianne in those days, those days before the first novel, the obnoxious lover, the abortion, the suicidal depression; before Maurice's professorship, Laura, Bernadette's widowhood, grandchildren.

Maurice had been left the Cambridge house by his father. It was near the Botanical Gardens where the old man had once taught him the Latin names of plants, just one more mental exercise among many. If he forgot what he was supposed to have learnt deprivation followed: no cake for tea, no freedom in the garden, no time with his mother. He grew anxious trying to remember. And a miserable, restricted childhood was only followed by a more restricted, exam-laden youth. 'When I met you I already felt about a hundred. You made me young again,' he said rather touchingly to Lucy once. He was not given to such admissions. He had been conditioned to tread warily. A moment later he might never have spoken.

For the first two years of his marriage his mother still lived in the flat she had made overlooking the garden, the flat in which Lucy was eventually to instal Turk. All round were accumulating signs of neglect: defective gutters, encroaching weeds, the whiff of dry rot. This was why there was never any butter on the bread until Marianne, dark, wild, not really 'nice' at all Marianne. And everything took time, especially Maurice's career, for at his father's death the urgency of knowing and understanding had left him, the old terror of not doing well. He was still only a junior lecturer then, distressingly humble. Cambridge was full of struggling young men just like him. So he rose slowly, so slowly, though with a strange inevitability all the same, for the dull and indispensable must finally be acknowledged. And Lucy learned how she must behave and, by and large, behaved reasonably well, charming the visiting professors, the politicians on government commissions, the old men of the college, Maurice's undergraduates.

'Are you listening?' Turk demanded. 'Loo? Where are you?' And then, because Lucy made no reply: 'D'you want me out?'

'Why should I?'

'You could do this place up, let it for a decent rent at last.'

'You pay a decent rent.'

'Not for these days.'

'Your rent helped us eat and buy wine and things for the children. Chris's hi-fi stuff. D'you remember?'

'You're behind the times. Don't you know what this hovel of mine would bring you in, tarted up, plumbing fixed? And I could afford to pay whatever you asked. You certainly know that.'

'Don't worry. If I wanted to, I'd ask for more. Only I don't want.'

They looked at each other. It was a ritual look, a sizing up. They had done it when they had first met, when Lucy had found a tall, bony girl weeping on the area steps and had brought her in, a total stranger, for gin and sympathy.

'Of course you'd miss the bloody noise,' Turk remarked. 'If I left. The typewriter at all hours.'

She has a beautiful, strong face, thought Lucy, remembering it that remarkable night lit by the harsh kitchen light-bulb. Tears, gin, uninhibited revelations ... So I took her under my wing, she told herself. Could she have resisted doing so, having known what it is to need shelter?

'She probably drove him mad with her clearing up,' Turk was saying. 'Endless bloody cleaning.'

'Who? Oh, Laura. She always kept the house tidy.'

'Not much of a home.'

'She's been a good mother.'

'Obsessive. The poor things were hardly allowed out for

9

years in case they dirtied their knees. Then the next thing they're bundled off to summer schools, abseiling, pony trekking . . . you name it, they do it. Not a minute to draw breath. Then back to that deathly house, not a chair an inch out of place, only to be washed and brushed and packed away to school proper. Not much of a family life.'

'Marianne, you're exaggerating.'

'Am I?'

They looked at each other again. They smiled. We've called a truce over Laura then, Lucy thought. And then: She must be forty-seven, forty-eight. Dear God, forty-eight. Where did all that time go?

'What a day!' she said, suddenly weary – feeling *my* age, she wondered? – 'Laura weeping and howling and then the most ridiculous phone call from Bernie about Oliver's house: what's it all about, what have I been up to, how, when, why, why, why? And on top more agonizing about leaving the Church because she wants to be a vicar or a woman priest or whatever they're calling them.'

'Leave the Catholics? Not Bernie. I always thought she'd be a nun.'

'She wanted to be once. Maurice squashed that, of course. He told her the whole idea was absurd, you know, in that voice he used sometimes, making her feel she'd let him down even to think of it. So after that . . . well, no more of the nuns.'

'But Maurice was the Catholic. Why was he against it?'

'I think that sort of commitment frightened him. He didn't understand it, it frightened him, and he didn't want Bernie having anything to do with it. Poor Bernie. He didn't stop to think of *her* feelings.'

'He went to Mass every week,' Turk said slowly, casting back.

'He said that was habit. I think it was. He'd been brought up to go. And he liked the choir.' Lucy thought: I remember trying to have an adult conversation about it. I wanted to know what he believed in. It seemed silly not knowing, when I was married to him, when it might have been something important in his life. But he wouldn't discuss it. He just said he went to hear the choir.

'It all means a lot to Bernie,' she said.

'Being taken notice of means a lot to Bernie. And now we're in for six months of stricken conscience, of wondering if her defection from Rome will break the Pope's heart, whether it's really God calling her. On and on. Loo, she'll drive you mad. You shouldn't put up with it any more. Tell her it's time she grew up. Christ, she's forty and has a daughter of nineteen.'

'She finds strength in faith,' said Lucy, and was aware she herself never had.

'She didn't when Maurice died. She went to pieces.'

'Are you going to contradict everything I say?'

'Yes,' said Turk. 'When you talk such crap.'

Bernadette rang again in the evening.

'I'm worried about Chloë,' she said.

'What about Chloë, darling?' Lucy was tired after the drama with Laura, after a hot afternoon in the garden.

'She's having a rough time. She says she doesn't like the course. She's talking of leaving before the exams.'

'Well, it's up to her.'

'Mother, that isn't very helpful.'

'No, I suppose it isn't. I'm sorry.'

'I wondered . . . couldn't you invite her for a week or two? She always loved staying with you. You could . . . well, point out there's only a year to go and she'll have the degree and . . .'

'Bernie, what a mad idea! Anyway, I might be in Greece.'

'Not this house? You're not going out there?'

'The least I can do is go and look at it.' I sound as if it'll come as a surprise, that I don't know what it's like, that I've never seen it before. Why?

'But you never go away.'

'I can begin.'

'But Mother . . . All on your own? And what about your cranky knees?'

'A warm climate might do wonders.'


'Your family imposes,' Turk said. They were in the kitchen drinking coffee while the sky darkened and darkened outside the window, the prelude to storm.

'Familes do. They ought to. There's no point to it all otherwise. We may as well live like moles, solitary and aggressive.'

'Perhaps what they really want is money.'

'They had Maurice's money.'

'If you sell this Greek house there'll be some more.'

'Chris doesn't need money,' Lucy protested.

'Divorces can be expensive.'

'And Bernadette's all right. She has a decent salary.'

'Those priests winkle it out of her, I bet. She'd clean out every account she had for that Father Brace.'

'And Alan,' continued Lucy stubbornly, 'never gave a toss for money.' She smiled at the thought of her younger son.

The first rumble of thunder reached them and the lights flickered a moment after. Lucy, sitting in one chair with her feet up on another, stretched her toes, cramped from her old gardening shoes.

'Don't you like my children, Marianne?'

Turk, hunched over her coffee, frowned into the cup. It was the last of the old Spode, inherited by Maurice along with the house and broken piece by piece over the years by Lucy, by Mrs Treece who 'did', by the children helping to wash up, by careless visitors, by cats, clumsiness or circumstance. There was history in it, that cup. It sat elegantly on a cheap willow-pattern saucer and Turk bent to look into it – looking back, looking forward.

'They think they know what's good for you. They'll soon put the pressure on over Greece.'

'Chris might. He likes to think he can manage me. Alan's never put pressure on, he's too lazy.'

'Emotional pressure. He makes you love him too much to resist.'

'But he'd be the only one to applaud if I went off to live there.'

'Would he? If he knew what it was worth?'

Lucy looked up. 'But *I* don't know what it's worth.'

'Loo, don't be naive. The Greek government's interested in buying it. It's a beautiful place on an unspoilt coast. It could be a hideaway for the seriously rich, a top-flight hotel, anything.'

'And it could be my home.' What a silly little flash of rebellion, Lucy thought, and too late – always so late. Her hand trembled suddenly. She put her cup down before she dropped it, turning abruptly to look out at the slatey sky, the flickers of lightning, the first drops of rain. 'I could go and live there. It's time I did something . . . ruthless.' She was not conscious of choosing the word and yet she had chosen it. It hung in the air a moment after she had spoken.

'But what on earth would you do in Greece, Loo?' Turk asked reasonably.

Adam said, on the phone from boarding school: 'I'd really like to stay with Gran.' He sounded much younger than fifteen, set about by these new problems. Laura, who was not an imaginative woman, suddenly remembered him at two or three, a quiet, happy child, playing with a bowl of water and plastic boats.

'Perhaps you can. Later on. I don't know what's going to happen in the next few weeks.'

'Nothing much, probably. Anyway, it won't be anything to do with me.' He didn't want it to be anything to do with him. He prayed it wouldn't be.

'I'd like your support, darling,' said Laura. She had ignored Lucy's advice. She had rung the school during the prep hour, dragging Adam from an essay on Bismarck to hear how she – how they all – had been abandoned.

'I'll see Dad in the holidays, won't I?' He sounded confident about this at least.

'I expect so.'

'And I can go to Gran's?'

'By yourself?' She needed him at home in order to burden him with every detail, every minute detail of failed marriage.

'Why not?'

They had always visited Lucy as a family. Duty visits? Chris and his mother had an uneasy relationship, affection mingled with exasperation. 'Why not do this . . . or that?' he would demand, and 'Stop organizing me, for heaven's sake,' Lucy would retort, and then the atmosphere would darken. He had wanted her to sell his father's books, to find a new builder when old Langridge kept her waiting for the new guttering, to get someone in to clean, even to employ a gardener. And Lucy shrank from this assault. She was handicapped by the knowledge that he meant well and that even in childhood he had been stricken by rebuff. When giving advice he always took a negative response as a personal insult. Like Maurice, Lucy thought. She could have pointed out that if she sold all the books she would have to dismantle the floor-to-ceiling bookcases and redecorate, that the shining boards took very little cleaning, that gardening was her joy, but she remained silent. He would only see her rejection of his ideas as a rejection of himself.

'Why not?' repeated Adam.

'I'll talk to Lucy,' said Laura diplomatically.

'Umm. Yes. Do. Do, please.' He had turned abruptly monosyllabic. A friend was plucking his elbow and it would be shaming to be found talking to one's mother except in an emergency. He was not sure marriage breakdown counted as an emergency these days. It was too commonplace. All around him in his class were the results of this apparently inevitable process.

'Bye,' he said. 'Supper bell.'

'I'll see about . . .' Laura began, but was cut off.

She put down the receiver with a sigh. She had an urge to ring someone else to impart her news. It never occurred to her she was not coping with a crisis. She might have been the only woman abandoned by a man that day. Luckily for Ginny, who was busy banging balls over a tennis net deep in the Dorset countryside, Laura felt her daughter was too young to take such news on the phone. She looked forward to a tearful reunion when term ended. Besides, Ginny might take her father's part. Ginny was more observant than Adam, and more critical. For a moment, remembering this, Laura felt the tears starting again and crouched forward on the chair as if, by absolute stillness, she could avoid them, just as Ginny, running for a wild backhand, was crippled by a stitch and folded up, not daring to breathe.

But: There's always Bernadette, Laura thought.

She rarely spoke to Bernadette. She found her personality frightening, dark and light at once, liable to flash out with sarcasm or be plunged in gloom or furiously energetic. Sometimes she seemed mortally offended by some chance word. But Laura felt Bernie should know her brother's iniquities.

'He just rang from some hotel,' she ended. 'He didn't even say he was sorry.'

Bernadette, whose own husband had been killed in a car accident four months after their wedding, leaving her pregnant, bewildered and remarkably angry, was unsympathetic.

'Surely you saw it coming?'

'No,' cried Laura. 'I thought he was happier. He'd been coming home earlier. He brought me flowers.'

Bernadette felt there was nothing she could usefully say. She was silent for a moment but then remembered all Lucy's strictures about not being unkind.

'Well, I'm sorry. I'm sorry for the kids. For all of you.'

She supposed marriages ended every minute these days, in spite of Father Brace's optimism. She felt nothing for Laura except a dim hope that now the break was made things would be better – the best anybody could hope probably. Since she worked as a legal secretary she saw a great deal of the emotional quagmire surrounding separation and divorce. This was periodically countered by Father Brace's touching belief in the sacredness of marriage vows and rather muddled views on sex and sin. Her own pitifully brief time with David was darkened by the quarrel they had had the morning he had died, a childish, acrimonious exchange over toast and weak coffee. She had been conscious ever since of not kissing him goodbye. So now, hearing what sounded like muffled weeping, she wrestled her better self uppermost and said, 'Laura? You're not crying, are you? Look, d'you want me to come over?'

'No. No, it's all right.' There was a pause. For tissues? 'I went to see Lucy.'

'Was she bracing?'

'The drink was. She had to drive me home.'

'She didn't mention this house in Greece?'

'What house in Greece?'

'Oliver Lussom's. You can't see what it's like from the picture in the paper.'

Laura took a deep breath to defeat the tears. The conversation had veered away from her, from Chris, and she felt overwhelmed suddenly. Did no one really care?

Well, she had never expected much from Bernadette.

'Who on earth is Oliver Lussom?' she asked bravely.


'My mother,' Alan announced to the Harvard professor he was entertaining in the Senior Common Room, 'has been left Oliver Lussom's house.'

'In-deed,' said the professor warmly. 'That's great news.'

'You see, my grandfather was Harold Cavendish.'

'The archeologist. I never knew,' as if he should perhaps have divined it. 'You should be proud.'

'Oh, I am,' but Alan glanced about, embarrassed, afraid to be caught boasting. 'Of course, I hardly knew him. He died when I was two or three.' He had a filmy memory of sitting on the lap of some old man who was intent, surprisingly, on making him a daisy chain. Rather touching, he thought now, in a great man. In any man? He could not picture himself making daisy chains though perhaps once he had, years and years ago, for baby Chloë . . .

'I've been to that house,' said the professor. He was rather anxious to get on with his dinner. He disliked dry sherry. Should he ask for something else? But all around him were glasses of sherry. He looked at Dr Flecker in mute appeal but Dr Flecker was concerned with Greece, not alcohol. His grave, thin face had come to life.

'You've been to Lussom's house?'

'I have. In-deed.'

'And what was it like?'

'Out of this world.' And absorbed by the vision that glowed before his inner eye, the professor took a whole mouthful of the foul sherry as if it had been first-rate, heart-warming Bourbon.

The storm was over but it was still raining. The house was unnaturally dark. The lilacs by the kitchen window moved wetly against the glass.

'Mother, what's all this about Greece?' Alan asked lightly.

'Greece?' She felt stubborn suddenly. It would be childish to pretend obtuseness, but also satisfying.

'Well, I read about Oliver Lussom. This house. It was in *The Times*. Why you, Ma? I never knew you'd met the man.'

'Why should you?'

Down the phone he sensed her sudden anger, as if he were a child again and had burst into the room without knocking, the room where she was completing private business. But: 'How are things your end?' she asked, and her tone had altered to one as light as his.

'Fine. I'm trailing a Harvard guy about, European history. He says he stayed with Lussom once. God knows why. The house sounds quite something. I'd thought it might just be a beach shack. You know.'

'Yes.' She could have meant anything.

'Have *you* ever been there?'

'Of course. Darling, is this inquisition going to last much longer? I've something in the oven.'

'You're being rather secretive about all this.'

'Not at all. I just want my supper.'

'But the house . . .'

'Is just a house. Alan dear, I must go. Marianne's calling.'

He tried to disperse his growing curiosity but found it tricky, like oil, spreading instead of being eliminated.

'Ma . . .'

In the kitchen Lucy said to Turk: 'Even Alan.'

'Told you so.'

'But then . . . you can't blame them being curious.'

Once, she remembered, she had believed she could push the children away as animals do, not callously but positively, urging them to their own lives. She had hoped to regain privacy and purpose. Are mothers never to be allowed private lives, she wondered. Young children naturally expect a parent to be exclusively theirs, but surely not still at forty-two, forty, thirty-five? Middle-aged, thought Lucy. My children are middle-aged. Good God!

'I feel a hundred,' she told Turk.

'Chris'll ring next. Wait and see.'

'If he does and you answer tell him I'm out.' Lucy made a clumsy attempt to rescue her toasted cheese where it dripped through the grill rack. 'You could have taken this out before it burnt.'

'It would have congealed. And by the way, why *did* Oliver Lussom leave you his house?'

'Only Oliver could tell you.' And I really don't know, she thought. I never met him again in all those years. There were just the letters. So many letters.

'I won't pry,' said Turk.

'You never do.'

'But I've never heard you talk of Oliver Lussom.'

'No,' said Lucy. 'I don't think I've ever mentioned him. Perhaps once or twice. Bernie used to watch his programmes. But he took over my father's site in the Peloponnese. You knew that.'

In the gloom they sat over the crumbs of their supper. They could hear the rain falling, persistently, whisperingly. At last Turk stirred, pushed away her plate.

'Coffee?'

The second time she passed behind Lucy's chair she stopped, bent to kiss her head.

'What sort of gift is it, Loo? Has he given it you to make you happy?'

'I don't know. I'll have to go there, I think, before I can answer that.'

The phone began to ring in the hall. Turk went on making coffee and Lucy gathered the plates and put them in the sink. After a while the ringing stopped.

'When are you leaving?' asked Turk.

# 2

LUCY was nineteen.

'There's not much for you out here,' said Harold Cavendish awkwardly, picking his way among words as he might pick among his stones. 'And too hot for anything this time of the year.'

Lucy nodded but made no comment. It was indeed hot and talking seemed to call for an unnatural effort.

She had missed the spring, the beautiful time in Greece, they had told her. Her mother's death had occupied April. She had not even seen English buds breaking, the new green, the primroses. There had been, in a sense, no measurable night and day, only long stretches of boredom, of penetrating anxiety, of helpless love and ultimately of helpless grief. Now Greece scorched under an August sun and Harold stalked his ruins with his daughter, the ruins he had waited so long to make his own, through war and civil war, through earthquake and bureaucratic delay. With the coming of cooler weather his greatest work would begin. And: 'There's not much for you out here,' was what he said to Lucy, for frustration was mingled with fright. What was he to do with her? He had forgotten puberty, knew little of young women except what Edith, strictly reared, had allowed him to know in twenty years of semi-detached marriage. 'Oh, that year I was in the Peloponnese,' he would say when challenged to remember what Lucy had been like at three, five, twelve. There had been so many years in the Peloponnese. And ten in Canada, while wars raged.

Lucy at nineteen had come as a shock.

'How you've grown up,' he had declared foolishly, meeting her in Athens. Of course, she had coped with Edith, the long illness, death, funeral arrangements. He, making excuses, had arrived for the service and had flown away again immediately. He had hardly glanced at Lucy. He had not cared to give way to any kind of emotion. He had behaved with a rigid, an absolute decorum. It was impossible to guess what feelings stirred him at the sight of the coffin. Perhaps none. He had seen Edith four times in the last six years. But he kept his eyes on the coffin and did not look at his daughter, as if putting off the moment he would have to assume sole responsibility.

In Athens, the moment had come.

She was slim, quite tall, pale, as shy as he had expected. A brown-haired girl in dull crêpe de Chine and a straw hat. She wore sensible, youthful shoes. She was appropriately polite. He soon found that her education had been sadly deficient – she knew next to nothing about the ancient world – and he was gloomily astonished. He had chosen her school with great care and paid a great deal for it.

'Well, you can't stay in Athens,' he had told her. What dangers might beset her in Athens? What Greeks?

'I really don't want to. I thought I'd live with you in Pylos.' She was a little shocked that he seemed reluctant to take her home. She looked on wherever he was as home because there was nowhere else now. Surely he didn't grudge her a few months at Pylos while she decided what to do with herself?

But at Pylos he said: 'No fun for you, my poor girl, out here in the back of beyond.'

He would have left her in England but there had only been his unmarried sister, deaf, eccentric, inhabiting a comfortless house. He hoped time would pass quickly until a suitable young chap took the girl off his hands. Maybe he could spend next summer in London, in Cambridge. There would be dances, tennis, picnics, the right sort of people.

'Perhaps I ought to get a job,' Lucy suggested, though diffidently, waiting until he had eaten a good dinner and was mellow, approachable, talking away about Telemachus.

'Nonsense. There's no need for that.' What job could she do in Greece? What job could she do anywhere?

'I'll have to train for something, Father.'

'Well, well. Maybe. But we won't talk about it now. Plenty of time.'

Lucy had been plucked from school, thrust from hospital to nursing home to graveside. A year of her life, she thought, a year between the end of that last term, the realization Edith was ill, and this beautiful, lonely, unspoilt place in the sun. Now she saw there would be no fitting in with Harold's life. He cared for nothing apart from this site, the stones on the surface, the stones beneath. He had battled for years for permission to excavate, battled for the money, manpower and academic interest. He had waited, fretting in the cold north, while the Greeks fought Germans and then fellow Greeks. In 1939 he had never imagined it would be the fifties before he lifted the first trowelful of earth. And I, thought Lucy, am just the daughter he's scarcely ever seen, not beautiful, not clever, not much at all really. He'll send me back to England when he has the chance. He'd send me tomorrow if there was anyone to offer me a roof and food . . .

'How you are like a flower opening,' Nikos, Harold's

driver, told her at the end of her first week on the site. He repeated it in Greek but with a subtle variation.

'What was that? What did he say?'

'I don't know, Father. It was too quick.'

'I must say, your accent is good. Coming on well.' He did not expect much from her, and her desire to learn Greek had pleased him.

They walked down to where little markers measured out the work to come. 'So important. So very important,' Harold said.

'A whole city?'

'A whole city, my dear. Here, under our feet.'

Lucy looked down. Her toes in their open sandals were dusty. There were only little pebbles, hard, beaten ground, a few parched but tenacious weeds. She was interested in the stones but they didn't speak to her, she knew nothing of their secrets, she could never read their fissures. She was so ignorant. Nothing she had been told at school seemed to have left an impression. Nothing in the articles on Harold she had collected from newspapers had fired her to learn more about the civilizations he pursued. How carefully she had hoarded them, showing them off shyly.

Now the light hurt her eyes when she raised them to look at the hills.

'We might have an outing,' Harold was saying. 'See some of the country.'

'Could we go to Delphi?' It would be as well to have a specific goal or they might visit every ancient site in Greece.

'To consult Apollo?' and Harold laughed, not unkindly. He was not given to jokes and those he tried to make were ponderous or feeble.

'I'd just like to go, I think.'

The stones were silent but the mountains spoke to her, the dry grass, the olives, the sea, the people. She would enjoy driving to Delphi.

'Next week maybe.' Harold nudged a marker with his toe.

'And I think I ought to have some new clothes,' Lucy added quickly, before he became too absorbed. 'I haven't got much for hot weather.'

'Clothes,' said Harold, startled. 'Yes, of course. Clothes.'

A minor road petered out where stone pillars marked a track rising between orange trees. There was no indication where it led. The car advanced cautiously, rocking over stones, dust rising. Ahead must only be the sea. In a moment it would surprise them, glittering below. Another bend and still nothing, only the silvery scrub, olives, the track winding away.

'This is one of the most beautiful houses I've ever seen,' said Harold.

But by now Lucy was tired of suspense and bumping up and down in the heat. Besides, she would never trust his recommendation. What did he mean by a 'beautiful' house? She sat back again on the seat – she had been leaning forward a little in anticipation – and sighed.

Then there was a pair of huge oil jars either side, as if to mark their progress. The car crawled round a gradual bend and under trees to a turning space by a flight of steps. There was nothing spectacular, only a low arched entrance, a massive door standing open.

'You must look at it from the sea, from the beach,' Harold advised, seeing her disappointment.

'Yes, Father,' said Lucy politely.

'It's called Paleochora. Do you know what that means?'

'Yes, Father.'

He offered her his arm and they began to climb the steps.

He had a square, strong face, a flattened nose, pugnacious. She thought she had never seen such grey eyes. Such grey, she was to remember all her life. She had never even considered it as a colour before. He was sitting in a wicker chair on a terrace with a view of a deserted bay sheltered by brown hills, and he was smoking, flicking the ash so that it fell over the balustrade on which he had lodged his sandalled feet.

'Lussom, my dear chap.' Harold stepped briskly forward, hand extended. The other man rose, smiled, crushed out the cigarette.

'I wasn't expecting visitors.'

'I know. Forgive us. We called on the off-chance, passing through.'

'Harold, nobody passes through Paleochora.'

'Well, I told my daughter this was the most beautiful house in all Greece and worth a small diversion. We're going on to Delphi.'

For the first time Lussom became aware of the girl. She was young and thin, in a plain yellow dress. She held her gloves and a small bag rather awkwardly and looked uncomfortable in her shoes. He had the impression that at any moment she might fling everything over the balustrade and run down, barefoot, to the sea.

'This is my daughter Lucy,' said Harold.

She had not expected to be noticed. She had been brought up a dutiful child, trained, discreet, no trouble. And yet she felt drawn in, included, protected by this man's affectionate glance.

She thought it affectionate but she had no experience. How could she tell? It seemed to her amused, warm, somehow even conspiratorial, as if he knew exactly how awkward she felt in her father's company, what sea of conflicts she swam in. Over lunch he asked her nothing about herself, made no condescending remark, quickly brushed aside Harold's mention of school, of the dances to come, the tennis parties. He only said to her at one point, while eating peaches, leaning forward and lowering his voice, 'You look as if you need to escape,' an unsettling

25

suggestion. And yet, if she could . . . if she could! Of course Harold laughed and said yes, how dull it must be for her plodding round ruins with her old father. The jollity was noticeably false. Lucy knew he had been vexed by this problem of her clothes. He had been embarrassed, even bewildered, by her request. He had forgotten she had no money of her own.

Shyly she raised her eyes and met Lussom's. She could not fathom his look. She had no experience. She saw what might have been mockery and what might have been tender concern. A strange heat enveloped her.

'It'll be unbearable at Delphi,' said Harold.

'There'll be a breeze in the mountains. Whose idea was it?'

'Lucy's. Well, why not? If she can stand the heat I certainly can after all these years.' He glanced at his daughter as if to confirm her resilience, her ability to take the midday sun. She looked flushed already, even here in the shade of the upper terrace smothered in vines, but maybe that was the wine, to which she was unaccustomed. Or the beauty of the place. Whatever one might think about Lussom's character he had impeccable taste.

'Stay here tonight,' he was saying, lighting a cigarette. 'Leave in the cool before sunrise. You've quite a journey.' He brushed away Harold's objections.

'We'll stay in Athens of course. I want Lucy to meet the Fieldings.'

'The Fieldings?'

'Mrs Fielding offered . . .' He could not explain what she had offered. He recalled her kindly, meaningful touch. She was still a young woman. Youngish. She knew, her touch had said, how to entertain girls bored to tears by Mycenaean potsherds. 'Mrs Fielding would like Lucy to stay, September, October perhaps. Plenty to do in Athens. And I'll be especially busy then. All these years waiting, planning, and now it comes to it everything only half organized. I hardly know where to begin.'

26

He's beginning by sending me away, thought Lucy. Nothing has changed. Nothing will ever change. I'm to be packed off to whoever cares to have me. He won't even talk about what *I* might want, about a job . . .

'May I go to the beach?' she asked, and waited, crushed by habit, for Harold's permission.

It was a perfect crescent of fine pale sand. In sudden ecstasy she took off her tight shoes and walked into the sea, holding up her dress. The water was warm. The sand moved between her toes. Then she turned and looked up at the house.

So it *is* beautiful, she thought.

There was such symmetry in the tiled roofs, the colonnades, the descending terraces. It might have grown naturally from the slope on which it was built, making such use of space and form.

I wish we could stay here, she thought. After all, it seemed she had done nothing in Greece but climb about in ruins. She would give up Delphi, give up everything for time in this place.

'It's perfect,' she said shyly to Lussom. She had found Harold asleep in his chair under the vines and had crept away to the upper terrace.

'Good. I'm glad I persuaded your father to stay. He's been wearing himself out lately.'

'He's so excited. He can't really concentrate on anything else.' In case he should think she was complaining of neglect she added: 'He thinks I'm not interested.'

Lussom had come to stand near her by the balustrade as if drawn by the view. And yet the view was only sea and hills, she thought, trying to assess it with sophisticated indifference. She looked down at last at the square brown hand next to her own. She had never noticed hands particularly before.

'And are you? Interested?'

'I try to be. But it doesn't . . . I can't . . . I can't

27

understand why it's so important to dig it up. I sometimes think it ought to be left alone. But I can't say that to Father, can I? It's his life.'

'It's mine too.'

'I suppose it is.' She wondered how deeply she had blundered.

Could he understand the hopelessness of her relationship with Harold? No, of course not. He must only see a father and a daughter, conventionally if distantly affectionate. All he had known about her before today was that she had existed.

Professor Cavendish's daughter, thought Lucy. His name had conferred a nebulous honour on her, stirring curiosity. But she had scarcely been anybody's daughter in reality, not even her mother's, for Edith had always felt too frail to cope. Since she was seven or eight Lucy had spent every holiday with friends. Perhaps ten times in her life she had been in the same room as Harold, usually a public room in a hotel. He had always seemed embarrassed and she had always been tongue-tied. And yet this was the man she now relied on for clothes, books, hairslides, her whole future. This was the man she called Father and followed obediently among the ancient stones.

'You'll like Delphi,' Oliver Lussom told her. 'But look at it in the early morning. Get there before anyone else.'

But I shall be with Father, Lucy thought. He'll give a lecture. He won't stop talking from the time we arrive.

She turned her head to look at the sea so that he wouldn't notice the ridiculous tears.

She woke late. It had been a long and hazardous evening, coping delicately with the unfamiliar. She had gone to bed drained by the effort of behaving well, of holding her own without disgrace.

She stretched her legs beneath the sheet. Sunlight filtered through the shutters. Shouldn't someone have called her? Shouldn't she and Harold have been on their way? A knock announced the maid Demetra and a tray of breakfast.

'The gentlemen are eating,' she told Lucy. 'Now you. Quickly, I think.'

The coffee was thick and strong. There was a fresh roll and honey. Lucy drank and smiled and smiled and ate. I *enjoyed* last night, she thought. She believed this now. At the time she had been drowning in adrenalin, her palms wet, her chin held up only by supreme effort. Alarming, sophisticated guests, unusual food, Harold's surreptitious worried glances ... But she had come through. She had even been complimented. The man Leftakis had kissed her fingers on leaving and one of the women had leaned a soft perfumed cheek against her own.

And Oliver Lussom had smiled at her.

In love we read so much into smiles.

The new bright morning, the sense of achievement came between her and the memory. He had smiled. It was enough. It signified some kind of approval. It might have expressed the affection she craved, it might not. She told herself, pouring more coffee, that he was ages old, a phrase from schooldays which brought back to her the comradeship of the dormitory, of Margot and Caroline, of hugging, kissing, comforting, teasing. He was ages old, perhaps thirty-five, perhaps more. But: 'We don't choose where we love or why,' she was to say to Turk years afterwards when they stood in church together full of forebodings while Christopher married Laura.

Lucy got out of bed and went to the bathroom. She had never seen such a bathroom, even in hotels. She remembered the great bath, the marble basin in Margot's house near Tours, but they had been grand and utilitarian, cold and hard and white. This was luxurious, the walls a bloody terracotta, towels like blankets. When she came to dress in the blouse and skirt and cardigan which was all she had apart from yesterday's yellow, she thought how her clothes belonged to the world she had left, a world of bus queues and chips and post-war exhaustion. They had nothing to do with the bathroom where she had just cleaned her teeth, with this place: sunshine, lemons, deserted sand, Paleochora.

'Ah, here's my sleepyhead,' said Harold, relieved. He had looked at his watch every five minutes for the last half-hour.

'Sleep well?' asked Lussom.

She smiled and nodded. Her voice failed her. He did not look ages old. For the first time she noticed not just his hands but his mouth, the freshly shaved cheek, that broad, ugly nose. She felt overwhelmed, as if each fresh observation cost her in energy, collapsed her lungs. She was afraid to look at him and longed to look at him all the time. When he said something ordinary and led her to look out at the hills, pointing, his nearness made her stomach contract sharply. And her heart.

Harold said, 'We ought to make a start, my dear. Or all our good intentions will go for nothing.'

Through the window of the car Oliver Lussom said, 'I hope Delphi lives up to expectation.' Lucy could only smile and look politely grateful.

'I hope so too,' said Harold, tapping Nikos on the shoulder. 'But Lucy couldn't have a better guide than her old father, could she?'

'Write and tell me about it,' said Oliver quietly to the girl whose wing of hair had fallen forward to hide her face.

And the car pulled away.

Delphi lived up to expectation because they did eventually see it in the very early morning, untroubled by heat, other tourists or souvenir sellers. They had had a puncture and had been forced to stay overnight in what Harold considered a hovel, a café with some rooms to let. This was a blessing in disguise, thought Lucy, who was beginning to see that most blessings would come this way with her father in charge. When she knocked at his door to see if he was coming to breakfast he complained he had been kept awake by the men drinking below, he would sleep another hour.

She asked Nikos to drive her the few miles left.

Gazing at the hills above the theatre, her nostrils filled with the resiny herbal smell of the brush, she had been moved to sudden joy. She thought it was the sacred place, the solitude, the mountains. Then she thought of Oliver Lussom and experienced that odd contraction again, that internal disintegration. She felt hot. She wanted, for no obvious reason, to cry.

I shall never see him again, she thought.

Had the oracle still been in residence she might have dared ask if this would indeed be the case. Between hope and despair she felt giddy. 'Write and tell me about it,' he had said. So she must. She must keep a contact, however tenuous.

At the café Harold had overslept his hour by another and so had lost moral superiority.

'Really, Lucy. Going by yourself,' was all he said. He was still not fully awake and the sun was already unbearable. He would not be disappointed to miss Delphi after all.

'I took the book,' Lucy told him. She showed him the corner of the guide sticking out of her bag. 'And Nikos has been lots of times before.'

'You didn't walk round with Nikos?'

'No. He stayed by the car.' She had been ready to insist. She had steeled herself for it. If not he would have paid her the predictable compliments, each one more daringly erotic, and then tried to touch her breasts or thighs. She thought him laughable, old and short and strutting and moustached. All the same she was glad when he met someone he seemed to know and went off to the shade to play cards.

Later, of course, Harold delivered his lecture on Delphi after all. It was in the car on their way back to Pylos. 'The

31

oracle was under the influence of drugs,' he said. 'Probably spoke gibberish.'

'But she had interpreters,' insisted Lucy. She thought the answer to her own question would simply have required a yes or no.

'How can you interpret gibberish?' demanded Harold. He was not, after all, in sympathy with every aspect of the ancient world. He found some things childish and some distasteful.

'So much depended on the replies.'

'Ambiguous. You can bank on it. Couldn't be wrong, could they? Supposed to be a god speaking.' Harold leaned forward and in his faultless, English-accented Greek said, 'Nikos, find somewhere shady for lunch.'

'Well, I thought Delphi was magical,' said Lucy.

She wrote: 'Dear Mr Lussom, Delphi was magical,' and the pen trembled. The letters wavered as if she had only just learnt to form them. She tore up the page and started again. 'Dear Mr Lussom, thank you so much . . .' She had sent scores of letters like this, stiltedly polite, shuffled from family to family because Edith was always being ordered quiet and sea air. 'Dear Mrs Harmsworth . . . Dear Mrs Alexander . . . Dear Madame Bonneaux . . . thank you so much for having me.' Only none of them had been as difficult as this, this trying to strike a balance between genuine gratitude and that kind of amusing adult lightness he would appreciate. She so wanted him to smile as he read.

And at the bottom she had to sign herself Lucy Cavendish in case, cruelly, he had already forgotten her.

The post came late to the old house along the coast from Pylos. Sofia the housekeeper told Lucy that that son-of-a-bitch Makis grumbled at how frequently he had to trudge the long track laden with letters and parcels. Museums, governments, academic institutions, Athens . . . Harold's correspondence flew back and forth. And Makis, wiping his brow, told Lucy her father was a great man, a great man, but his, Makis's, legs would not stand it.

'You son-of-a-bitch,' said Sofia every time. It was a phrase she had learnt during the war.

'I am an old man,' Makis would retort. 'I have tired legs.'

Shrivelled and stooping, he would press letters into Lucy's hand. 'All these young men. Young men always writing. What does the Professor say?'

'Young men?' asked Lucy, bewildered.

'You son-of-a-bitch,' said Sofia, and chased him away down the track.

Never young men, thought Lucy, only friends. Later she would never say 'only'. She would be sustained and nourished by friendship. It was just that summer that she felt detached from the past. It blurred and grew remote. Afterwards she thought it must have been grief for Edith. Or falling in love. Or both. In Greece she read Margot's news with indifference as if Margot had been a stranger, even though there were photos of the house near Tours, of Monsieur Bonneaux by the dovecote with a calf on a rope; even though Margot had written 'I miss you' in English on the last page, a most un-Margot-like eruption of sentimentality.

In Caroline's letter from the vicarage there was a note from Caroline's mother. 'I do hope everything will work out. It must be difficult being the daughter of such a brilliant man.' Is he brilliant? Lucy wondered. It wasn't a word she would have chosen, but clever people were often called by it, mistakenly, she felt. The vicarage seemed far distant, containing no brilliance at all, only ordinary, struggling people, the vicar always failing over a sermon or mending his bicycle, Caroline making spotted dick, the twins with jam-jars of sticklebacks or shoebags writhing with grass snakes.

'I can hardly remember England,' Lucy told Sofia.

33

'And a good thing,' replied Sofia.

'It must be the sun or something.'

'The sun! The sun must make the Professor forget your dresses. You must have new clothes.'

'I know. But he says he'll see about it later.' Lucy's Greek had improved immeasurably. It was something she could do with her time, learning Greek. And time hung heavier and heavier.

'We'll have to go to Athens,' Sofia declared, although she had never been and was unlikely to be allowed there with Lucy.

'Father's mind is on other things.'

'Pooh! His mind's all over the place. Stones, bones, bits of old pot. Old pot!' And Sofia laughed rather scathingly, Lucy thought. 'There might be jewels, gold. Instead, little bits of this and that, tiny, unimportant.'

'I think everything's important,' said Lucy loyally.

The following day the news came that Makis was ill. Sofia said mysteriously, 'Perhaps his wife has tried to poison him.' From beneath her hot black cardigan she produced a single letter and handed it to Lucy. 'More friends,' she said.

It was a white envelope with unfamiliar writing. Lucy held it away for a moment as if it were dangerous, explosive. It's from Oliver, she thought. In her mind she referred to him now as Oliver, the name repeating itself until she had to close her eyes and force herself to think of something else. She walked down to the perimeter of the site where the first pegs and lines and marker posts impeded progress. She sat on a piece of fallen column and the stored heat struck through her. As she had come to expect, heat flowed from other directions too. Was love always accompanied by such abrupt risings and fallings of temperature?

It turned out to be an unexceptional, ordinary letter. How could it be otherwise? Yet the man being what he was, words broke away here and there, a glint of humour showed, and he ended: 'You must visit me again. Perhaps

34

next time you'd like to swim. Your father and I need a few days together before he starts work. Tell him to come over and bring you with him. I have a boat too. The coast is best seen from the sea.' He signed himself Oliver.

Lucy folded the single page and replaced it carefully in the envelope. Dazzled, she imagined the love letter he might one day write to her. And he would sign it, she knew, like this, just Oliver, a splash of precipitate ink across the paper, as striking, as individual, as impatient as the man himself.

She got up slowly, a little shaky, and set off across the burning ground to where she could see her father in conversation with a small man in a white suit. On the site Harold was always affable, always approachable. Out here among his stones and bones he might even, one day, look at her with love instead of anxiety. She saw him notice her when she was still quite a long way off, as he would notice anybody trespassing between his pegs, and he raised a hand. She could imagine his smile, his murmur to the man in white: 'My daughter, you know.'

'Father . . .' she began.

'Lucy dear, this is Mr Stefanidis.'

She shook hands warmly. Joy had made her bold. She still held the letter, folded small between her fingers.

'Mr Stefanidis has come from Athens to . . .'

'You won't forget I must go to Athens to buy some clothes? I really haven't anything left to wear. They've washed my last good dress to pieces.' She smiled at Stefanidis who spoke limited English and only saw that she was pale and charming in that awkward, rather graceless English way.

'Lucy, really, this isn't the time . . .'

'But it really is desperate. And we've been invited to Mr Lussom's. I'd love to go. I could swim, he says, and I love swimming.'

Harold, seeing Stefanidis smiling – at the youthful appeal in her voice? – did not know himself manoeuvred.

He did not credit her with guile. He felt the appalling heat rising round him from the stones, the baked earth, and the thought of the sea, that lovely house, appealed as instantly as he supposed it had appealed to Lucy.

'Well, I don't see why not,' he said. 'I need Lussom's advice on a few points.' He made it sound as if in seeking advice he was conferring an honour.

I knew I should see him again, thought Lucy. It was as if the oracle had spoken after all. That she was contriving to nudge Fate in her own direction was unimportant, for the inevitable must be inevitable, only needing now and then a small lie, a helping hand, to come about.

'I'm so sorry I interrupted. Are you an archeologist too?' she asked Stefanidis cheerfully, in Greek.

Harold nodded in approval. He believed that in the end he would be quite reconciled to the sensations of fatherhood.

# 3

Adam rang.

'Hi, Gran. Heard the news?'

For a moment Lucy's heart lifted. What was it? A prize? A merit for maths, consistent effort, the hundred metres?

'News, darling?'

'Dad's swanned off and left us.' He used the old-fashioned phrase carefully as if he hoped to elicit more sympathy, while still keeping his voice cheerful, showing he did not really need it.

'Your mother told me.' Lucy felt her heart sinking back, sinking lower.

'Mother's in a state, isn't she?'

'You'll have to expect that.' Damn Laura, she thought, disregarding the only piece of advice worth taking. She must have rung the school after all.

'I suppose . . .' The assumed lightness of tone had vanished. He sounded gruff, his voice breaking back into a croak of uncertainty. 'Gran, could I come and stay when we break up?'

'Of course.' But then, remembering, she found herself forced to add gently: 'If I'm not in Greece, darling.'

'Oh, I'll come to Greece,' said Adam.

\*

'You wouldn't think a fifteen-year-old boy would want to spend time with his grandmother,' Lucy remarked to Turk. It was still raining and she could not garden. A fine persistent rain. . . We might be in the West Country, thought Lucy, recalling her honeymoon under low blankets of cloud, the grey, determined drizzle.

'He has fun with you. And you don't nag him all the time.'

'Oh, I could understand it when he was eight. Or even twelve. But he's a man now. Almost.' He has to shave once a week, she thought, and he has those large, knuckly, young man's hands, so moving for no reason at all.

'You represent security.'

'I try to. I don't always feel as if I do.'

'And it's not only Adam who depends on you.'

'Being depended on is sometimes like being crucified,' said Lucy.

'You encourage them.'

'I only listen.'

'But you *always* listen. And when I point out how they depress you with their troubles you say that's what mothers are for or some shit like that. Oh, I know, I've needed you too. I've leaned and you've propped, God knows how many times. But . . .'

'I thought you generally propped me. Anyway, it all started when I was Adam's age and had no proper family and went from friend's house to friend's house like a perambulating poor relation. Caroline – you remember Caro – had the most marvellous parents, so funny and affectionate. They treated me like another daughter. I think they understood about Father, what he was and what I wanted him to be. They knew from the start I'd be disappointed so they made sure I knew their family was my family. . . what was it? That I could lean and be propped. And I thought, one day, one day I'll have a family of my own and then . . .'

At any moment Bernadette might ring with more questions about Greece, about Oliver. She would keep on until she had all the missing pieces, the whole story to which this was just the end. If it is an end, thought Lucy.

Then next day the post brought a pathetic letter from Ginny. She had heard third-hand that her father had run off with someone else's mother. Is it true, she implored Lucy.

'Read that,' and Lucy passed the looping scrawl to Turk. 'The child's in deepest Dorset and somehow gets to know the sexual adventures of half Bishop's Stortford.'

They were having a sandwich for lunch. Turk was still in a dressing-gown and bare feet, looking disreputable, her hair standing up in tufts. The dressing-gown had been left behind by someone years ago and was home-made, a shaped candlewick bedspread, sleeves like bat wings.

'Poor kid. Laura's neurotic, you know.'

'I don't think Laura's anything to do with this,' said Lucy, touching the letter where it lay, a sad scrap, by a dish of tomatoes.

'Why did Christopher marry her?'

'I don't remember. They were in love, of course.'

'You had misgivings at the time.'

'Yes. Perhaps.' Lucy cast back and back to those pre-wedding weeks. The weather had been oppressive, lightning at mid-morning, a terrible humidity, only a few drops of rain, hard and huge. 'Chris was like a man bewitched. D'you remember? He scarcely ate.'

'No, I don't remember.'

'He said . . . he said he couldn't wait.' Now, so long after, she could not get into the words the intensity of feeling they had once expressed.

'I don't suppose they did,' said Turk. 'Waiting went out in the sixties.'

'No, not sex. It wasn't to do with sex. It wasn't that sort of possessing.' It was as if Chris believed, thought Lucy, that with the marriage vows he would enter into a sacred guardianship of this creature who was his whole concern.

She had been so appealing, a lovely lost child, confused by the early deaths of her parents and a piecemeal upbringing tossed between relations and school. In those days her prettiness had had an elfin quality. She had worn flowered Indian dresses, left her long hair loose. She had clung to Christopher with what Lucy feared was only pathetic gratitude as the drowning, in need, cling to whatever seems solid.

But marriage is not a heavenly guardianship, she thought. It's bloody hard work.

'Ginny love,' she said down the phone to the school. 'I'm sorry they had to winkle you out of lunch but I've just had your letter and it worried me.'

'Oh, I don't mind. I've got a match this afternoon. I ought to miss pudding anyway or I'll never be able to run for the ball.'

'Darling, I don't think Daddy's gone off with anybody else. He just doesn't want to live with your mother any longer.'

'Polly said . . .'

'But how could Polly know? Darling, be sensible.'

'Polly's mother's friend used to work for Daddy's firm.' It came out in a sing-song as if she had learnt it by heart.

'Oh,' said Lucy, taken aback. 'Used to,' she emphasized. 'She doesn't any more then. So how could she know?'

'Well . . .'

'I just wanted to tell you not to worry. You'll see Daddy in the holidays.'

'Shall I?'

'Of course.'

'But not at home?'

'Probably not. Wherever he's living. Or here.'

'That would be nice,' and Ginny brightened. She could see the hands of the headmistress's clock beside the phone ticking on towards match time, a match she knew she could win if only a few balls were sent to her wobbly

40

backhand. The thought of avoiding the inevitably grim atmosphere at home and spending time with Lucy, her father making a surprise visit, made her light-hearted again. I *will* win, she thought.

'Laura ought to be shot,' said Lucy bleakly to the wall, putting down the receiver.

Bernadette, whom Lucy seldom saw these days, arrived in the middle of the drinks party.

'What's going on?' she asked Turk who answered the imperious pealing of the bell dressed in a white silk vest that finished a long way above her knees.

'What d'you suppose?'

'Are you going to let me in?' She thought: What an outfit for a woman her age.

'Bernie, how lovely,' and Lucy was there, leaning to kiss her cheek. The room behind was full of people, the clink of glasses, exclamation, laughter. Lucy was in a dress of purplish splendour. It was not a colour Bernadette associated with her mother. It occurred to her that she had not seen Lucy partying since Maurice died and had supposed she never did.

'I haven't called at a good time, have I?' she said without contrition.

'Couldn't be better. It's only a lunchtime fling. I cram everybody in and let them get on with it and they all leave as soon as they feel hungry. All I can manage in my old age.' She smiled at Bernadette. She might have meant it.

'Mother . . .'

But Lucy had caught a short, bald man by the elbow. 'John, you remember Bernadette.'

'Little Bernadette?' He swivelled, snatching his glass out of someone's way, suddenly looking startled as if he had not expected a middle-aged woman.

'I'm afraid I wasn't expecting a party,' said Bernadette weakly. He put a glass of wine in her hand. He introduced her to a woman called Alicia who spoke at length on anthropology and dishwashers. There seemed no obvious means of escape.

'Years since I saw you. What are you doing with yourself these days?' John asked.

'I'm thinking of taking Holy Orders.'

He blinked, drew breath. A moment ago he had been remembering her running naked in and out of her paddling pool, a child of three or four.

'Well, I admire you,' he said.

'I wish Mother did.'

'But Lucy's not religious, is she? She can't have any objection.'

'Oh no, she hasn't any objections. She's completely indifferent.'

He wished she were easier to talk to, more relaxed, a little flirtatious perhaps. He wished she suited his party mood.

'Roger,' and he shot out a hand, 'Roger, this is Lucy's daughter. Look after her while I get a refill.'

'Oh, God,' said Turk across the room. 'I'd better go and rescue Roger.'

'Is that Bernadette?' asked Lucy's friend Nina, peering. 'Darling, how grim she looks. And overweight.'

'Nina . . .'

'Can't I speak the truth after all these years? What are friends for?'

'Even friends must be careful how much of the truth they ever tell,' said Lucy.

In the next half-hour she was aware of her daughter beached here or there, holding a glass, not drinking, hardly speaking. The dark, heavy face did not smile. I suppose she's mine, I suppose I gave birth to her, Lucy thought, but although she cast her mind back she remembered only the moment after delivery, the tiny, screeching thing, black hair smeared into peaks.

People were drifting away, talking about lunch. The front door opened and closed, opened and closed.

'Mother, you look terribly pink,' accused Bernadette when the house was theirs at last. She had only just seen the collection of empty bottles on the kitchen table.

'I need to sit down,' said Lucy. She swept up some leftover edibles and sank into one of the armchairs exiled to the dining room. She kicked off her shoes.

'This can be my lunch,' she announced.

'But Mother . . .'

Here we go, thought Lucy. She put something into her mouth at random. Chewing, she could keep silent, could refuse the challenge. She was sorry not to have a happier relationship with Bernadette but . . . but. We're so different, she thought. The difference often seemed so monumental that there were no words to express it. From an early age Bernie, taking her cue from Christopher, had seen that her mother needed restraining, tidying. 'You never finish anything,' she had exclaimed once, finding half a knitted sock and an incomplete recipe for game pie in Lucy's sewing basket. For a perilous moment, indignant but still amiable, Lucy would bow to convention. She would abandon the eccentric hat she had been going to wear for speech day, would dust the many places Mrs Treece avoided, would buy sober shoes with low heels. But then . . .

'I've never seen you in purple before,' Bernadette said, watching Lucy eat two smoked salmon rolls at once. 'Green. You always used to wear green.'

'Not all the time.'

'When I was small you did. Turquoise. Emerald. At school I always knew where you were. Everyone else's mother seemed so dull.'

Dull, safe, anonymous . . . What agonies of embarassment I caused, Lucy thought. In photographs Bernadette looked solemn and anxious, a passive child who enjoyed routine.

'How's Chloë?' Another anxious child, Lucy felt.

'That's why I came. It's about Chloë.'

'She's all right?'

'I think so. Apart from wanting time out to rush off to Chile or Brazil or somewhere. There's this boy . . .'

'Nice?' Lucy brushed crumbs from her lap.

'Nice? I don't know. I haven't met him. But he's unsettled her. She's changed.'

'Love is generally unsettling,' Lucy said. Her toes ached. The new shoes? She wondered where Turk had gone. Turk never liked Bernie much, she thought, not even when Bernie was quite young and unobjectionable. 'You know, if you want something to eat you'll have to look in the fridge. Or the cupboards. I've an appointment with Whybrow this afternoon.'

Whybrow was the solicitor. Bernadette sat down suddenly in another of the heaped-together chairs and looked interested.

'About Greece?'

'Partly.'

'What an extraordinary thing to do, leave you a house.'

'Was it?' Lucy ate a little crescent crowned with gherkin.

'Did *you* make them?' Bernadette was moved to ask. They looked Lucyish, ill-formed and brightly coloured, a culinary mishap.

'Good heavens no. Turk orders them from that place in Trinity Street. Or is it Bridge Street? They're usually very good.'

'Mother, you aren't really thinking of going to Greece? The heat will be unbearable. And there'll be tourists everywhere. I hoped you might ask Chloë down . . .'

'We've been through this.'

'Tell her the degree's important.'

'But perhaps it isn't.'

'I've found another tray of those bloody crab puffs,' Turk announced, coming in with it in her hand.

'It's this boy . . .'

'Have one,' and the tray was thrust at Bernadette.

'Bernie dear, she's a woman now. She has to choose for herself.'

Bernadette did not think of Chloë as a woman. Even now she saw her with a brace, eating egg sandwiches by the rockpools of Cornish holidays.

'I don't know who he is,' she said. 'He isn't at the university. I don't know where she met him.'

'These things all happen in their due season,' said Lucy. She thought Bernadette, who rarely wept, might have done so if Turk had not been in the room. She would never weep in front of Turk.

'What things?'

'Well,' and Lucy licked her fingers, 'colic and measles and crises over the tooth fairy forgetting, and then later the false friends, the spots, the will-he-ask-me-out-won't-he evenings. Next it's love affairs and marriage and children. And miscarriages, fibroids, divorce.'

'Oh, Mother.'

'It probably won't come to anything,' said Turk. She had counted twenty-four crab puffs. They would have to eat them for supper.

'But it's something already.'

Poor Bernie, thought Lucy. She suspected she would make the worst kind of mother-in-law, always obtrusive while constantly declaring she would hate to interfere.

'Marianne, is there any of the wine left?'

'A bottle under the sink. I saved it.'

'We'll open it then. It's just what Bernie needs.'

'But Mother . . .' began Bernadette.


'She always wore you out,' said Alan. He had taken Lucy for lunch in the rather fashionable little restaurant only yards from her front door.

'Mentally yes, absolutely.'

'Physically too.' He could remember periods in his childhood when Lucy had had daily tussles with Bernadette and, at the closing of the door, had folded up into a chair as if wounded. 'Oh, Bernie's always been a nuisance,' was all Christopher said. 'The quiet ones always have the worst tempers when roused,' pronounced Mrs Treece who watched it all with interest. For a child once alarmingly religious – 'Spiritually absorbed' Maurice called it, rather amused – Bernadette grew alarmingly wild as a teenager. Lucy thought: Wait till you have children of your own, then you'll find out what this is like. Just wait. But for now it was she who waited, for the storm to pass, for the elements to be subdued. Constant tantrums, outrageous behaviour, all-night parties . . . 'She's barely seventeen!' Maurice cried when Lucy tried, unsuccessfully as usual, to bridge the gaps. At seventeen *he* had collected beetles. He had been on a walking tour with his father.

Then suddenly, as if youth were cut off with scissors, Bernadette was twenty and married. Too young, warned Lucy's inner voice. She was beset by new fears. What next? she wondered. They were still in stormy waters. What seemed to Maurice blessed calm might only be the long, smooth swell preceding the typhoon. In the church Lucy prayed, in spite of being certain no God was listening. After the wedding Mass, so stultifyingly long in such heat that they felt they had crossed deserts step by painful step, she found she could barely walk. It was Turk who held her up as she tottered into the dusty amber afternoon. She was aware only of distant thunder, Bernie leaning to be kissed, David's anxious young face.

'Ma, you're miles away,' Alan reproved. It was typical of Lucy to behave like this, he thought. In restaurants, at college gatherings, any important function, she would suddenly go off into a trance. And what was it she was looking at? Future or past?

'Oh, I was thinking of Bernadette. Thinking of the accident. Poor David. And Bernie growing more and more religious, just how she used to be at eleven or twelve.'

'That sums it up nicely. She's never behaved like an adult.'

'I wish I knew what sort of life she really wants.'

'She doesn't. How could you?'

'I don't know what any of you want.'

'It's only Bernie who goes in for morbid soul-searching. She takes everything so seriously.'

'And you don't. Or you pretend not to.' Lucy straightened the cutlery, smoothed the cloth. She did not look at him. 'The job doesn't give you much pleasure, does it? And you don't have much luck with women.'

'What a funny thing to say.' He felt a sudden alarm.

'Of course, it's none of my business.' She smiled at the waiter as the salmon arrived.

Alan watched her. She was indestructibly Lucy and his mother. She never changed. As the thought came and went he saw her hands picking up knife and fork. They were square and large. In his childhood they had always been a little roughened because she dashed at the housework Mrs Treece side-stepped and never bothered with gloves. Also she sewed and gardened and frequently, for Maurice proved incapable, wielded hammer and saw, patched plaster, wallpapered. Now they were ageing, the veins more prominent, a little rash of liver spots across the knuckles. In the past they had soothed or smacked him and now he found they startled him, reminding him of his mortality.

'I'm sorry,' Lucy said. 'I sound like a miserable old woman. Bernie's turned me sour. It'll pass off in a while.'

'Isn't it to do with testosterone or something?'

'What?'

'Old women growing aggressive.'

'It's Bernie, not hormones, in my case.'

He laughed but he was unsure. He didn't think her distraction was only caused by Bernadette.

'You're just tired,' he tried. 'When I rang, Marianne told me you'd had forty people to drinks yesterday.'

'And Bernie. She positively goggled with disapproval.'

'I can imagine.' He could. He added, not meaning to be unkind: 'Have you noticed she sounds just like Father when she's sermonizing?'

Lucy smiled. Her son smiled back. For the briefest moment they heard Maurice's voice, a little hooting in middle age as he grew slowly deaf.

The waiter removed the debris of the salmon.

Alan said, 'Tell me about this place in Greece.'

'There's nothing to tell.'

'But you've been there?'

'Years ago. Nineteen fifty something. Years.'

He could not tell if she were being deliberately evasive. Her manner was often vague.

'Mother, why did he leave it to you?'

Now he had grown serious she studied him seriously. He had a lean, strong face, a good pronounced nose. His dusty-looking hair sprang up untidily. She could recall brushing it and brushing it when he was quite little, with no effect whatsoever.

'I don't know,' she said.

'But you must know.'

She saw, across the room, the waiter carrying her strawberries. 'You know, I hadn't seen the man for decades. Not since I was nineteen.'

'That makes it all the odder, doesn't it?'

'Of course I'd heard from him.' She received the plate of strawberries with another charming smile, picked up her spoon. 'There were letters.'

'You wrote to each other. All this time. And you never mentioned it.'

'Should I have? I don't expect you to tell me every time one of your friends sends a postcard.'

'It must have been more than postcards. He left you his house, didn't he?'

The strawberries were sweet and full of flavour. Like mine from the garden, thought Lucy, pleased. She heard someone three or four chairs away cry 'Gazumped!' with extraordinary passion. Then there was a sudden clatter as if something had been dropped in the kitchen.

'When I was a child,' she said, 'I used to think that might be the chef laying about him at the scullions.'

'In a modern restaurant?' And Alan laughed.

'Why not? In France once I saw a waiter run amok with a broken bottle. Even the local gendarme retreated before him. Monsieur Bonneaux said someone must have criticized the way he served the quail.'

Alan watched her scrape the last of the strawberries from her bowl and wished, as he had often done as a child, that his mother had not spent so much of her life in France with Margot's family, becoming so French in her eating habits. He could imagine her picking up the bowl and licking it. She would have done so in the kitchen at home.

'How solemn you look,' she said.

'I still don't understand your relationship with Lussom.'

'Relationship. What a cumbersome sort of word.'

The coffee arrived. Opportunely, thought Alan. He had felt the sudden pricking of nerves that told him there was dangerous ground ahead.

'Mother, they're not all for you,' as Lucy raided the little dish of mints.

'But I shared everything with you when you were small, always had nothing myself or the smallest piece. Now you're grown up you'll have to fight if you want any, I'm going to indulge myself.'

He tried to look amused. It was not like Lucy to be mischievous. He looked gravely at her familiar face, the soft grey hair pushed loosely, impatiently away from the high forehead, those hands now busy unwrapping silver foil. At the beginning of lunch he had thought he knew her so well she could hardly surprise him. Now he found her a mystery.

'Darling,' she said. 'I didn't mean it. Have a chocolate. You look quite strange.'

He received a mint into his hand. 'You wrote to each other,' he repeated. 'Often?'

'Often enough, I suppose.'

The mint tasted oddly bitter, not quite as he had expected. A foretaste of things to come, he joked grimly to himself. For he was touched by a premonition that from now on everything would be subtly different and that nothing he had counted normal would remain so.

# 4

OF course it wasn't Sofia who was allowed to help Lucy choose new clothes in Athens. 'Good heavens,' said Harold. 'Sofia's only a village woman.' He made arrangements with the Fieldings who lived in the very shadow of the Acropolis.

'I'd really rather have Sofia,' Lucy protested, appalled at the thought of exposing her underwear to strangers.

'But what would everyone think if I sent you with Sofia? She's never been further than Kiparissia.' Harold sounded affronted. It was really for Sofia to be affronted, Lucy thought.

Nikos drove her to Athens. It was a long hot journey but Harold had imposed a time limit, there could be no lingering, either for food or for love-making. For a while Nikos tried to talk to her over his shoulder but neck-ache and the state of the road defeated him. Lucy ate her lunch out of a paper bag. The hours passed.

The Fieldings lived in the Plaka, in part of a very old house. Edward Fielding was in Greece to sell tractors to Greek farmers, an improbable task, Lucy felt, demanding iron optimism. And, like the tractors, the clothes Bunny Fielding picked out were too dear and too sophisticated.

Even the shop women, anxious for sales, shook their heads.

'I don't think so,' Lucy said each time. She felt exhausted by the effort to be polite. Her face flushed, her hair tangled, she grew damp. 'I don't think so,' reject after reject. But what really saved her was that she truly did look awful, like a child dressing up.

'No, I don't think so either,' sighed Bunny. She still struggled to appear bright and interested and hopeful but it was a failing struggle. She wished she were sitting on her bed lighting a cigarette, easing off her shoes.

In the end Lucy went out alone and came back with the simple dresses, the shirts and skirts she needed.

'I'm sorry you and Mrs Fielding didn't get on,' said Harold. The joy of the English language was that 'get on' in this instance could have been interpreted any one of three ways, possibly more.

'But we did,' Lucy felt obliged to insist. 'I like her. She's very kind. It was just . . . she didn't know what suits me.'

Plain things suited her, and bold colours. In later years there would be egg-yolk yellow and the turquoise and viridian that caused Bernadette such anguish. Now there was primrose and almond and white. 'Lovely, lovely,' exclaimed Sofia, unpacking. 'Charming,' said Harold, relieved to see nothing outlandish. She wouldn't disgrace him, he thought, though there was still the faint suggestion of English schoolgirl. Her eyes shone with a schoolgirlish excitement, he noticed, when he told her they were going to Paleochora for a week.

'There'll be other people staying, of course,' he added regretfully. 'He always liked big house parties.'

'Archeologists?'

'Or actors. Diplomats. Journalists. Who can tell?'

'Don't you like him, Father?'

'Like him?' Harold sounded surprised. 'He's brilliant in his field, you know. Brilliant.'

'Poh!' cried Sofia later when Lucy found her dipping a pot into the runnel of water that was the house's only supply. 'A week of luxury. Maids. Hot baths. You won't want to come back.'

Perhaps not, thought Lucy.

When the car had climbed the hill and had drawn up by the steps, the silence was broken by the whirring of insects, nothing more. The door opened on a cool and empty interior beyond which the terrace overlooked the deserted bay. Lucy, stunned by the step from light to shade, saw the man enter there even as she blinked, saw him hesitate even as she was doing.

She felt the by now familiar heat. He's too old, she admonished herself again, too old, too old. But when he reached her and she looked up shyly, holding her breath, he wasn't any age. He was simply a man with whom, unaccountably, she had fallen in love.

The sea floor was undulating sand and small round pebbles. Lucy dived down and down until her lungs ached, and then burst upwards into the sunlight, gasping.

'Lucy's having a wonderful time here,' Harold remarked, gazing down from the terrace at the small speck in the water.

'I hope so. She hasn't had much fun recently, has she?'

'I find it difficult to know how to entertain her.'

'Oh, I didn't mean since she came to Greece,' said Oliver mildly. 'I meant Edith's death. Such a miserable illness, all those weeks in hospital. And she'd only just left school, left her friends.'

'Friends?' Harold had never thought of friends. 'Well . . . but she left school *last* summer.'

'And spent the next six months – seven, eight? – in sick rooms, one nursing home or another.'

'I sometimes think all she did at school was a bit of tennis and some singing.'

'Friends are important.'

'I've no doubt. But girls that age . . .' He realized again he knew nothing of girls that age. Besides, of Lucy's friends he had met only Margot, plump, sunny Margot who spoke English with a French accent and French with an English one. He had not cared for her. He could not conceive of her being important in any way, more important than parents, than Edith. And the dying Edith had the right to command her daughter's attention. In such circumstances friends must wait, quite naturally disregarded, not even allocated walk-on parts. Harold's feelings on this point demonstrated his attitude both to friendship and to family obligations. He would never have acknowledged that Edith had shied firmly away from motherhood in almost all its aspects, that he himself had consistently avoided all responsibility but the paying of bills.

It was four o'clock. He had not slept after lunch. He had discussed the site, the implications of its exposure. As usual, Lussom had deflated his balloon of enthusiasm. He disputed dates. Small things but irritating, as sandflies are irritating and eventually drive one to quit the beach. Harold told himself he valued the man's opinion but he had always had trouble with opinions that didn't coincide with his own. As in the case of parenthood he made quite wild assumptions, one of which was that a younger generation never ought to question the wisdom of the Grand Old Man.

'I must doze, dear boy,' he said. No, I don't like the fellow, he thought. He lowered himself into one of the accommodating wicker chairs and closed his eyes, showing that he meant business, he meant to sleep.

After a while he certainly appeared to be asleep. Lussom finished smoking and left the terrace. One of the maids crept out and crept away again. In the silence hardly an insect stirred. But Harold's eyes opened now and then to stare at the thick canopy of vine leaves overhead. He was genuinely weary but his brain refused to compose itself, to accept oblivion. He thought of his site, the work to be done. Years of work. Years of dispute? This ridiculous tussle about dates ... well, the truth would be dug up eventually. He would be proved right. Or wrong?

There was no wind. The vine leaves did not stir. His eyes opened on them and closed and opened again.

Indignation was no soporific.

Oliver had gone down to the beach. Quite far out Lucy was bobbing by the rocks, treading water. She must have seen him but she seemed intent on her own pursuits, ducking under, coming up in a flurry of splashing, vanishing suddenly round the point.

'You've been in the water long enough,' he called. In answer she reappeared, or so he thought, but he had no means of knowing if she had really heard, or had heard more than mere sound, no sense attached. Her ears must be full of water, he thought.

But it was a weakness that had overtaken her, as debilitating as cramp. For a moment she doubted she had the strength to swim to the beach. She looked down at her hands, pale and wrinkled from prolonged immersion, and thought they trembled. He was sitting on the sand waiting. He was unavoidable.

'You must be scorched,' he remarked affably as she emerged. He watched as she picked up a towel as if he expected to see her shoulders and thin back red with sunburn. 'You shouldn't have stayed in all that time.'

'I s'pose not.' She could not help it. Her voice came out small and tight,

'I'm sorry. Do I sound like an old nanny?'

'Yes.'

He smiled, lying back. 'And of course you have enough of that from Harold.'

No reply to this suggested itself. She rubbed at her hair. How must it look, lank and darkened? She knew she had spots on her forehead, high up, usually covered by her fringe. She had hoped such imperfections were of a transitory kind but had recently noticed spots on the chin of one of the archeological wives, a woman of thirty-five, a mother. Respite might not come with age, then. She sat cross-legged, the towel round her shoulders. As her hair dried in the sun it would take on a lighter shade. Perhaps the annoying fly-away ends would be gold. Then, thinking she must look undignified, she straightened her legs and leaned casually to brush the sand from them, looking steadfastly out to sea.

She could hear his breathing. Why should his breathing disconcert her? Was he falling asleep? And though her eyes were fixed on the intense blue beyond the rocks she could see the brown of his outflung arm, the white mark where his watch had slipped a little, the short clean nails. Unbearably moved, she shifted an inch, turning her head away.

'Your father's no idea what to do with you, has he?' Oliver said. She was acutely aware he had opened his eyes and was studying her. All he could see, she hoped, was her hair drying into gold feathers.

'He tries hard.' She had no idea why she must defend Harold. It was just a gesture, feeble but none the less required. She had sensed this man's faint contempt. She could not say if it was personal or professional, but it existed. She felt obliged to go on the defensive.

'You're bored to death.'

'I'm not.' She wasn't. 'When the digging starts I'm going to help. Not with digging. With the recording, cataloguing, all that.'

'Will he let you?'

'Why shouldn't he?' But when she had asked him he had been evasive. 'Why shouldn't he?' she repeated.

'God knows. But Harold's a touchy character. Imagination and humility aren't among his virtues.' He was sitting up now. Sitting up he was too close. His hand touched her arm. 'He seems to think you lived in total isolation back in

England, no friends, no social life. What he'd really like is for some obliging male to take you off his hands. It's another way to buy out of responsibility. He stumps up for a wedding, kisses the bride, pats the bridegroom on the back, and hurries back to his digging.'

She said nothing. He had withdrawn his hand but she still felt its touch. Her arm burned where his fingers had passed.

'There's no need for him to feel responsible. I'm supposed to be grown up.' She didn't sound it, she thought. 'I ought to get a job.'

'Doing what?'

'I don't know. Something. Anything.'

'Has Harold any suggestions?'

'No.' She took a breath. Raising her head, she shook her drying hair, parting it with her fingers, letting the sun reach the damp fronds beneath. It was to show him she didn't care, didn't care about the frustrations of her relationship with Harold. Then she spoiled it by saying, 'He won't discuss it.'

Oliver stood up. 'We might as well go up to the house. We're going out tonight, remember? The village's saint's day. There'll be a procession. And dancing and eating.' His hand clasped her wrist, pulled her up. For a moment she felt dizzy. It's so silly, she thought, so silly.

'Hallo,' said Harold as they reached the terrace. 'Did you have a good swim? How brown you look.' Her hair had dried into a tangle. Her costume showed off an angular body, still unfinished. He could keep intact his image of her as a child. But then her voice surprised him, warm and low, as she stooped to kiss his forehead. It was an unexpected gesture too. It was as if an excess of happiness had made her impulsive.

'I saw an octopus,' she said. 'It looked enormous.'

'They live in the rocks,' he told her automatically, unnecessarily. 'You must be careful.'

He did not enlarge on this. It was difficult to know if it

57

was the octopus he warned her against or something else, something undefined, more menacing, that might lie in wait for her. He didn't know himself. It had been Edith's job to spell such things out. He only felt a faint unease, out of which came these ambiguities.

'Be careful,' he said again. He patted her hand.

He was comforted by the thought that such gangling innocence could hardly stir any man's desire, especially Lussom's.

'I always am,' Lucy declared. She was astonished by his warm hand over hers.

He had never seemed affectionate before.

The village was all coloured lights, candles, torches and tinny music.

'We can eat and watch the procession go by,' Oliver had said, leading them to the most prominent restaurant where, naturally, they found him a table although all the tables had been booked for this particular night for weeks. Did he often come here, Lucy wondered. And if so, with whom?

'Many women. There are many women,' Aphrodite the maid had told her, making her bed while Lucy brushed her hair.

'What sort of women?'

'Oh, women.' None were safe, she implied. 'Once there was a lady professor. And one was the mistress of a minister.' She yanked the sheet taut and tucked it under. 'English, Americans, Greeks, French.'

But where did all this go on, Lucy thought. In his room under the noses of the ignorant husbands? On the beach, within sight of the terraces? Though she wanted to know everything about him she didn't really want to know everything about this, it seemed dishonourable, even sordid. She hoped it wasn't true, but even part of it being true might rock this precarious happiness. As Aphrodite spoke she felt herself falling.

But: I don't care about other women, she told herself. In the adult world one had to put up with a few such imperfections just as one had in childhood. They were simply different imperfections. In the long run, with luck, they would prove as unimportant.

The food was excellent. There was celebratory wine. Even Harold grew flushed and expansive. The carnival atmosphere, the passing floats and holy images, encouraged casual applause and casual participation. It had never occurred to Lucy that religion could be cheerful. The good-natured crowds, the candles held aloft, the prayers, were a revelation. She thought how Rev would enjoy it instead of his stark formal services, the dreary hymns, long intervals balanced awkwardly on the moth-holed kneelers.

'You remember Caroline?' she asked Harold. 'We were at school together.' Right from the beginning, she might have said, eight-year-olds in stiff new tunics tied with the yellow house sash. St Edmund's. Who was St Edmund? Still, she had been drawn to Caroline by his yellow, shining out in a sea of blue and purple. St Thomas's? St Catherine's? In a week or two, like the senior girls, they would talk about Eddie's, Tom's, Kate's. That first day fright and ignorance stuck their tongues to the roofs of their mouths. They could hardly get out the words of the hymn. They were overwhelmed by instructions. Someone, beyond shame, was sobbing at the back. Lucy and Caroline, sharing the sash, sharing the hymnbook, sharing the clutching anxiety, were happily to share a class and most things ever after.

'I don't recall . . .' began Harold. He knew none of her friends. He would probably forget he had even met Margot.

'Her father was a vicar,' Lucy said.

'I don't think so.'

'You met them at Mother's funeral.'

59

Then he most certainly would not remember. He shook his head firmly. It seemed extraordinary to him that there should have been strangers at Edith's funeral.

His amnesia disconcerted Lucy. It also deprived the remark she had been going to make of its point. If he refused to remember Rev it would be silly speculating on Rev's probable delight in a Greek holy festival.

'You mustn't let Harold snub you,' Oliver told her as they walked in the wake of the candles to the main square.

'I didn't know I had been,' she replied, but it sounded so naive she added quickly, 'He's hopeless about names and faces.'

'When he chooses to be.'

The press of onlookers was unbearable. There was a band, some singing, several priests. Lucy was saved from being swept away by Oliver drawing her into the shelter of his arm.

'They hold a service on the beach,' he said.

'They're all so happy.' Yes, Rev would approve.

'Aren't you?'

'Yes.' She had never known happiness shot through with so much anguish. Desire and dread seemed inextricably mixed.

'Don't let Harold put you down.'

'I don't know what you mean,' she said and then, because she sensed again that hidden current of contempt: 'You don't like him.'

'Look. Harold among his ruins is superb. Self-opinionated beyond belief, but superb. Anywhere else, coping with everyday life, being a father, he's little better than a baby. I don't have to like or dislike him to see that. So leave him where he's happy and go off and make a proper life for yourself doing something you want to do. Don't hang about here waiting for his permission, or his blessing, or for a sign he's going to make up for twenty years of neglect. He couldn't if he tried. It's too late now. Accept the fact he's got nothing to give you, pack your bags and move on.'

It was as if one of Harold's columns had toppled, crushing her. She could not breathe for a moment. She thought she must cry.

'I'm sorry,' said Oliver. He slid his hands up her arms and drew her back against him. 'Poor Lucy.'

'I thought you'd been trampled to death,' said Harold, emerging from the crowd with his panama askew and his stick held before him in exaggerated self-defence. He thought Lussom, gamely holding on to Lucy to stop her being stampeded away, looked oddly solemn. And Lucy looked solemn too, and tired. But then she had swum for at least an hour this afternoon and in all that heat.

'I think we've seen all we want to,' he said. 'Perhaps we should make our way back to the car.'

# 5

ALAN, propped on one elbow, ran a finger down the spine of the girl in bed beside him.

'Suppose someone left you a house in Greece . . .'

'I'd go and live in it.' No hesitation.

'Even if you were in your sixties?'

'Christ!' She laughed then, and smothered the laugh in the pillow. She could not imagine being sixty. Although she squinted into the future she could not see herself so far away, not from this angle, the angle of age twenty-one and horizontal in this man's bed. 'Well . . .' she conceded at last. At least she sounded as if she meant to give the problem some serious thought. 'I suppose it depends.'

She turned over, putting her hands behind her head and staring at the ceiling. He gazed at her perfect young breasts but dared not touch. He felt as inhibited as he had trying to see Bernadette through the bathroom keyhole in the days when a naked sister was all the nakedness he was going to get. He remembered the dread of being found there by Lucy, by Mrs Treece. He remembered the fury at seeing nothing, or a passing pinkness of steamed flesh which was as good as nothing. And afterwards Bernadette, who had heard him there, put soap in his eyes.

'Depends on what?' he asked. This girl liked him to look at her. He continued to look but not to touch, which met with her approval.

'Well,' she said again. He leaned closer and thought about kissing her cheek, but kissing her cheek might be interpreted as a gesture of affection. She had not asked for affection. She did not appear willing to receive any. He leaned away again. Last night she had frightened him with her humourless, controlled response. In the daylight frightened seemed too strong a word, but he could only substitute appalled. Hardly better really. He could not come to terms with her clinical attitude: to her body, to his, to sex itself. There was no mystery. She made the right moves, allowed him to make his, and waited for the inevitable outcome.

And Alan had always hoped his love-making might make women happy.

'So what do Greeks do with their old people?' asked the girl suddenly. Perhaps she felt she had been stared at enough.

'I don't know. They stay in the family probably. In the old days . . .' He was aware the surest thing about the old days was that they were old. Perhaps now, even in Greece, the elderly needed home helps and hip replacements and sheltered housing. Perhaps everywhere family ties were loosening, or had broken.

'So? Is there a family? I mean, sixty's fine but what about seventy, eighty?' She wrinkled her nose as if old age was something she could smell, even at such a distance.

'Eighty?' He could not imagine Lucy at eighty. It would have to creep up on him so that he grew used to it before he realized . . . before Bernie rang and said, 'What'll we do for Mother's eightieth?' He thought of Lucy's tall, angular figure crouched, scrubbing a floor – which was an odd vision to pluck from memory for Lucy had rarely done such a thing. And since Mrs Treece had died only Turk

63

had ever picked up a scrubbing brush. He said: 'She does have a family. In England.'

'That's not much good then, is it?' The young voice was relentless.

'No. No, it isn't.'

He wondered if he could slip his hand . . . but no. He didn't feel he could perform again to such exacting standards, text-book standards, time allowance implicit, no scope for diversions. There would be no warmth, only the body heat of physical exertion. She would not smile. Does all your generation take sex so seriously, he wanted to ask, as if it ought to be done because it's good for you, like working out with weights or eating high fibre cereal.

'So you'd sell the house?' he asked. His mind looped back to Lucy. He recalled that never once, all the years he had observed them together, had he ever been aware of the slightest sexual desire between his parents. But that's probably normal, he thought. And anyway, that was *that* generation.

'What house?' asked the girl.

Lucy couldn't persuade Turk to go with her to Paleochora.

'You don't need a nanny, do you, at your time of life?'

'You haven't been listening.'

'Why should I? You're talking drivel.'

'It would do you good. A real holiday. The book's nearly finished, isn't it?'

'So you keep telling me.'

They were outside, drinking coffee. There was a small paved area under an unstable wooden arch draped with honeysuckle.

'Listen . . .' Lucy began again.

'Are you afraid to go alone?'

Lucy put down her cup. She had never, she remembered wryly, ever concealed herself adequately from Marianne.

'Perhaps I am. I don't know. I haven't been there for so long.'

'Memories?'

'Too many.'

'Good or bad?'

'Good, I think.' But they both knew this was almost irrelevant. Good memories could be as crippling as bad.

'You could always say you don't want it. Or just sell it,' Turk suggested. 'Give the money to some college or other. The Oliver Lussom library or bursary or bicycle shed.'

'How Oliver would laugh,' Lucy said, unexpectedly. It was as if she wasn't really hearing what was said to her, just responding to the pauses, aware it was her turn. 'He'd say I was losing my nerve. He tried so hard to toughen me up.' And once, protect me, she remembered. 'What's it called now? Streetwise. He wanted me independent, self-reliant, streetwise.'

'Which you weren't.'

'Not for years.'

The morning was very still, no breath of wind. They could hear traffic, schoolchildren, a dog barking. Years ago, on just such a morning, she had sat here and told Maurice she was expecting a baby. Which baby? And why such a time and place? She watched Turk pouring more coffee. Strong hands, badly kept nails. Though Lucy's were larger, Turk's hands had always been the stronger, they gripped or shook or held on, held up. Now I know which it was, it was Alan, thought Lucy. It was Alan because he was a shock, I hadn't wanted another. I spent a week thinking how not to have him. Sleepless nights, fright, guilt, resignation. There was no way I could get rid of a baby.

But why tell Maurice under the honeysuckle arch?

'I never understood why you married Maurice,' said Turk as if she read Lucy's mind, spotted him there. 'Why?'

'Because he was there. I thought he was solid and reliable.'

'Solid. Wasn't there anyone else?'

'No. And at the time I needed what Maurice had to offer.'

'But he made you miserable. Anyone could see that.'

'Could they?' Lucy was startled. Had all that carefully concealed unhappiness been visible, after all? 'Well, the children didn't see it,' she said. Had the concealment been for them, then? Or for herself? 'And Chris said Maurice was the unhappy one. He said I never talked to him.'

'There wasn't much to talk about, was there?'

'Besides which,' continued Lucy, her eyes fixed on some distant point, 'besides which, we had rows. Not many, but enough. Rows and then silences, silences and then rows. Chris said it was bloody silly.'

'But he was grown up, flown, snug with his flower child. What right had he to judge?'

But children do judge, Lucy thought. She looked at Turk and wondered what it felt like to be childless, to have missed the bearing, the feeding, the total and constant anxiety, the unquantifiable joy. But one is judged, she thought, and becomes the focus for a legion of vague resentments, for slights and embarrassments, for sins of commission and omission, for scaring away boys, for wearing green at school concerts . . .

'Anyway,' she said ridiculously, 'Maurice is dead.'

The sun was growing too hot. 'There'll be a storm,' said Turk.

'Come to Greece,' Lucy tried again.

'Dear Loo, if you've ghosts to lay run away and lay them yourself. I can't help you.'

'I just meant . . . come.'

'No.' Turk shook her head. 'I'll just stay here, keep the place ticking over. There's the book, remember?'

'Happy ending?'

'Not so you'd notice. You know I don't believe in tying all the knots.'

Is there a knot to tie at Paleochora, wondered Lucy. And will I know what it is after nearly fifty years? Oliver, what have you done? What did you want to do? What did you hope to achieve?

Far away, she heard the phone.

'That'll be Laura again,' Turk said. 'Wanting more psychotherapy.'

'Let it ring,' said Lucy.

Whoever rang, it wasn't Laura. That same moment Lucy poured another coffee, waiting for the faint warbling to stop, Laura was meeting her daughter at the station.

She had been careful to dress for the occasion, to dress down. She had not wanted to look unapproachably smart. She had been undecided for a time and then had settled on dark blue trousers and a shirt. But: Fancy bothering to look so grand just to meet someone at the station, thought Ginny, automatically registering they were new trousers, a new shirt, and that her mother inhabited them stiffly, self-consciously. They were not really Laura's style. She felt Laura's embrace was self-conscious too, as if there was an audience to be charmed and impressed. Rather red, a little startled, Ginny struggled for dignity by pouring into speech.

'Beth was with me all the way. Well, nearly all the way. You remember Beth, don't you? She had her hair cut off this term and she looked so *funny*. You know, funny odd. And Matron kept thinking she was someone else. By the way, don't read my report till this evening unless you really feel strong. I thought . . .'

'*I* thought we'd eat in town,' Laura intervened.

'Do we have to?'

'I thought you'd like to. We could look round the shops afterwards.'

'Shops? Oh, Mummy. I'm in uniform. I don't want to walk round anywhere in *uniform*. I don't know why we have to wear it to come home, it's so childish. Other schools let their boarders leave in anything, but not summer dresses and white socks and *blazers*.'

'But you look so nice,' Laura said thoughtlessly. You look your age, she could have added, not like those frightening waifs, twelve dressed up as twenty, I see every day catching the school bus at the end of the road.

'Nice!' cried Ginny. She was scraping her sports holdall along the platform, walking backwards. 'But who wants to look "nice"?'

I need to tell her about Chris, thought Laura, who had spent all morning rehearsing how she might do so and now found she had apparently missed her cue. Ginny, whose only desire after a term away was to change into old jeans and sit in her favourite tree in the garden until her world had readjusted itself, was obviously mutinous at the idea of lunch in a smart restaurant.

'Do we have to?' she demanded twice while Laura inched into the traffic.

'I thought you'd like a treat, darling.'

But Laura's restaurants, Ginny knew, required too much concentration – to deal with the cutlery, the menu, the eccentric combination of flavours. As she had expected, Laura's only concession was to let her remove the blazer, for the day was stiflingly hot. This still left the indignity of clumping in among a dozen grown-up diners in huge brown sandals and short white socks. Ginny felt herself on fire. Her placid, uneventful life was punctuated by these moments of acute embarrassment, most often caused by her mother. They loomed as large and meant as much as real catastrophes. If not in restaurants then at the tennis club, sailing, buying clothes . . . everywhere she went she was waiting for the instant of humiliation, the stinging in her cheeks, the sense of being diminished. It never got any better. When Adam said, 'Oh, just grin and bear it. You know what Mother's like,' she tried and tried but could not bring it off. She couldn't grin. She couldn't bear it.

Sometimes she knew there was no possibility of bearing it unless she discovered the secret of transmigration: one day she would close her eyes and open them to find herself tall and willowy and seventeen and somewhere else.

'I'll have smoked salmon,' she said. She expected this to please Laura, who often grumbled if she took too long to make up her mind.

'Are you sure?'

'Well, I don't think I like mussels' – and they would be difficult to eat, surely? – 'and the pâté looks strange.' She had seen it pass, prettily arranged.

'Oh, all right,' said Laura.

Ginny sat back. She could sense irritation in the air like electricity. 'You look ravishing,' she remarked. Laura sometimes responded to flattery. 'Rav-ish-ing. Beth says . . .'

So if Laura had hoped to affect the poor abandoned wife, weeping and desolate, she had failed, in spite of the shirt and trousers, in spite of her pointedly subdued greeting on the platform. Ginny was so full of school and the journey and this ubiquitous Beth and Matron and Miss Prickert – was that really the name? – that Laura's quietness passed unnoticed. And now it was smoked salmon and more tales of Miss Prickert – or was it, surely, Pritchard? – and something about a girl called Lettice climbing out at night to meet a boy in Frome.

'I didn't know girls were still called Lettice,' Laura remarked feebly. And she had never imagined girls Ginny's age climbing anywhere to meet boys.

'Well, she is. We call her Sal sometimes, short for Salad.'

'Oh,' said Laura.

After the salmon, rack of lamb. Ginny tackled it as she tackled the warmed-up meat-in-gravy served every Thursday after hockey practice in the winter and tennis practice in the summer. There was about the same amount, she noticed. What Gran would call insufficient for a growing girl.

'How's Gran?' she asked. The carrot strips were abominably hard. She pushed them to the side of the plate.

'Gran? Oh, very well. But darling, there's something I must talk to you about.'

Ginny put down her knife and fork. That was *it*. And it had cost all that money, enough to buy a feast of bacon sandwiches. She and Adam could make some tomorrow evening, take them out to the summer-house and pig in the tarry private twilight between the folded deckchairs, the old badminton nets. She felt she adored Adam. She encouraged the girls at school to droop over his picture. For a day or two a great wave of this pride and affection would sustain them. Then they'd spend the rest of the holidays bickering comfortably, telling Laura they hated each other.

'Ginny . . .' Laura bit her lip. 'Virginia.'

'You mean about Daddy?' Then, scanning the nearest tables: 'I think I'll have that.'

'Have what?'

'That fruity thing.'

Laura didn't bother with coffee. She led the way back to the car. The heat was oppressive. The glass of house wine had given her a headache. Or was it trying to play this unsuitable part that had caused pain? Holding the steering-wheel so that her knuckles showed white, she blurted out: 'Daddy won't be home this evening. He's gone to live . . .'

'Yes, I know.'

Laura wanted to put her head on her arms and weep. 'How could you know?'

'Well . . . it's complicated.'

Ginny was sitting a little hunched, fearing one of Laura's outbursts. Even now there was the red mark on her forehead where her school hat had pressed all that time in the train. Her freckled arms looked painfully thin and her hands were covered in inky messages and had grubby bitten nails. She wasn't the sort of girl to climb out of windows and run after boys in Frome.

'Darling, we'll just have to make the best of it. We're going to have to manage without him,' Laura said, and put a hand lovingly on Ginny's wrist.

But Ginny had not yet abandoned the ruthless logic of the very young.

'*You* are,' she said unkindly.

Lucy was rescuing some scones from the oven, as she rescued most of her cookery, when she heard the front door open. It opened slowly as if someone was being furtive, and there were hesitant footsteps on the tiles.

'Gran, are you there?' called a gruff anxious voice.

'Adam!' cried Lucy.

He looked hot and guilty. 'I caught an early train,' he said off-handedly as if no other explanation could possibly be needed for coming on to Cambridge when he should have got off at Bishop's Stortford.

'But isn't your mother going to meet you? She'll be at the station.'

'Not till twelve-thirty.'

'You'll have to ring her.'

'I suppose so.' He sounded as if he hoped Lucy might take on this disagreeable task. He added: 'All my bags are on the front step.'

She helped him pile them in the hall, then got him a mug of tea.

'I like your hair,' she said. It was extremely short and made him look older, although all his myriad spots were pitilessly exposed.

'I like yours.' He gazed lovingly at her soft, disordered style. No style at all, Lucy would have said.

'You know, I'm flattered you've come to visit, but what are you up to? Your mother won't be very pleased.'

'She said I could stay with you.'

'Yes, but *after* giving her a hallo kiss and five minutes of your time.'

71

'She only wants me there to moan on about Dad.'

Lucy thought this was probably true. She kept what she considered a diplomatic silence, piling her crisp scones on to a plate.

'Bloody books,' said Turk, coming in with a gin bottle in one hand and a wastepaper basket in the other. 'I'd like to retire.'

'Hallo,' said Adam shyly. 'But what would all your readers do, no latest Marianne Cochrane?'

'You here? Why aren't you at school?'

'Term's finished.'

'Home, then.'

'I made a sort-of-diversion.'

Turk threw the empty bottle into the basket for the bottle bank and tipped the paper into the kitchen bin. 'Last ten pages. Twenty times corrected, twenty times condemned. Any fags in the drawer, Loo?'

Lucy opened a drawer in the dresser and revealed a mess of string, scissors, matches, elastic bands and unidentified keys.

'No. 'Fraid not.'

'Then I'll have to go out.'

At the closing of the door Adam looked slightly relieved. He reached for a scone but it crumbled dryly in his mouth, impeded his vocal chords.

'Darling, you're making a mess,' Lucy admonished.

'Can't help it. Mother says . . . Mother said Marianne was a bad influence.'

'On me?'

'S'pose so.' Adam was gummed up with scone and the feeling he was trespassing where he had no business. He felt compelled to go on, however, to see what happened. 'She said there were terrible men always coming and going. And sometimes women.' He glanced up, wiping his mouth, to judge how Lucy was taking it.

'D'you want another before I put them away?' she asked.

'They're like pumice, Gran.' But he took one anyway.

'Turk's private life is entirely her own affair. It always has been.'

Adam mumbled, dropping more crumbs. Once he had accepted Turk without thought, in but not of the family, always there but not necessarily involved, walking on perhaps to shift the scenery. Then Laura's hints had made him curious. He was at the time of life to be curious. He thought her mystery might be contained in her two names, Turk and Marianne, the two sides of her. Innocently, he ascribed the gin and the cigarettes to Turk, the foul language he had sometimes heard, the acerbic exchanges with agents, publishers, journalists . . . He found Marianne voluptuous, licking butter off her fingers after demolishing artichokes, physical, feminine. She was far more feminine – he did not define this at any time – than his grandmother, for instance, who could give a good imitation of the sort of woman who helped build the Empire or explored the Orinoco. Lucy appeared to be holding herself in, or maybe was held in, generally, by some model of emotional corset. Marianne suggested she had no inhibitions worth speaking of. If she was old it didn't matter, he had found. She stirred something in him. He was afraid of her.

He had subdued the scone. It was gradually clearing from his tonsils. He wondered why Lucy, who always seemed so capable, was apparently unable to cook. His mother could cook. She took trouble. If she ever burnt things or they flopped or fell or tipped on to the floor, she must put them in the bin before anyone knew. He had never experienced less than total triumph.

'Dad and Mother don't have a private life at all, do they?' he said, his mind having wandered on. 'When you've got children what you do sort of rebounds somehow off all these other people who have an interest. Ginny and I get in the way really, don't we?' He sounded cheerful about it. After all, it was how it should be. In choosing to have children one accepted such restrictions. He swallowed carefully, testing his inner parts for strayed scone. He wondered if he would now starve till lunchtime and whether he could stay with Lucy for lunch, or whether Laura would swoop down and bear him away to emotional maelstrom and baked beans.

'Do you *mind*?' Lucy asked. He looked quite happy about his father's defection. She thought of it as a defection. Desertion would have suggested malice, intentional and final severance.

'About Dad?' Adam leaned his elbows on the table. Concentrating, he looked grown up. He looked . . . he looks like Father, thought Lucy, astonished.

'Yes.'

'I think I *mind*,' he replied slowly. After all, it affected him, might affect him, in ways he could only guess. There was Laura's hysteria for a start. To avoid it he had already refused to get off a train at the correct station. 'I do mind, but it wasn't unexpected, was it? He'd half gone already, hadn't he? He used to leave for the office so early and come home so late, and for years we've never done much as a family, we've always gone away separately or to friends.' He paused, his blue eyes clouding suddenly as if some memories, in spite of his casual manner, were more painful than he could reveal. 'Mother was always pushing us to go out, join clubs, do things. You know. Poor Gin had to go and play tennis at that awful place down the road. It was always tennis or ballet or swimming or something. And then it was two weeks away with Mother and a week in Cornwall with Dad. Nothing together. It's been like that for ages. Ages and ages. So all this didn't exactly come as a shock.' A thought struck him. 'It didn't come as a shock to you, did it, Gran?'

'No, I don't think so.'

'What I really want . . . ' He touched his spots in a ritual of nervousness, one after the other. 'What I *don't* want is to talk about it. And Mother will talk. You know she will, Gran. Can't you tell her I'm staying here with

74

you for a week or two? She said I could come if you'd have me.'

'Which leaves poor Ginny right in the soup,' said Lucy.

'Gin could come too.'

'Then your mother would be alone.'

But Adam felt and looked unsympathetic. He had walked to the window to make sure the garden was unchanged, and was staring at the washing on the line: underwear, tea-towels, pillow-cases. 'I think she's better without us,' he remarked. He did not enlarge on the meaning of 'better'. He could not have done so sensibly however much he tried. But he knew what he meant. And he knew Lucy knew too, although she only sighed and came to put an arm briefly round his shoulders, a loving and adult gesture, not compelling him, as Laura would have done, into a crushing embrace as if he were still seven years old and not five feet eleven and needing to shave once a week.

'It's peaceful here,' he said.

'Darling, I'm going to Greece next week.'

'Can't I come?'

She looked out, like him, but it was not the garden she saw, not this garden anyway. The memory of Paleochora rose and grew clear, clearer than she had allowed it in years. There was the bay and the fine sand, the cobalt sea, the path climbing between the scratchy aromatic shrubs, the terraces, the big cool rooms.

'Perhaps you can,' she said.

# 6

THE week was almost over. Lucy no longer woke hoping for novelties, surprises. Oliver and Harold shut themselves away every morning, every evening the smoke of their cigars, hanging over the terrace, made her feel sick. They talked and talked, allowing her only a word of her own here and there, like a small child dipping her toes in the ocean.

'What is it they say?' demanded Aphrodite, bringing Lucy coffee. 'How excited they get.'

'Father hates to be told he's wrong,' said Lucy.

Every day she swam before breakfast and again in the late afternoon when the heat had relented a little and the sea was as warm as a bath. She swam vigorously now, no longer bobbing indolently by the rocks. Afterwards she came to collapse on the sand, breathing hard, feeling tearful. From above, she thought, she was just a speck, an unimportant speck. She could imagine Harold remarking with satisfaction: 'How Lucy enjoys it here. A real holiday for her at last.' Pressing her face into the towel she felt the hot tears squeeze out. She drew difficult breaths, suffocating in a smell of sun oil, salt and wet hair. Since the night of the festival Oliver had scarcely spoken to her. Tomorrow more friends were arriving from Athens.

Today is half over already and it's my last whole day, she thought. She had no appetite for lunch. But Oliver said, 'I thought we'd have a boat trip this afternoon. I told you, didn't I, the best way to see the coast is from the water?'

'Yes,' said Lucy.

'We'll leave about three. You'll still be able to swim. We'll find a bay for you. Your very own.'

For a moment she waited for Harold to object. It would be like him to decide to come, to talk and talk . . .

'Good. Off you go. I'll be able to close my eyes in peace,' he said. She wondered afterwards if he had been deceived by the 'we'. Who had he thought was going?

'Are you sure, Father?' she asked.

'Oh, I don't like small boats,' he told her. 'And I like my shut-eye.'


Oliver rowed easily. The water was flat calm. Lucy sat in the stern and watched the silver drops trickle from the oar blades. She did not look up. She avoided looking up for so long that her eyelids ached. She couldn't think of anything she would rather be doing, of anywhere she would rather be. And beyond the bay at Paleochora were other bays, stretches of pale, deserted sand, and out to sea nothing but the distant hull of a fishing boat riding out the long, hot afternoon.

At last there came a small perfect crescent of a beach under a strange jutting promontory.

'Come on,' said Oliver.

The sand was still too hot for bare feet. 'Come on where?' asked Lucy, hopping, pushing up the brim of her hat, wishing she had sunglasses. There was nothing but a goat track through the scrub.

'Up there. Come on. Climb.'

She climbed, but slowly. Perspiration ran into her eyes. Once Oliver reached back his hand but she ignored it, smiling up vaguely to show him the gesture was appreciated but wasn't necessary. After all, she was Harold's daughter. The heat, the stones, the little thorny bushes and stinging, spiky grass were nothing to her. At the summit she stood panting. Not another step, came the brain's instruction, or you'll die. When she had enough breath and her eyes cleared she understood why they had come up here. There were hills, trees, a fishing village along the coast, deep water deeply blue. The boat, drawn up on the sand, looked like a painted toy.

'I like this place,' said Oliver.

When they went back down the sand was less fierce. They swam for half an hour, lazily, quite apart, and they hardly spoke. All the same it was as if he touched her, the preliminary touches, soft and easily mistaken, still a fraction away from the forbidden places.

'I could stay here for ever,' said Lucy.

'You'll come again.' He sounded certain, as if he had already decided for her.

'Shall I?'

In the young hope is vigorous and splendid and sustaining.

The friends from Athens were a bald, self-opinionated little man and his elegant, much younger wife. Lucy, who had been packing, avoided them until almost the last minute.

'And this is my daughter,' Harold announced as she came into the room.

The woman looked Lucy over. She saw a slender, tall girl with brown hair held back by a slide, a clean young face, good clothes. Because such an innocent was obviously not a rival she received a smile with her handshake.

In the car Harold said, 'I can only say I'm glad they arrived when we were leaving.' He was looking out of the window as they turned between the stone pillars into the road. It was not often he showed her his feelings. He reached for Lucy's hand where it lay limply on the seat between them. He thought she looked much older and, most strangely, piercingly unhappy. He vaguely supposed that children felt disappointment acutely.

'All good things come to an end, eh?' he said gently. She nodded, but did not speak.

'Write to me,' he had said, and she had no means of knowing if he meant it or was simply being polite. She waited a day and then wrote a brief note of thanks, putting in a line or two about the dig where some students had arrived and were coping badly with the heat, the food and Harold. And that's that, she thought, as she sealed the envelope. Why should she expect any reply?

'You've grown,' said Sofia.

'That's not possible.'

'You're brown.'

'I've swum every day.'

She glowed. Without and within, thought Sofia. Though she and Makis did not speak, they exchanged meaningful glances. Don't ask me what the old man thinks – he never notices, said Sofia's eyebrows.

Lucy thought: It can't last. It can't. But it seemed to be lasting long enough, making her alternately ridiculously happy and ridiculously unhappy, making her long for a word from him and despise herself for longing.

'More diggers,' Sofia cried every morning now.

'Greeks?' Lucy would ask.

'English.' It was an English dig after all, but Sofia was not quite sure about the English. The young men seemed pale and anxious, awkward, easily burned.

Something, at any rate, was being achieved. They had already uncovered part of a staircase. Lucy walked down to see it early in the morning before the September sun grew too hot. She had expected anything but what she found, a broad, curving marble step of ceremonial proportions.

'What is it?' she asked. 'The entrance to a temple?'

'Maybe,' said Harold.

For a moment she glimpsed the substance of his dream. His city really was under her feet. In this apparent solitude thousands had traded, prayed, fought, cast votes, composed love songs. Yes, she thought, having found one step he must go on and find the next and the next.

'You ought to go and see,' she told Sofia, returning to the house.

'Poh. Old stones,' said Sofia. Then, softly, and with the blank expression of the conspirator: 'There's a letter. It came five minutes ago. Only five minutes.'

He wondered if she could spare a few days to visit Paleochora after the twenty-first. He had to entertain the daughter of a visiting American professor in a house full of elderly academics. The girl would be relieved to see another young face. They could explore the coast, the villages, or simply swim and talk.

But what will we talk about, wondered Lucy.

Harold said, 'That sounds very pleasant, dear.' His staircase was descending to the wrong point in time. He feared Lussom had been right after all. He had been misled by the remains on the surface. He had misinterpreted the clues.

'You don't mind?'

'Not at all. Go and enjoy yourself.'

'Go. Go!' cried Sofia. 'Get away, far away. What kind of life is it for you here?'

'There are lots of young men,' Lucy pointed out. Every day Makis remarked on them, showing his teeth in what she interpreted as a wolfish smile.

'Them!' Sofia dismissed them. 'Dirty clothes. Dirty hair. Trowels. Go. Go. Enjoy yourself while you can.'

'I'm only invited to keep this other girl company,' Lucy reminded her. Anxiety welled up in her: that she would fail in this apparently simple task and Oliver would think less of her for it.

'Someone your own age,' flung out Sofia, already making for the door. 'Someone to talk to. There's no one here for you to talk to, is there?'

Lucy went back to the typewriter where she had been copying some of Harold's notes. She typed slowly, trying to use more than three fingers. After a while, when she felt she couldn't face another word, she laid her arms on the keys and her head on her arms, exhausted.

Love-sick, Sofia would have told Makis, if she had seen.

The car drew up beside a small hire bus. There was no one about.

'There'll be someone here,' Lucy told her driver, getting out. He too got out and stood, looking resigned, finishing off a cigarette.

The front door was ajar. Suitcases were lined up inside on the tiles. She could hear voices in the distance – on the terrace?

'Lucy,' and Oliver was crossing the room to take her hands, to lean and kiss her cheek. 'You're early.'

'Nikos had to take Father to Athens so a boy from the village drove me. We nearly killed a donkey and two old women. He's crazy.'

He had stepped back to look at her. 'You look pale. Has he given you a fright? Look, you'd better come and meet these fossilized old dears. They're just about to leave.'

'But I thought . . .' She was confused, by his closeness, by his words.

'Oh, they're leaving a day early. Something to do with ferry times and flights from Athens.'

'What about the daughter? The American girl?'

Oliver led her out to the terrace where a group of elderly men were talking furiously, as if they must get things said before they were confined in the bus and rendered speechless by dangerous driving, as she had been. They greeted her kindly but conversation barely faltered. They told her she must be proud her father's was a household name. They meant academic households, university campuses, the places they knew best. Voluble to the end, they passed out to where the bus, turned round, loaded, its engine running, waited to hurry them away round hairpin bends.

'The daughter,' Lucy repeated as Oliver came back into the house.

'Miss Schwartz? You *do* look pale and wan. You'd better have a drink. She didn't come.'

'Didn't come?'

'No. After all that she just didn't come.'

It was like Harold's staircase. One descended step by step but not necessarily to the expected destination – simply to an obvious one.

# 7

LAURA left a message at Christopher's office for him to ring her, and when he did she told him Lucy wanted to take the children to Greece.

'Good old Mother,' said Christopher.

'But ...' began Laura who could think of so many objections they could scarcely be separated, tumbling over in her mind, rendering her inarticulate.

'Let her take them,' Chris said. He thought it ironic she had contacted him only to enlist his co-operation against Lucy. As if nothing has happened, he thought, as if we are still living under the same roof. Only a day or two ago she had probably been crying on the phone to Lucy, or sitting weeping at her kitchen table. He could imagine her doing that. Now Lucy had surprised her and she was indignant. The tears had failed her. All the time Lucy had had her mind on something completely different.

'You were always inconsistent,' he said before he could stop himself, thinking the moment the words were out: But she's consistently inconsistent, I'll give her that. 'You told me last time we spoke you'd like someone to take the children for a week or two while you came to terms with

. . . with all this.' He didn't want, he found, to refer directly to the divorce for which he'd just asked.

'I meant a week in Cambridge. Or with friends. I didn't mean Greece.'

'What's wrong with Greece?' And then, aware that after all there might be pitfalls: 'Is Mother going to pay?'

'She says so.'

'Then what's wrong?'

'We don't even know what this house is like.'

'For God's sake, Laura . . . just accept. Say thank-you gracefully, pack the kids' bags, wave them off. Accept.'

Chris had always accepted whatever Lucy had offered. 'Mothers like giving,' he had said to Laura. He seemed unaware such generosity might involve sacrifice or that as an adult he might, with matching generosity, refuse it. He still saw Lucy as the bringer of good things, the bearer of the cornucopia.

'This house,' Laura pursued. In the past it had been she who always complained the summer holidays were too long, who strove to exhaustion to keep the children occupied even when they would far rather have idled about the garden. 'This house could be anywhere.'

'But we know where it is.'

'I don't.'

'It's near Pylos. Well, somewhere near. Up a bit.'

'It's all so mysterious. And I can't seem to get through to Lucy at all. She doesn't listen to what I say.'

'Excited probably, the old darling. Shame she'll have to sell really. But it's as well she gets a bit more cash behind her before . . . you know. Nursing homes. All that.'

'All what?' Laura had been miles away, swimming off a deserted beach somewhere up a bit from Pylos. For one thing she had established, digging facts out of Lucy as Harold Cavendish had once dug them from the unyielding Greek earth, was that there was a beach below the house, a perfect little beach of pale sand.

'Private nursing homes cost the earth. It's as well to be

prepared,' Chris said. 'I'd let the children go. They'll never get another chance, will they?'

Chloë was dressed in black.

'You look like an old woman,' said Lucy, who had given up tact long ago. Of course it wasn't true. No old woman could have such a figure, such legs, such hair.

'Oh, Gran. It's what everyone wears now.'

'Why be like everyone?'

Lucy was clutching a trowel and gardening gloves. At the far end of the lawn Adam was trying to tie the hammock between the two old pear trees, Turk instructing.

'I wasn't expecting you. Your mother said . . .'

'Oh, Bernadette. I can imagine what she'd say. She never listens to what *I* say.'

Chloë's hair was waist-length, fine, very dark. She was very like Bernie, Lucy thought, but in a more insubstantial way. Bernie on her wedding day perhaps, almost ethereal in a cloud of tulle.

'I'm sure she tries. She worries . . .'

'She worries about God,' said Chloë sharply. 'She worries about her relationship with God. She worries if Father Brace has enough to eat. That's all. That's it.'

'You're wrong, darling,' said Lucy firmly. She took Chloë's slightly resisting arm and led her indoors.

'You here too? It's like a family party. I thought you were off abroad,' said Turk, following them in.

'Not yet.'

'God. Widow's weeds.'

'I've already said that,' Lucy told her. She saw Chloë's dark, bewildered look. She had never liked being teased. The air about her prickled with resentment. Had there been a quarrel with Bernadette to bring her here like this without even a phone call to say she was coming? Poor scrupulous Chloë, always so well-behaved, so old-fashioned . . . until now? And should I be glad or sorry I've become a place of refuge, Lucy wondered. She also

85

wondered if sheltering her grandchildren would set her at odds with her children. She received a brief mental picture of Laura's delicate face, the eyes enlarged in appeal. Laura had become her child the moment Chris had brought her home. She'll grow dramatic, she thought, when I ring about Adam. There might be tears of rage. Rage at what, though? Adam, Chris, Lucy?

'May I stay the night?' Chloë was asking. Her voice was a little harsh as if she had already steeled herself to being turned down or only suffered to remain after humiliating debate.

'But of course. Why ever not?'

'I just brought a toothbrush.'

'Fine.'

Upstairs Lucy opened the door to the small guest bedroom, the one in which Chloë had always slept since the cot, pressed back into service for the grandchildren, had been repainted and put up under a picture of Dick Whittington. There was a view straight down the garden and today, in the bright sun, the sash was thrown up so that the elderly curtains billowed in the draught. They could see Adam carefully testing the hammock and then, satisfied, lying back with his arms behind his head.

'It all looks different,' Chloë said.

'There's a new bedspread. That's all. It's years since you slept here, you know. It comes of your mother having moved so close.'

'I suppose so.'

'Adam's bags are only in here for the time being. I don't think he'll be staying, poor lad. I haven't rung Laura yet,' and Lucy glanced at her watch, seeing the hour approaching. 'I really must. Anyway, he can decamp to the Big Front if his mother's going to leave him here.'

'Bernadette told me about Uncle Chris.'

'It wasn't unexpected.' Lucy sounded brisk. She hoped no morals had been pointed, no sermons preached.

'Wasn't it?' Chloë's eyes still scanned the room for

changes. Now and again she stared from the window as if to surprise any in the garden, but the garden looked as she remembered it: roses, delphiniums, white lilies. She had watched her mother playing croquet on that lawn, making a four with Maurice and Lucy and Uncle Alan. She had watched avidly, every movement, every stroke. She had adored Alan.

'It's dreadful at home,' she confessed suddenly. 'You'd think Bernadette would talk to me as if I were an adult. But she doesn't. I might as well be eight. Even younger. We have arguments all the time.'

'About what?'

'Everything. My clothes, my boyfriends, my attitude. My not going to church. Can you believe it? She won't listen when I try to talk about *her* attitude. To me. To everyone else. All this fuss about being ordained. She thinks you don't care what she does and Father Brace will care too much. I said nobody could imagine her as a vicar, it was too absurd. It is, isn't it?'

'Perhaps. Poor Bernie. She needs a purpose in life.' I said this to Maurice twenty years ago, Lucy thought. The same words. Poor Bernie, never happy, never settled. 'I think we need a glass of wine,' she added.

It was as well lunch was cold salmon and salad. I'll just make more salad, Lucy thought. They would have to be frugal with the fish. She hurried Chloë to the kitchen to take her mind off Bernadette and found Turk there already, opening a bottle.

'Laura,' Turk said ominously. Her eyes scarcely flickered towards the kitchen clock.

'I know. And Chloë must ring Bernadette.'

'I shan't bother,' Chloë said. 'She won't care. She thinks I'm staying with Rick.'

It occurred to Lucy she would never get used to this feeling of impotence in family matters. She had once thought mothers, holding all the threads, could weave them smoothly, no rough places, no loose ends. Even as toddlers the children had shown her this was impossible. She held threads but they crossed and broke and spoiled the pattern.

'She does love you, you know,' she said gently to Chloë. The statement struck her as pathetic and not likely to be well received.

'She doesn't show it.'

Lucy assembled glasses.

'May I have one?' asked Adam, appearing on the threshold, flushed and cheerful.

'You're still practically a baby,' said Turk.

He grinned. He realized he was taller than she was, taller than Chloë, taller than his grandmother. He was coming on then. He felt a general satisfaction.

'He'll have to sleep it off in the hammock,' said Chloë, to whom he was still just an adolescent cousin with pretensions.

Afterwards it was Turk who used the word 'swoop' to describe Laura's flying visit to remove Adam. That Adam himself, though silent, was remarkably distressed at leaving wasn't lost on anyone present, even Chloë, who up till then had only treated him with disdain.

'But you'll let him come to Greece?' Lucy asked at the door. She kissed Laura's cheek although Laura tried to avoid it.

'We've been through all that,' was the reply.

'It can't be a problem. They'll be out of your hair for a while. And Ginny would love it. She could swim and walk and read . . .'

'Children don't read any more,' Turk told her when she returned to the kitchen. 'Don't you ever look in the papers? They play with computers and watch videos.'

'Ginny reads. She always has done. She *devours* books.'

'Loo, accept it. Laura doesn't want her children gadding off to Greece. She probably thinks they'll fall off a cliff or get abducted or come home with jiggers.'

'Yet Bernie's probably offering up novenas twice daily in the hope I'll take Chloë.'

'Bernadette never worried herself over salmonella, clap or athlete's foot. And she's never seen you as a bad influence either. Laura worries all the time.'

'Clap seems an outdated word,' was all Lucy said.

She was putting the coffee-maker on the ancient gas stove. It was something she had acquired long ago in France during one of the last holidays with Margot. It was battered now, having made her breakfast coffee for half a century. Dear Margot, she thought. How Laura would have hated your marvellous earthy family, Papa drawing wine from the barrel for us to taste, Louise letting young Jacquot kiss her in the dairy for a bet, five cats in the kitchen, Grand'mère slicing truffles.

At the bottom of the garden the hammock hung limply. It seemed to Lucy an emblem of defeat. She hadn't even, while standing physically between them, been able to deflect the ill-feeling between mother and son. And by now, having negotiated the worst of the town traffic, Laura would be beginning a tirade against Chris while Adam, disgusted, stared woodenly out of the window and Ginny, helpless in the back, bit her nails.

Damn, Lucy thought. Damn. Damn. And there had been no tears of rage but only a dry, trembling anger. Laura's face had been quite white. Her cheek had felt cold and paper-thin. If anything Adam had been whiter.

From the hammock, where she went to sit with a second glass of wine, she could see Chloë at the bedroom window. The girl opened it a little wider and lodged herself on the sill. She had done that at seven or eight, Lucy recalled. In those days someone would have called out to be careful in case she fell, and she would have withdrawn solemnly, biting her lip in vexation. An introverted, secretive child altogether. She had appeared overwhelmed by Bernadette who was so restless, so intense. At family gatherings Lucy had always separated them by the table's length, putting

Chloë next to Alan. She knew Chloë loved Alan passionately.

'Ready for lunch?' she called up now.

'I'll come down.' Chloë waved. For a moment the dark hair swung out over the void. Perhaps there was a smile.

In the kitchen the coffee had boiled. 'Is that for me?' demanded Turk.

'You said you didn't want anything to eat.'

'I might change my mind.' She looked reflectively at the salmon as if experiencing its life battling currents and predators only to end in such ignominy.

Chloë appeared. She looked as if she never smiled. It was my imagination, then, thought Lucy. It was the child Chloë I saw, happy long ago.

'Are you in love with Rick?' she asked.

A startled look, wide, amazed eyes, warned her she had spoken aloud. She had not meant to. She saw Turk's pained expression, heard the soft, exasperated 'Oh, Loo.'

'I don't know,' said Chloë slowly.

'I'm sorry. Of course I shouldn't be so curious.' Lucy busied herself with the food. 'Help yourself. Don't wait for Marianne. She can't make up her mind.'

Chloë sat down, leaned forward. As she did so her hair fell across her cheeks like a curtain, silk, concealing.

Shutting us out, thought Lucy.

The phone rang. Lucy went to answer it. At first nobody spoke.

'Look, you might enjoy this sort of thing but at my age I haven't the time to waste,' she said. She remembered you shouldn't speak to anonymous callers.

'Gran, is that you?' asked Ginny cautiously.

'Virginia! Is anything the matter, darling?'

'Adam wants to run away. He says he's going to. There's been a horrible row.'

'A what?' There were voices in the background, indistinct but shrill.

'A row. Mummy cried a lot and Adam shouted.' There was a breathy pause while somewhere else – another room? – the voices subsided to a low, angry murmuring. 'Gran, what can I do?'

Lucy thought: What can *I* do? She felt helpless and far distant, like someone hailed from another mountain and baffled by the chasms between.

'Lucy? Is that you, Lucy?' came Laura's voice. 'Lucy, I can't do anything with Adam.'

'Lolly, he's upset. Just leave him alone for a while.'

'He says he'd rather live with his father.'

'That's only for effect.' Even as she spoke Lucy knew this conversation was futile. She felt the threads tangling, slipping away. Soon there would be snags, unravellings and frayed edges.

'The things he said . . .' Laura began but then her voice choked off, resumed abruptly to say, 'Don't be so stupid, Ginny,' followed by a muffled sound, muffled but continuing. Ginny crying?

'Adam's growing up. You can't expect him to behave like a good little boy.' Lucy pressed on, but without conviction. Even good little boys can't cope with hysteria, she thought. 'Look, let me take them both to Greece. Take the pressure off. You and Chris'll have a chance to sort things out.'

'What things?' And there was a breathy silence. More tears, thought Lucy. She could see them, running over Laura's hands and into the receiver.

'Lolly? Are you still there?'

'I don't know what to do,' came the thin, tremulous voice, half-drowned.

'But I do,' said Lucy.


'She say she's catching the five-fifteen at the bus station,' said Turk. She was waiting for the kettle to boil.

'Five-fifteen to where?'

'No idea. Derby? Nottingham? Somewhere up there.'

'Rick's place perhaps,' said Lucy.

The day which had promised so well had deteriorated to unbearable sultriness. Chloë had spent all afternoon in the hammock reading one of Turk's books. Now she was upstairs packing her toothbrush. Shut in her room anyway, thought Lucy, remembering Bernadette calling and calling, suitcases in the hall, taxis at the kerb – and only silence above. Then at the last moment Chloë would appear and slowly descend, not speaking, to kiss Lucy goodbye.

'It'll work out,' Turk said. She took the kettle from Lucy's hands and poured, clanking the spoon violently round the pot as if determined every leaf should play its part.

'The one certain thing,' said Lucy, fetching cups, 'is that nobody's ever grateful for advice.'

'Why should they be?'

'I worry so, Marianne. I mean, what's to become of Bernie? She isn't happy. I don't think she's ever been happy.'

'Darling Loo, you can't force her to be happy. She'll blunder on exactly as she wants, whatever you do. It's only natural. And Chloë will become a complacent middle-aged woman with wrinkles and liver spots. And Bernadette will grow old still telling everyone how unappreciated she is. And you won't be around so it won't matter to you any more.'

'It matters now. I've often thought ... if I'd been a different kind of mother to Bernadette she would have turned out a different mother to Chloë.'

'Or might not. I wish you'd leave off this soul-searching. If, if, if ... You did your best with Bernadette. I was around a lot of the time, remember? I saw you. She never lacked love or attention.'

'She lacked understanding.' Lucy was not going to back down.

Turk could have said: But she's so difficult to understand and after a while one simply grows exasperated and can't bear to struggle on. Walking through brambles blind-folded would be more rewarding.

'Here.' She handed Lucy her tea. She would say nothing about Bernadette or brambles. 'I think I might have triumphed over the last chapter.'

'You've finished?'

'No-o. I've tied a few ends.'

They heard footsteps overhead. Lucy leaned back and closed her eyes. Years of fret and optimism, she thought. Alternating bouts, now one, now the other. Fright at the thought of Bernie sleeping around indiscriminately, thank-fulness she seemed to have steadied on meeting David, fright again when at twenty she'd promised to keep only unto this one young man as long as she lived. But before all that even . . . Bernie as a child, brooding or overexcited, top marks or detentions, up down, up down.

'What was it sent Bernie so frantically religious?' she asked. 'Maurice never forced the children to go to church. He should have done. We'd promised. It was the rule in those days. Father Webb used to come round and complain sometimes. Then Maurice would complain to me about Father Webb and wouldn't go to Mass for weeks, not even if the choir was tackling a bit of Bach for a treat.'

'She was a morbid child,' remarked Turk.

'Oh, I know. All those martyrs, death by pressing, crucifixion on the wheel or whatever. Perhaps she shouldn't have been exposed to any of it.'

'You get that sort of stuff in convents.'

'You did then.' Lucy had found the sisters excellent in every respect but they had never blenched at the detailed and bloody description of suffering. No one suffers now, she thought. No one changes their faith for love or prom-ises to raise their children the way all the Father Webbs insisted. At some point a wall must have come down. She remembered Bernadette had done the Stations of the Cross for punishment, coming home late smelling of the school chapel: incense, polish, moth balls. It could never happen now, surely. 'Prayer as a punishment!' Lucy had cried to Maurice, shocked. Maurice had been simply amused. Bernie had been surprised at such indignation. 'I prayed Sister Xavier would fall off her bicycle,' she said.

'I'm off, Gran,' announced Chloë from the doorway. They could hardly make her out because her black garb blended into the shadowy hall behind.

'No time for tea?' asked Lucy.

'No, thanks. It'll take fifteen minutes to walk to the bus. I don't want to miss it. There isn't another for two and a half hours.'

'You could always come back,' Lucy told her. 'Come back and have something to eat.'

'Oh, I wouldn't bother you again. I'd go for a burger or something. Goodbye, Gran. Thanks for everything.'

They heard the street door open and close.


Lucy's friend Nina, who was as astringent on the subject of Bernadette as Turk, had a much younger lover whose knees, Lucy noticed, were covered with downy golden hairs.

'I wish someone would leave me some property abroad,' he was saying, relaxed in his deckchair, one arm trailing, plucking at the daisies on Nina's minuscule lawn.

'It's a responsibility,' Lucy told him. This had not actually occurred to her before today and she spoke with a sort of guilty surprise. She suddenly imagined Greek bills coming through the letter-box.

'It's an opportunity.'

It would be for him, she thought. He would soon find someone else to deal with the bills. Nina, for instance. This was not a bitchy thought, simply a realistic one. Lucy found him unnerving, partly because she couldn't imagine him making love to Nina and rather despised him for doing so. Surely he could capture a woman infinitely more charming, more desirable? More his own age? Not that Lucy wasn't fond of Nina, who had been her friend for years and years, had rallied round in crises, had stood up to Maurice.

Perhaps I'm jealous, she thought.

Yet she could not seriously contemplate Toby as a lover. He was too much the little boy. Invariably cheerful and indolent, he was thoroughly aware of the charm he could exert without effort – from the depths of a deckchair, looking across at her with childlike intensity.

'Greece, Lucy dear. Greece! I know for a fact if I were bequeathed anything at all it'd be a hut in a Norwegian forest or some unspeakable modern one-bedroomed flat in Bonn.'

Lucy decided, not for the first time, that deckchairs were altogether too awkward. The one she occupied was old and sagged threateningly so that her behind was inches off the grass and her knees poked up inelegantly. She felt as if any sudden movement would cause the whole thing to give way and fold up.

'You'll sell, of course,' Nina said, coming out with a tray on which were the long-awaited drinks and two bowls, one of ice and one of some kind of contorted, worm-like snacks.

'I'm not sure.'

'But didn't you say it was a big place? How could you keep it up? So far away, Loo. I mean.'

'There are planes, you know,' Toby pointed out, and he undulated a hand, presumably to indicate flying. 'Airports all over Greece.'

'Don't be so silly,' said Nina brusquely. 'It's a marvellous surprise. Heavenly. But a bloody nuisance.'

'Perhaps Lucy doesn't see it as a bloody nuisance,' retorted Toby, but a little doubtfully in view of her mentioning responsibility so recently. He looked bored suddenly. He found any talk of responsibility irksome. He had none of his own, at least none that impeded him in his enjoyment of life. He had a small income from money

95

invested for him by loving parents, both now dead, supplemented extravagantly by Nina who had done well out of three good marriages. He was not aware of being a parasite. He had a sort-of job and a sort-of commitment to getting on in life when opportunities presented themselves, which they did with astonishing frequency. 'It just wasn't Toby's thing, darling,' Nina would tell her friends afterwards when life had fallen back into its lazy routine. As nobody had expected it would be, this declaration always seemed superfluous, but it showed a touching loyalty of which it would have been churlish to disapprove. Besides, it was obvious Toby kept her happy both as companion and lover. The difficulties he faced in this were not to be underestimated. And he made extraordinary efforts with her children who were his own age and who, for a considerable time, had been determined to despise him. He was, in fact, something of an all-round success.

'For heaven's sake,' he exclaimed mildly, heaving himself up and scattering his daisies, 'let poor Lucy do what she wants with her Grecian villa without a lot of dire predictions.'

'I haven't predicted anything,' Nina protested.

'You said . . .'

'I'm trying to be practical.'

Don't quarrel on my account, Lucy wanted to say. She assumed a thoughtful expression as if to confirm she too saw it as a serious problem. Which I don't, she discovered. At least, it was not the Greek bills that were troubling her. Other forces, more subtle, might trouble her shortly, but not the domestic details of water, telephones, swimming-pool filters.

'You're jealous,' Toby was saying. This appeared to be his final statement. He seldom argued long, and never with sophistication. Instinctively he often dropped on the truth. He reminded Lucy of a dog that unerringly picks out the handkerchief with the handler's scent on it.

'Why should I be jealous?' asked Nina.

Why should she, wondered Lucy. She looked at her carefully, while trying to appear not to, in an attempt to come to some conclusion. She had always admired Nina. If Nina crumpled they must all crumple, she felt. For Nina still exuded the strength and energy and optimism which are often lost quite early on in life. She was sixty now, maybe a little more. Lucy couldn't remember. She could only remember that Maurice had never liked her. 'Always dragging some dreadful gigolo about,' he had said. Even then the word was outdated. But he has chosen it carefully, Lucy thought. He means to be cruel.

Now she thought: If I had my hair streaked like that I'd simply look as if the hairdresser had made a mistake.

'We could use the house for holidays,' she said, for she recognized it as the solution someone was bound to offer sooner or later.

'Still, such a big place . . .' It seemed to enlarge each time Nina spoke. 'What a worry. Chris was only saying how he wishes you'd move out of the terrace into something smaller and more convenient. What on earth would you want a mansion in Greece for at your time of life?'

'Whatever made you think it was a mansion?' My time of life indeed, thought Lucy. 'When on earth did you see Chris?' Her startled eyes met Toby's sympathetic ones. He raised his fair eyebrows slightly to signal his despair of families ever behaving rationally.

'I met him in London. Didn't I tell you? Last week. No, the week before. Henry's old firm always ask me to the annual dinner. Silly old-fashioned courtesy. I shan't go again.'

'But surely Chris wasn't there?'

'Isn't he tall, dark and handsome? He does you proud to look at.' She implied he might not do Lucy proud in other departments. She gazed fondly at Lucy but was thinking of Chris in a push-chair, an attractive child but grumpy. 'It was at the station. We were both on the same train and didn't know it. We shared a taxi.'

Chris had been critical of Nina all his adult life. 'She's vulgar, Mother,' he would protest occasionally. Like Maurice, he tended to rake up old words to show the depth of his disapproval. 'I don't criticize your friends,' Lucy would say calmly. He thought this irrelevant. Perhaps it was. If he pursued the subject she would refuse to be baited, would carry on rolling the pastry or poking the fire or reading a book. For Nina might be ostentatious, infuriating, forgetful and reasonably promiscuous, but she was not vulgar in any sense Lucy understood.

So now was she to imagine Chris, on the brink of a business meeting, exchanging pleasantries with a woman he disliked?

'He thought I ought to sell my house?' she asked.

'He seems to think the day isn't far off when you won't manage the stairs. I told him, good God, that's twenty years away, dear. But he always was a worrier. Handsome but stuffy, darling.' And she smiled to take any sting out of the words, handing Lucy the contorted worms.

'These are disgusting,' said Toby, throwing his on the grass. 'Aren't there any olives?' He took the bowl away from her and started indoors. He hoped the interruption might put Nina off her stroke. Off dangerous subjects, he thought. He could see Lucy beginning to have a feeling of unease. Shopping would be a safer topic, or Nina's gruelling sessions at her health and fitness club – he suspected she really only lay under a sunlamp – or the imminent arrival of the third grandchild.

'He never likes my crackly things,' Nina remarked sadly, picking up half a dozen worms from the grass and eating them slowly.

'Chris has never said anything to me,' said Lucy. It was this that gave her the unease. 'I can't believe he'd talk to you about it in a taxi.'

'Well, he seemed quite serious.' Nina was casting her mind back, but everything she could remember confirmed it.

'I'm not eighty. I'm not decrepit,' Lucy protested.

'I know. I know, dear. I told him so. I said: Your mother's busier than ever, WRVS, church jumble, poetry society accounts, gardening club. And d'you know what he said? What church? Mother never went to church. And what poetry society? She can't add up, either. Quite put out. I don't think he has any idea what kind of life you lead.'

'I don't think he has.'

'And when I said: Anyway, Marianne would never leave, look how she's stuck through thick and thin, marvellous friend, wouldn't blink at pushing you about in a Bath chair, he went very huffy, hardly spoke until he dropped me at the Dorchester. He's growing like his father, darling. I hate to say it.'

Toby returned, striding out triumphantly with the olives. He was tall and athletic. Lucy supposed he had a great deal of spare time in which to keep himself fit and all the vanity in the world to encourage him to do so. She felt suddenly motherly towards him and gave him a tender look. After all, he was rather sweet. He would have made an easier son than Chris, less critical and certainly not given to musing on the day she would be incapable of climbing the stairs. Or perhaps not. Perhaps as a son he too would be difficult, would be touchy.

All relationships are fraught with dangers, she thought bleakly. Like jungles.

# 8

LUCY saw her arms parting the water as if they were someone else's: slender, brown, young. Below her the sea floor was laid out like a garden with paths of small pebbles and isolated fronds of weed like small trees. This was not like swimming at school or in the dingy municipal baths. This was bliss. She turned to let the sun beat on her face.

'I love this place,' she said again – how many times now? – to Oliver as she emerged and sat down on a towel next to him. He had swum already, had gone to sleep in the shade of the ancient bleached canvas umbrella, and he only grunted, his eyes still closed.

Lucy rubbed her hair.

'How lucky you are,' she said.

'You speak as if I won Paleochora in a raffle.'

'But some people could struggle and struggle and never bring it off,' she told him. He had told her about the building of the house, the long labour and difficult birth. She could only admire him, for daring, for tenacity. On the other hand, his money had been inherited – at least, the money that was to build Paleochora. To her this was luck. Without it she could not see how vision could have become reality.

'I worked hard,' he said.

'I know.' She was afraid he thought she was criticizing. But all she had meant was that she had noticed fate was more arbitrary than just. If pattern and purpose existed, they were difficult to discern. She thought of Caroline's father, dear Rev, so modest, so persevering, and the succession of unattractive vicarages in which he was expected to do his best.

'I should be in Athens,' said Oliver.

'Then why aren't you?'

'Because I wanted to spend these two days with you.'

She wondered how to take this. If he had been her own age ... but he was not. Always she was left groping helplessly after his real meaning, afraid he was teasing, afraid he was laughing.

'When did you know the American girl wasn't coming?'

'The day after I'd written to you.'

'You ought to have written again.'

'I suppose I ought.'

She sat quite still, knees drawn up, looking out to sea. She didn't question his behaviour, she had so wanted to be with him. Now she suddenly realized she might be required to give explanations later, that Harold might come – by some unspecified means – to hear there had been no American girl after all. Slowly the implications unfolded to her: of lying or of not telling the whole truth, of brazenly admitting she had stayed alone with this man. Only we're not alone, she thought, there are the maids, the housekeeper, the gardeners. Anyway, what am I doing wrong? But she could not pretend to be as innocent as that.

Her happiness was dissolving. In a moment it would be irrecoverable, seeped away like water through the sand.

'Look at the gulls,' she said. 'There must be a shoal of fish beyond the rocks.'

He didn't look at the gulls. He looked at her. She could

feel him looking as if he had given her a physical blow between the shoulder-blades.

'Are you glad you came?' he asked.

'Oh yes,' she said.

Though it was the truth it gave her no comfort.

In the late afternoon they walked miles, brushing through the scented scrub, following goat paths, shepherds' paths. They walked apart so that when they talked it was over their shoulders, up or down hillsides. It was as if they were skirting the problem by skirting each other.

She was afraid to be too near him. He could still take her breath away. She dreaded the sensation of helplessness. She knew that sex was a mystery to her, only the theory straightforward, as theory often is.

'It's late,' he said at last. 'Can't you go any faster?'

Soon night would fall, the cool blue darkness that never seemed dark the way even summer evenings in England did.

'May I come again?' she asked like a small child.

'If you want. You may not want.'

'But I do.'

She toiled a little behind him now, growing more tired. Sometimes she took off her hat to ease her hot brow and once, squinting up, she saw the house in the far distance, white against the brown hillside.

'You've fallen in love with it,' he remarked, coming back for her.

'Yes.' She was sitting extracting a pebble from her sandal. Her toes were dusty. Unimportant things like this seemed all there was to distract her, take her mind off the disintegration of the day, the silly, childish, unformulated hopes.

A minute later they went on. The path was wide enough for two now but he went ahead. She thought he was strangely serious, as if he had a great weight on his mind. She felt it was probably to do with Mycenaeans. She too felt a heaviness, unbearable and stifling. She was relieved when at last Oliver called to her and she looked up and saw the lights already shining out from Paleochora, much nearer than expected.

He hardly spoke at dinner. He seemed preoccupied. He smoked erratically, strolling out to the terrace before coffee came in. Nothing is what we expect, thought Lucy, sitting on alone, leafing through magazines she could hardly see, words making no sense, pictures meaningless. In a little while she said goodnight from the safe distance of the doorway, smiling to show him everything was normal, that she could be relied on to behave politely and unobtrusively.

'Goodnight,' she said, and her smile seemed to take all the strength she had.

One of her fugitive hopes had been that he might kiss her goodnight. But kisses were chancy things. She remembered a boy at Margot's party, the rubbery discomfort, the resentment at being crushed, disregarded, expected to be amenable. When she had extricated herself he had been mildly abusive. At least that had put paid to her apologizing. If there was a lesson here she wasn't sure what it was. Margot didn't seem to have such problems, for instance. Or maybe the boys she kissed had better technique.

Lucy thought of Rev's dictum that all problems are more easily solved in the morning. She decided that tomorrow she would feel perfectly capable of asking Oliver to drive her to Kiparissia where she could catch a bus back to Harold, or failing this to make some suitable arrangement. There would then be no need of any shadowy guilt to hang over this visit, she could keep the vestiges of her happiness intact, could even rescue a few of the old hopes, usefully vague, even though she knew now – as she supposed she must always have known – they would never be realized.

She slept uneasily and in the early hours woke and lay wondering where she was. The morning seemed far away.

She felt that returning to Harold was, in spite of everything, the very last thing she wanted. Apart from anything else, he had no interest in her. He saw her not as an individual but as an idea. 'My daughter,' he would say, introducing her to his colleagues. And because she wasn't pretty or clever or well up in Minoan burial practice, that was all he would say, relieved because she was unexceptional.

If she didn't get up, she thought, she would cry.

Outside on the terrace there was a cool breeze, the smell and sound of the sea. She hugged herself, climbing the steps between the great stone amphoras to the terrace above, to the shelter under the vines where Harold had slept out his afternoons.

'Lucy?' Oliver was in one of the chairs. There were cigarette stubs in a saucer on the ground, an empty glass and discarded book.

She hesitated. Far below she saw the glitter of the sea moving between the rocks. Or thought she did. After what seemed to her a lifetime he put out his hand.

It would have been unnatural not to take it.

He woke before her and roused her gently.

'Slip away,' he said. 'Aphrodite will be about.'

How many times had Aphrodite found a woman in his bed? 'There are so many,' she had told Lucy. 'Wives, sisters . . .'

'Noll . . .' She could not remember now how she had come to call him this, suggested or invented it, making it her name for him.

'You always sent me away,' she was to write to him twenty years later.

'Because I'm not good for you. I never was. You deserved better,' he replied. It wasn't the first time he had told her this, and she wondered if he really meant it. She had never known with Oliver.

'Noll . . .' Even then she had known it was not exclusive,

it was a name used by other women who were also dismissed before they were discovered by Aphrodite.

Afterwards, when she was a grandmother and looked back, she remembered nothing of what they had said. She remembered instead the cool grittiness of the stones on the terraces as she ran, barefoot, back to her own bed.

# 9

AT the airport Ginny felt sick. Lucy waited while she visited the Ladies in the hope of settling the matter one way or the other. Adam grumbled, but under his breath. He would like Lucy to think he'd reached an age where he could tolerate the peccadilloes of kid sisters, might even be sympathetic. Alan, on the other hand, who had driven from Oxford on a whim to see them off, said, 'Oh my God!' and slouched off round the shops buying barley sugars and stomach settlers and the late-twentieth-century equivalent of smelling salts.

'She'll be all right,' said Lucy. 'It's only excitement.'

'She didn't eat all yesterday,' Adam told her. 'Mother kept on and on about strange men and not eating lettuce or something. Poor Gin said her ears were numb.' Yes, he felt astonishingly sympathetic. In fact, he had never felt so sorry for Ginny before, watching her plucked raw by Laura's tongue, reminded to do this, ordered not to do that, to use sun cream, not to swim out of her depth, to avoid men who whistled.

Had any man ever whistled at Laura?

'Gran, what was Mother like when you first met her?' By this time they were waiting for Alan to bring coffee and for Ginny to reappear from her third visit to the lavatory. Adam had organized the hand luggage and sat by it, one foot keeping the whole pile stable. He looked down with a certain satisfaction at his size nine shoe. Size nine and rising, he thought.

'Your mother?' Lucy sounded taken aback. 'Oh, she was lovely. Fragile. Pretty.'

'And Dad loved her?' He was not sure he had intended it as a question.

'He was besotted,' said Lucy truthfully.

'You don't mean he wrote poetry and stuff?'

'I shouldn't think so. But he adored her. No question.'

Adam noticed a baby several tables away whose screams were so lost in the general din that it looked like an enraged little old man impotently opening and closing his mouth. He was aware of a fluctuation of emotion in himself, as if his actual stomach or liver sank and rose. He'd noticed this happening recently. It was like the feeling he had always had when told he could turn over the exam paper. There were so many things he didn't know about and wanted to know about but – and this was what seemed to cause this peculiar fright – never would. Adulthood was not to be more than a partial revelation after all.

'I wonder what happened,' he said.

'When?' Lucy was wondering about Alan and Ginny.

'Between then and now. Dad and Mother when they married and . . . well.' He moved his foot a little and the flight bags listed ominously.

Alan, arriving with the tray, knocked into them and there was instant collapse. 'Sorry. Can't you sling it all under the table?'

'I think I'm better,' announced Ginny, reappearing and standing as if she awaited an inspection to confirm it.

'You'd better not have any of these,' and Alan shifted the plate of Danish pastries nearer Adam.

'I wasn't sick.'

'All the same . . .' Alan looked at Lucy for help but she

was putting sugar in her coffee and looking vague. She was certainly not listening.

'Perhaps it's hunger,' Ginny suggested. She felt guilt at having cast a cloud of anxiety over the day and would have liked to make amends. And it wasn't fair, anyway, that Adam should eat two pastries while she felt her stomach was shrivelled and in need.

'Ma, tell the child she'd better not eat. She'll be ill on the plane,' said Alan.

'There are paper bags on the plane,' Adam pointed out.

'Perhaps not, darling,' Lucy murmured, putting a consoling hand over Ginny's that effectively stopped a raid on the pastry plate.

She's distracted, Alan thought. But distraction for some reason suggested a rather chaotic state. Preoccupied, then, he decided. He wondered what it could be. It seemed unlikely she was anxious about the journey, she wasn't setting off into untrodden wilderness, and she had the children for company. All the same, this bloody house.

'Time to go, Ma.'

And of course at the gate he faltered, hating goodbyes. He felt a strangeness in the moment.

'It was sweet of you to come,' Lucy said. Her cheek was warm against his. 'You've got the number?'

'I think so.' Automatically he patted his pockets. 'Well, everyone else has it. Laura, Turk . . .'

'I'd rather hear from you than Laura,' she confessed.

'Dear Ma. Am I the only one who doesn't bring you problems?'

'Oh, I don't mind problems. But I can never help. You've no idea how tiring it is being an onlooker.'

'I've never thought of you as an onlooker.' He was startled.

The children, waiting dutifully a little way off, darted worried looks. The crowd had thinned. They would soon be left. Alan thought: I can't kiss them at their age. He walked to shake hands with Adam as this seemed one way out of the predicament but then could think of nothing for Ginny but an avuncular pat on the head which would certainly be resented.

'Perhaps we should shake hands too,' he said with an apologetic smile.

'How silly,' said Ginny. It had not occurred to her that anything in their relationship had changed. As she kissed him she noticed with surprise the lines on his forehead and the few grey hairs. He had always seemed so much younger than her parents or Bernadette that she had expected somehow to catch him up as soon as she had left childhood behind.

'Hurry,' he said. 'They won't let you through.'

Of course it was his mother's angular athletic figure that paused in the far distance and turned, raising an arm. He returned the salute with affection. On the way to the car park he discovered the barley sugars on the seat where they had first waited but felt too embarrassed to claim them and walked on quickly, head down, like the boy he had once been keeping out of trouble.

It had been a long journey. The children grew exhausted by it in fits, reviving at each change of transport but depressed again by delays and then, as the day wore on, by the very strangeness of it all.

'Look at the orange trees,' said Lucy as the taxi carried them the last fifteen miles, but it was she who looked, her eyes tired and sore from staring.

'We're nearly there,' remarked the driver brightly, but it was a phrase sullied by use at inauspicious moments in the past: on wearisome trips by car or train, counting cows and telegraph poles, singing fitfully to counteract queasiness. Adam groaned. He was beyond being pacified with falsehoods.

But it was not a falsehood. They had long left Kiparissia behind. We're nearly there, thought Lucy, nearly there. What a struggle the day had been. Perhaps they shouldn't have flown to Athens, they could have . . . and this long drive. Heat, orange trees . . . there was the sea. Another village. She decided she recognized it, then that she didn't. All day words of Greek had been coming back to her but she hadn't used them, she hadn't been ready for them. Her spirits were somehow dimmed. It was like hiding her eyes before the birthday cake came in and then being afraid to look in case there was no icing and no candles.

'Paleochora,' announced the driver. They turned between the stone pillars. Lucy, sitting with Ginny in the back, felt a sensation of vertigo.

'Are we there?' Ginny struggled awake. She had been in a stupor for miles. Her hair was plastered to her forehead and she looked indescribably tired, like a child who had been through war or earthquake.

'Almost,' said Lucy.

'Really there?' But when she looked out there was nothing but parched spaces dotted with trees.

'Oh, go back to sleep.' Adam's weariness made him gruff and masculine. For a moment Lucy recalled how Maurice too had grown touchy over trifles, speaking brusquely to hotel porters, making, she had felt, an exhibition of himself. He had hated travelling.

'Is that it?' asked Ginny.

And they had reached the turning-place by the steps. The oil jars are still there, thought Lucy. Like Harold's staircase, this one might lead to unexpected discoveries or to nowhere, who could say?

'What a funny house,' said Ginny.

'I thought it was going to be old,' said Adam. An atmosphere of disappointment began to settle.

'I think it was finished in the late thirties,' Lucy told them. 'Just before the war.' She was finding that even with the children she must keep up this pretence of knowing little, of having forgotten, of being unnerved by this unlooked-for inheritance.

'Gran, there's a pool,' cried Ginny, miraculously re-
vived. 'I can see it. Look.'

'There used not to be. We always swam in the sea.' She
forgot to be vague.

'May I go down and see?'

'Oh, Gin, for heaven's sake . . .' But Adam followed
her, trying to look as if he were only going to keep her out
of trouble.

'Mrs Flecker?' A tall, stout woman with rigidly permed
hair appeared at the top of the steps. 'Mrs Flecker, welcome. I am Evangelia. I am the housekeeper.'

She should really have been waiting outside with a great
bunch of keys, thought Lucy. Then when she let me in it
would have been a symbolic gesture. Instead the door was
open and the eye was drawn as always across the cool, dim
spaces to the sunlit terrace beyond.

'I'll just pay the driver,' said Lucy, and turned back.

He did not smile at her. He made no comment. She
knew perfectly well she was paying too much and besides,
he had been disagreeable over the possibility of Ginny
being sick. None the less she was pleasant to him. None
the less he gave her his card and pressed her to ring him
for the return journey.

'But perhaps I'll stay for ever,' she told him, irritated
because he was immovably morose.

At this he actually laughed, though not very politely. It
was such a ridiculous statement.

'No, no,' he said. 'No. How could that be?'

And he turned the car and drove away, still smiling.


Nothing and everything had changed, as in a dream where
known landscapes take on surreal overtones. And overall a
shabbiness she didn't remember at all, caused, Evangelia
said, by five years of careless occupation by the archeology
students from Athens. 'Young men, smoking, drinking
. . .' and she spread her large hands as if she might display
them, Lilliputian-like, to Lucy. 'Computers, papers,

books, boxes, office tables . . .' And even on the terrace, the same though without the wicker chairs, discarded in old age for hideous plastic things with metal legs that might have come from a hotel, there was evidence of institutional abuse.

'Where are the big pots?' asked Lucy. It was the first Greek she had spoken and her hands described the great bellied urns as she stood where they had been.

'Gone. Gone,' said Evangelia. She shook her head mournfully but did not elaborate, as if the fate of the pots had been too cruel, even unspeakable.

Below, the children were running down the path to the beach. There nothing had changed apparently. There was even a small boat drawn up on the pale sand as if it had been waiting there since Lucy's last visit.

'The pool was properly landscaped,' said Evangelia, showing her.

'Yes,' said Lucy. It was self-evident that someone had taken a lot of trouble. From the house the pool was invisible. Evangelia led her to it and from it with a more buoyant step and explained that the students had not been allowed to use it, it had been drained while they were in residence as a final discouragement. It was normally filled with sea-water pumped up cunningly from below.

'Yannis has filled it for you,' she said, and gazed at the dazzling surface with satisfaction, as if only now things might begin to return to normal.

In the house the cases had been brought in and stood neatly arranged in the middle of the floor. There was only one maid now, Evangelia said, not enough for such a house. Forty-five years ago things might have been different. Housekeeper, cook, maid . . . 'I am all those things,' she told Lucy. She could not stand on her dignity though she stood on it as often as the girl, Mini, allowed her to, for only to Mini fell the truly menial tasks. Such as the cases. And she had left them like this because she hadn't known where to take them next. There had been a dispute over rooms. At first the children had been put together. 'But they're too old,' Evangelia remarked. 'Your nephew is a man.'

'Almost,' said Lucy.

'So everything is changed. And you are in here, Mrs Flecker.' Evangelia opened a familiar door.

'What a view. How lovely.' As if she had never seen it before.

When Evangelia had left her she sat down suddenly in a chair as if her legs had failed. She felt overwhelmed. She was not sure any more what she was doing here. She thought she could hear Turk's voice somewhere far off among other indistinct murmurings asking, 'Why did he give it you, Loo? What did he expect you to do with it?'

God knows, thought Lucy. Then she wondered if the problem – which other people defined in various ways and she hadn't yet defined at all – was more to do with her inability to cope with such a startling present than Oliver's motive in giving it to her. Maurice, never flush with money, had once bought her a fur wrap for Christmas and she had been at a loss how or where to wear it, it suited neither the person she was nor the sort of life she led.

There was a discreet knock at the door.

'I've made you tea,' said Evangelia, bringing in a tray. She simply smiled at Lucy's amazement, as if to demonstrate how absolutely ordinary and everyday all this was to her.

'I wasn't expecting it,' Lucy managed. And how welcome it was, she thought, almost disappointed in herself for being comforted by tea among orange groves.

'Whenever he was home,' Evangelia told her, deftly arranging cup, pot, sugar bowl and the little dish of lemon slices, 'Mr Oliver took tea at four.'

'A bit what?' Turk demanded. She was wrestling to part top and bottom of Lucy's coffee-maker.

'Well. So much sex,' said Bernadette.

'It's what I write.' Top and bottom parted abruptly and old coffee grounds fell out all over the table. 'It's what sells.'

'I sometimes think,' and Bernadette assumed an expression of worldly distaste, 'that everyone's obsessed by sex these days.' But the distaste might have been for the coffee grounds which Turk was scooping into her palm.

'Pass me that cloth, will you?'

'Don't you think so?'

'Haven't noticed.'

Bernadette was dressed in dark colours as usual. Her wardrobe was mostly black, brown and charcoal. She wore a small gold cross round her neck and her hair was scraped back in a pony-tail just as it had been when she was twelve.

'I recall,' Turk said, feeling she might as well stir the depths and see what could be forced to the surface, 'you were obsessed with sex yourself. Your mother used to sit up worrying. I used to make coffee in this bloody thing *then*. And she smoked my fags. You can tell how she felt. She never smoked normally.'

Bernadette turned bright red. She had always blushed unbecomingly. Mrs Treece had always wondered why, she held that most young girls should have a pretty blush or two in their armoury, the weapon of innocence and modesty. Bernadette invariably looked as if she had been suffocated, the whole of her face vermilion, her eyes watery. 'A sad affliction really,' Mrs Treece told Lucy. 'How I feel for her, poor dear.'

'It was only a few months,' Bernadette asserted. 'And I wasn't obsessed with anything.'

'It lasted years. Three years at least.'

'But nothing happened.' It was impossible to tell from her tone whether it was sex, or some greater calamity, that had never occurred.

'Loo never knew where you were.'

'But I always told her.'

'You lied.'

The coffee-maker hissed on the gas hob. Turk and Bernadette both looked at it. It had been present at all the crises in this house – all those, and that was the majority, acted out, endured and overcome in this kitchen. There had been lies of all kinds, no doubt, and a good few home truths.

'I suppose there was something you wanted?' Turk asked as it began to tremble. 'Something to do with your mother?'

'No.' Bernadette sounded rather surprised at this herself. 'No. I wanted to know if Chloë had rung.'

'Rung here? Why should she? She knows Loo's away.'

'No messages?'

'Nothing.'

Turk put the last good cup in front of Bernadette. Then she hunted out the sugar bowl with the cheap bent spoon that had 'Yarmouth' on the handle.

'Oh, I remember that,' Bernadette exclaimed. 'It rained and rained. Chris had chickenpox. They were all waiting for me to get it. We came home early and Daddy was furious.' Furious with the weather, the embarrassingly infectious children, or Lucy's sensible decision to retreat to the comfort of her own house?

'Before my time,' said Turk.

Bernadette stopped fiddling with the spoon. She had forgotten anything had happened before Turk. Surely Turk had been with them always? But you were always there, she wanted to say.

'Are you sure?'

'You were ten or eleven when I moved in. You were about to have a brace fitted. You'd have thought it was the end of the world. I don't think there were that many kids with them then. Only the worst mouths got the treatment. Or perhaps only the best dentists bothered. I don't know. I can remember the caterwauling.'

'I didn't wear it long. We changed dentists and the next

one had other ideas.' At the time she had thought it was her prayers that had brought about this happy variation in orthodontic opinion. 'Chloë had to wear one,' she added, but it was probably not history repeating itself. Chloë's had been discreet and painless, a modern wonder, and the improvements staggering; or so Bernadette had been told.

'Lost Chloë, have you?' asked Turk.

'I thought she was in Nottingham. I thought she was with her friend Liz. Then I tried Richard's flat – Rick – but nobody was ever in. I got through to his mother in the end and she said he had a temporary job on some American campus. I don't know what. I don't think she did. But she didn't think Chloë was with him.'

'Chloë would have told you. About America.'

'Would she? We've had some battles recently. I might be the last person she'd tell. I don't like this Rick much. I met him once. I think he bullies her.'

'Did you tell her that? Watch out or she'll stick to him come hell and whatnot. My parents tried to frighten someone away so I married him.'

There was a pause during which it was possible to hear the birds outside in the cotoneaster by the window, and the faint hiss of the persistent rain. Then Bernadette pulled herself together and said quite calmly, 'But I didn't know you'd ever been married.'

'Well, it didn't last.' Turk put her lips to the coffee. It was immensely strong, just as she and Lucy liked it. We must have poisoned ourselves with enough of it down the years, she thought. Cups had punctuated hours spent waiting for doctors, for the phone to ring with news of birth or accident, for the police once, for the fire brigade twice. All the disruptions of a normal family?

'But I never knew!' cried Bernadette.

'You never saw him. He threw off marriage like a child throwing off clothes. Couldn't get out quick enough. And neither could I by then.'

'I'm sorry.'

'Why? It was a long time ago and ridiculous even while it lasted.'

'But why did I never know?' Bernadette groped back and back for a clue, for the moment when Lucy might have said . . . Only Lucy had said nothing. And I never asked, thought Bernadette. If she'd wanted to ask questions there had been a score of others suggesting themselves. I never did, I never did, she repeated. Turk had simply been part of the background of life, along with the rattle of the typewriter, the haze of cigarette smoke, the deep, private laughter late at night in the kitchen.

'We had three good months,' Turk was saying, 'three so-so, and three bloody ones when I found he was keeping a tally of post-grads who'd given in to his charms. After that I left him and couldn't find a room and ended up with blisters howling on your mother's basement steps. I was nineteen.'

But Turk at nineteen seemed an impossibility, like red eggs. She had always seemed frighteningly grown up, more than Lucy even. Bernadette cast back but the memories were faint except on this point. Dark hair, tremendous eyelashes – false? – that deep, rich laugh. There she was in a kimono eating toast, and pouring wine for Lucy, and arguing with Mrs Treece who hated anyone 'cluttering up' when she was doing her chores and who had always thought Turk, in that mysterious phrase, no better than she ought to be.

And Maurice had disliked her from the start.

'That woman,' he had called her. Sometimes, out of the children's hearing, he would qualify the noun. 'Your stocks of descriptive filth are pretty low, aren't they?' Lucy had once said, exasperated. Over Turk she was immovable. He could rage on that it was his house, that he wanted the flat empty, that someone had told him . . . Had Lucy any idea what went on under her own roof? 'I thought it was your roof?' said Lucy maddeningly and then carried on with whatever she was doing: darning, sewing on name tapes, writing a letter.

'Daddy didn't like you,' said Bernadette. She had been aware of the rows, infrequent but shattering, Lucy tight-lipped, Maurice at his most strident, but she had never really known if they were differences over Turk or the usual emotional disturbances of married life. Her own married life could give her no pointers here, having been so brief, its one quarrel so deeply regretted.

'I think he might have hated me.' Turk had taken a long time to reply but if she too were sifting through memories she was sifting effortlessly. Her brow was smooth. Her eyes smiled.

'But you stayed.'

'He never told me to leave.'

'Because Mother wanted you to stay.'

Maurice had gone into that first book, written in a frenzy of . . . certainly of something. 'Everything by the look of it,' Lucy had said, and laughed. Cynical, sexy, darkly funny, the book appeared to soar away with a life of its own. Returning from literary entertainments, Turk would complain she felt like the mother of a debutante watching her child whirled by on the arm of some delight-fully eligible young man: the object of the exercise achieved did not diminish a sense of loss. Lucy had recog-nized Maurice at once in his minor role and was glad for him when the book did so well. He himself was unaware such immortality had been conferred and as he had not read a page could not think what the fuss was about.

Mrs Treece had been circumspect, shaking her head over copies she found strayed on to her kitchen table. Mr Treece would not approve, she told Lucy. He was very particular. And he'd seen some of the reviews. 'Not that I don't wish Miss C all the best but I couldn't be seen between the covers,' she declared finally. Lucy supposed she couldn't and helped, stirred by sympathy, with the cleaning of the bathrooms. On reflection, she thought, it was just as well. Mrs Treece was almost certain to recognize Maurice, of whom she had conflicting opinions.

'He liked to take the high moral ground, your father,' said Turk to Bernadette, lighting another cigarette. 'Then he had a feeling of security. He could look down on the rest of us, poor imperfect fools, but there was nobody to look down on him. Did you know he screwed some woman from the University library once a week for years?'

'No,' whispered Bernadette.

'I saw them together once at Blaine's. It wasn't a place middle-aged dons went to often so I suppose he always took her there for a drink and a sandwich, thought it was safe. I didn't tell Loo. She had other things on her mind. You, for instance. And Alan and that Susie girl. Then later she told me she'd known for months. I think Nina played informer. She never cared for Maurice.'

Bernadette tried to revive herself with coffee. '*I* didn't know,' she said. She felt humiliated. She had not imagined until today that she knew so little.

'I don't think Loo broadcast the news. I do remember we had frequent progress reports from Nina afterwards. Mrs Treece used to say, "God watches everyone," but Nina had beadier eyes than God. Maurice never stood a chance. She had a huge circle of friends and kept herself well briefed: who, what, where, when. Loo just laughed.'

'Laughed?' Bernadette's voice had faded away. She seemed to struggle to produce sound at all and her eyes looked watery as if with the unbelievable effort.

'I don't mean laughed nastily. She just didn't care.'

This time they heard bicycle bells and someone reversing badly, punishing the gearbox. The rain still fell, sibilant, monotonous. The kitchen had grown dark, as if it were almost night or winter instead of August. Turk smoked on. She wondered what sort of shock she had inflicted. Knowing Bernie, the mountain would eventually be made out of the least likely molehill.

'I knew they argued sometimes. But it never seemed

very serious. I thought it was normal.' Bernadette struggled for breath.

'For God's sake . . . there wasn't any drama. Maurice had whatever it was he wanted and Loo decided to stick it out. He couldn't have been seriously unfaithful if he'd tried. Some of that moral high ground had got stuck on his shoes after all probably. And he and Loo got along by and large. They agreed about a lot of things.'

'What?'

'Your friends. Alan's reports. Laura.'

I'm giving a rather false impression of unity, Turk thought. But it was easy to criticize someone else's marriage. Such marriages, judged failures by outsiders, might be surprisingly ripe and quick from within. She knew, for instance, that Maurice and Lucy had not slept together often after Alan was born, but that did not necessarily mean they took no pleasure when they did. It had irritated Maurice that he had a wife with the temperament of a mistress and a mistress with what he considered the correct passivity of a wife, but he kept this to himself.

'I never thought Father . . .' Bernadette could not bring herself to call him Daddy this time. She had always thought it sounded endearing from someone her age but now she repudiated it. It described a different Maurice perhaps from the one Turk had revealed.

'Nobody did. And in a way everyone pretended he hadn't. It was what Loo wanted. I don't think they ever even discussed it. Anyway, it wasn't long before Nina came hurrying round with tales about you, and that girl of Chris's before Laura, can't remember her name.'

'But what happened?' Bernadette disliked stories without endings. She liked to tie a neat and satisfactory knot.

'About Maurice and his once-a-week Eleanor? Oh, all of a sudden she got a job at another library. Don't know where. Abroad, I think. It was probably something she'd always wanted to do, and Maurice wasn't offering any exciting alternatives.' Turk stretched, and the tip of her cigarette glowed in the kitchen dusk. She added after a moment: 'I expect he thought he'd had a passionate affair, looking back on it afterwards.'

Bernadette still felt bewildered. It was not that all these facts about her parents had been so terrible, just that she wished she had not remained ignorant of them until middle age. She felt that her perception of Maurice, her attitude to his always-slightly-bullying tone to her, would certainly have been different had she known. She might even, she thought, growing resentful, have managed to love him better. She always worried that he had failed to see how much she cared about him, but his lack of response made her think the fault was in her, that in quantity or quality her love must be defective.

'. . . and I don't think I'd ever heard Lussom's name except spoken by the announcer on the television,' Turk was saying. 'Your mother said nothing.' And then, as if to brush it aside: 'Well, it was up to Loo, wasn't it?'

'She knew about the house. I think she'd known for a long time. But she didn't tell anyone,' said Bernadette, and the words came out in a miserable bleat, like a small child confused by adult falsehoods.

'Would it have made a difference if she had?'

'I don't know. It just seems odd.'

'Poor Loo. Must she make everything public?'

'We're not public,' Bernadette protested. 'We're her family.'

The telephone rang. Turk stubbed out her cigarette and listened for the third ring when the answerphone would take over.

'That might be Loo now. To say she's there,' she said.

But the journey to Paleochora, she now realized, had begun long ago, years and years ago, and might not yet be over though Lucy was at this minute sitting down to eat under the Greek vines.

# IO

HAROLD was anxious about his daughter. She was in a fever of obvious happiness one moment and weeping the next.

'Love,' said Sofia cheerfully, for why should love be a disaster? 'The dear girl. She is in love.'

It was a state Harold had never experienced.

'With whom?' he asked coldly.

'Who can say?' answered Sofia.

For a while after this he peered suspiciously at every young man, American, English, Greek, who crossed his path. It occurred to him that the whole site was littered with young men as thickly as it was with the unrevealed artefacts of the past. And they were all totally unsuitable as companions for Lucy. For a short time this fact dispelled some of the anxiety – surely Lucy would never form an attachment to any of these? He remembered the expense invested in her education, the careful vetting – Edith, undoubtedly, had always been careful – of the friends with whom she spent the holidays, the constant reinforcement – Edith again, he took for granted – of all the old rules of behaviour. And anyway Lucy was never out of his sight long enough to be doing anything she shouldn't. He was conscious of her presence all day from breakfast, when they were uncommunicative over poached egg and Oxford marmalade, throughout the hours of note-revising and cataloguing and labelling with the new young secretary from Athens, to their dinner in the late evening when they spoke mostly of the food or the weather. But gradually his unease increased again. After all, there were so many young men. He began to regard the site with disfavour, as if he had found a perfectly well-behaved, ordinary woman guilty of successive love affairs.

'Would you care to go to Athens?' he asked Lucy one morning.

'Athens?'

He thought, suddenly struck by her pallor, that she must be thinner, her eyes looked so huge. He had never properly noticed her eyes before. They were not his eyes, nor Edith's. They were a clear and lovely blue.

'You've been looking tired,' he said. 'And it's not much fun out here, is it? Now Evdoxia's arrived she can easily cope with all the office work. So I thought ... what about a trip to Athens? You could stay with the Fieldings.'

He was certain it would be a great treat. He expected endearing, even excited gratitude. He smiled across the table at her but she was not even bothering to hide her horror.

'I'd rather not, Father.'

'Aren't you well, dear?' If it were something female Bonny Fielding could do something about it, he thought optimistically.

'Oh, I'm perfectly all right. But I don't really think Mrs Fielding would want me. I caused her all that trouble over the clothes.'

He had forgotten. It all belonged to some awkward, unfortunate moment in the past, to his period of mourning for Edith, to those months of disruption and disturbed emotion. He had put it thankfully out of mind.

'Clothes? Don't be silly, Lucy. I'll send a letter tomorrow.'

'I'd rather not go. I like it here. I like helping,' Lucy tried.

Harold tossed down his napkin and stood up. 'But Evdoxia's paid to copy up my notes, dear. Now, don't be obstinate. You look quite peaky. And Sofia says you haven't been eating.' He might have shared none of her meals, he had not noticed for himself. 'It's not so hot in the city now. You'll have fun. Eating out, lots of new faces, concerts, that sort of thing.' He patted Lucy's shoulder kindly on his way past to the door. 'You go to please your old father.'

Mentally, he had already begun on his letter. He had wasted only two lines on conventional greeting before he plunged in boldly with 'Poor Lucy has not been well, I'm afraid. I have been at a loss what to do for the best. However, it occurred to me . . .'

He hurried away to get it all on paper before he forgot.

The Athens trip was to last a week. It was the only concession Lucy could wring, Harold having held out for a fortnight. In later life, coping with children, Maurice's social obligations, Mrs Treece's varicose veins, Lucy would view a week as but a lightning flash, would cross the days off the calendar in continual astonishment, they fled so fast. At nineteen a week might have been a decade, especially in the company of the Fieldings.

'Well, I must say, you've definitely lost weight, dear. Your father said you'd been suffering from the heat,' Bonny remarked, meeting her at the ferry.

'I haven't been ill,' Lucy insisted.

'Run down, poor thing. That's what Harold said. His letter quite worried us. Perhaps . . .' and she mentally ran through the list of delights she had planned, 'perhaps we ought to take things easy. Dancing till late won't help you get your strength back.' She rolled the gold bracelets up and down her arms as she always did when nervous.

'I've never been dancing.'

'Haven't you? I suppose not. What with your mother
. . . Well, maybe some dancing then.' In a burst of emotion
Bonny put her arm round Lucy's shoulders. They walked
awkwardly across the quay, linked physically but in all
ways out of step. It was a relief to reach the car.

'It's kind of you to have me,' Lucy said dutifully.

Bonny smiled in answer and then retreated behind her
sunglasses.

'But I haven't been ill,' Lucy added. She wondered
what exactly had been said in Harold's letter.

'No, dear. Perhaps not. But we really must look after
you.'

It was David Fielding who thought he could read between
the lines.

'I bet old Harold's rushed you off in case his students
paid more attention to you than to their trowels. He
wouldn't want that, would he? He's got to find that blasted
city or die.'

'No.' She blushed and blushed, trying not to let him see.

'I bet.' He took her hand. 'It would be nice to see a
smile,' he told her.

She smiled seldom. She said she felt weak. Bonny began
to look at her more closely, suspicions rising like bubbles,
and, heavily conscious of being in loco parentis, was driven
to call the doctor. He said he thought Lucy was suffering
a reaction to Edith's death.

'But that was in March,' Bonny said.

'And here we are at the end of September. No time at
all. To lose a mother, Mrs Fielding.' He took her hand.
'Think. Think.'

'I suppose she had to be brave,' Bonny conceded. She
had not known Edith, had not even seen a photograph.
The woman might have been a Tartar or the loveliest soul
on earth. 'Her father wouldn't have been much help of
course,' she added, certain of this at least.

'Exactly. You must be patient. Very patient. She is exhausted with bravery,' said the doctor firmly. In the absence of any indication of clinical disease this was an explanation that would do very well.

'You're sure it's not food poisoning? Or ... or appendix?'

'She has no pain. No temperature. She is simply low in spirit, tired out. She mourns her mother. Now the excitement of coming here to her father is over, she thinks back, she grieves.'

'But what can I do?' asked Bonny. She pushed at her bracelets anxiously.

'She may be happier at home. Here she feels she must try too hard to please everybody.'

'I'll send her back then,' Bonny said briskly. She saw Lucy as a parcel she would be pleased to rewrap and despatch.

Her husband came home to find arrangements under consideration: ferry, taxi, bus?

'Well, what did the doctor say?'

'He says she's mourning for Edith.'

'He might be right.' He did not think the doctor was right at all.

'I thought she might be pregnant.'

'Good God! By whom? She's been with Harold ever since she got here.'

'He doesn't keep her in a chastity belt presumably.' Bonny leaned forward to look in the dressing-table mirror, puckering her lips. 'I'll have to do my face. The Halliwells are coming at seven. Are you going to change?'

'Pregnant?' He couldn't think of changing. He remembered Lucy's pale face across the breakfast cups.

'There again, she might just be exhausted. Harold exhausts *me*. Or really and truly suffering for Edith. The woman was ill for months. It couldn't have been pleasant. Anyway, I'll leave you to ring Harold. You can tell him the doctor's ordered rest.'

'Why do I have to do it?'

'Because if I do he'll go sentimental over Edith.'

'Never. When was he ever sentimental over anything?'

'Just do it. Tell him to send a car to meet the bus.'

'The house isn't on the phone.'

'Ring the café in the village and ask them to send a message. He'll ring you back from there.'

There were still three days left of the original much-disputed week.

'Give my love to Harold,' Bonny said heartily, kissing Lucy goodbye.

'Was he very angry?' Lucy asked.

'Disappointed. David said he was disappointed. And worried. He'd hoped you'd have a good time, fun with the young people. Still, you'll come again.'

'I'm sorry to have been so much trouble to you,' said Lucy.

'There's no future in this,' Oliver said. He was leaning on one elbow looking down at her.

'No.' She didn't open her eyes.

'I mean it, Lucy.'

They had swum and now rested in the shade where the rocks formed a natural shelter.

'Have you thought what you're going to tell Harold?'

'When I got off the bus I left a message at the café that I was staying in Athens after all. They wouldn't bother where I was ringing from.'

'He'll find out.'

'He might not. I could say I felt ill on the bus, that you rescued me. After all, I could phone here, couldn't I?'

He touched her face. Had he been wholly responsible for this transformation?

'You ought not to lie,' he said. The ironic smile that followed this statement, and which she did not see, was for the inappropriateness of his giving any kind of moral instruction. 'I wish . . . ' he suddenly began.

Her eyes flew open. 'I only want to be with you,' she said.

'But you can't be with me. Apart from anything else, I should be in Athens. And next week in Rome.'

She sat up. The drops of sea-water that still glistened on her shoulders ran gently down to her nipples. Then she leaned forward and folded herself in the old childlike way, hugging her knees, her head laid sideways, the hair across her cheek and in her eyes.

'Oliver . . . '

I shall never call him Noll again, she thought.

Harold sent the car to Paleochora with instructions to bring Lucy back at once. He told himself he did not doubt her story but he could not concentrate on his work all morning, conscious of an obscure unease.

'A chapter of accidents,' he told Bonny Fielding when he rang her from the café. 'She sent a message here but they must have garbled it. She's not herself, poor child.'

'Harold . . . ' Bonny began but was at a loss how to continue.

'So it was Lussom,' said David later. 'Still working the old charm. But seducing schoolgirls? Hardly his style, is it? You don't really think . . . '

'It's for Harold to think,' said Bonny. 'And she's nineteen. Don't let that innocent little miss look fool you. I was married at nineteen, remember?'

'Well, I don't think the innocence was put on.' He saw it as a gauzy cloak clasped around Lucy's frail shoulders.

'Men are easily fooled,' said Bonny.

At breakfast over the English delicacies, the elderly English paper, Harold cast wary glances at his daughter. She seemed to have changed overnight into a difficult woman. And she certainly didn't look well.

'Perhaps you'd like to go home for a while,' he suggested.

'Home?' She stopped breaking up the crust of her toast. 'This is home.'

'I meant England.'

'But where? Aunt Margaret?'

'No. No. What about . . . ' He was determined England must provide a solution. 'Well, that Margot girl.'

'She lived near Tours. Anyway, she's in Switzerland being finished.'

Harold frowned. 'Who else?'

'There is no one else.'

'Those people at the funeral.' He had pretended not to remember, had certainly not wanted to remember. A tall, thin, balding clergyman? A girl, badly dressed and untidy, whose hand Lucy had held at some point as the drowning hold to wreckage.

'Caro.' Lucy sensed the inevitability of exile. From Greece she would return to grey drizzle and queues and coupons. She would exchange Sofia's olives and cheese and tough, tasty bread for spam and margarine.

'I think I'd better write. A month perhaps,' and Harold folded the paper with an air of accomplishment as if Rev had already been warned of Lucy's imminent arrival and any further communication would be simply a formality. 'Just until Christmas.'

He was conscious of Lucy's look of resignation and reproach, and felt uncomfortable, felt the weight of his responsibility. Had he been right to bring her out here? Was he right in sending her back? To what? He didn't like the look of this post-war world. Such changes and yet still rationing . . . 'I don't know where it will end,' he said aloud, and then, embarrassed, tapped the newspaper with his knuckle. 'Lot of nonsense. Socialist claptrap.'

'Do I have to go, Father?' Lucy's head was bowed over her plate. She looked as if she had a pain.

'Christmas,' he said firmly. He made it sound a word of infinite promise. 'We'll be together for Christmas in

Athens.' And he laughed a little, to show her what fun it might be.

She was silent. He looked at her unhappily but she gave no further sign of resistance. Her only hope, though he couldn't know it, was that Caroline's mother, who refused no one in need, would refuse her. She had recently moved to a sprawling, inconvenient country parsonage where Rev was apparently grappling with damp, prejudice and ageing churchwardens.

'You do promise about Christmas?' Lucy asked.

'Of course.' Harold smiled. He would get Evdoxia, such a charming and competent girl, to compose the letter to the vicarage. He saw himself writing it out, amending the odd word, signing it.

His promises, as Lucy knew, had always been easily made and as easily broken.

Caroline's mother, Joyce Horringer, wrote by return that they would adore having Lucy back. How they had all missed her. '*Back?*' queried Harold. He was unaware of the Horringers' past kindnesses, the holidays, the weeks or months Edith had felt unable to cope. Stranded in Canada during the war, he had got on systematically with writing a book, organized, undistracted and ultimately triumphant. Although he had written regularly to England he had sent little more than reports of his own progress. He had never asked after Lucy except to hope she was well. Edith replied spasmodically, and these replies were full of medical matters. He never read them thoroughly. Some never reached him at all, victims of the many hazards of war, and so, in sequence or out, they made little sense, and the doctors' pronouncements with which Edith invariably ended the final paragraph seemed increasingly arbitrary.

'I suppose you know these people well,' he remarked to Lucy, a little put out by Joyce's dashing script, words frequently colliding, whole sentences underlined. A vicar should be all right, he was thinking.

'Of course I do.'

'She sounds emotional. And there's this postscript. A whole page. "Tell her to bring lots of woollies." I didn't know what it was to begin with. It looks like wollies.' He peered at the offending word, perfectly serious, and clicked his tongue at it in reproof.

'I haven't any warm clothes,' Lucy told him.

'What about in the trunk that came out with you? The cabin trunk? It's still in Athens.'

'But that was school clothes, ages old. Things I'd grown out of and didn't know what to do with.'

'Still, there might be something.'

'Tunics. Green knickers,' said Lucy.

They always seemed to return to this vexing subject of clothes, he thought.

'Well, October in Dorset. You'll need a coat. We'll have to ask Sofia.' He disliked being thrown back on Sofia after all he had once said, but she might know a local tailor, he was thinking. A winter coat for a parsonage in the country would not need to be fashionable.

Then the sound of typing, rapid and businesslike, reached him from the distance.

'Evdoxia,' he said. 'Now there's someone who'll know.'


The vicarage smelled of fried bacon and mice and dry rot. It contained only the furniture brought from the previous, more humble house, and the big rooms were bare and echoing, the bang of a carelessly closed door transmitted from attic to cellar.

'I can see you've had the sun, dear,' was Joyce's greeting.

'Lucky you,' struck in Caroline. She felt herself large and unattractive next to Lucy. Lumpy, she thought. There were bound to be comparisons. For the first time new doubts crept in: how resilient were friendships, how blind, how forgiving? It seemed a long time since school.

'Like the old days,' exclaimed Rev, whose doubts were

131

all to do with organ pipes and death watch beetle in the bell chamber.

It was not like the old days at all, thought Caroline. She dreaded a month of difficult silences and petty bickering. Affection will turn to ashes, she thought. They had been foolish to expect the old Lucy who had been part of those old days. The Lucy they had fetched from the station was entirely grown up and completely changed. She could no more be pictured in a maroon felt hat or a house sash or gym knickers than the vicar himself. There's been too much water under the bridge, Caro told herself, a phrase she had heard old Mrs Miller use to Miss Forbes while cleaning the church last Saturday, and which, as she was thinking of Rev at the time, had seemed ineffably sad. He would never do better now, she had been thinking, than this tucked-away and fossilized place. He could never pass for one of the new and thrusting generation marked out for a big city church, nor would he ever be offered an easy administrative sort of job at the cathedral, which would suit him best. Instead he must struggle with all these people who seemed forever ranged against him, critical if even a vase were banished from its accustomed place or he dared to wear a different stole than the one put out for him. Too late, poor Rev, his daughter thought. Too much water under the bridge.

Joyce, not so distracted by the dogs, the twelve-year-old twins and an old lady with a message for the vicar, that she didn't notice Caro's gloom, said, 'Take Lucy upstairs and show her where the bathrooms are.' The practicalities of life, she thought, help occupy the troubled mind.

'Dreadful Victorian gothic,' said Caroline to Lucy, leading her up into deeper gloamings above the considerable twilight of the hall. 'Can't you imagine vampires?'

'It's enormous,' cried Lucy.

'Impossible to heat, impossible to furnish, Rev says.' Caro sounded quite cheerful about it. They had all come to terms with these impossibilities long ago.

'This is your room. Next to mine. Mother thought it might be nice for us to be near. There are miles of passages between here and the twins. And the bathrooms between like caverns measureless to man or whatever it was, white tiles, everything oversize. And freezing.'

The bedroom had a deep gothic window overlooking cedars on a ragged lawn. The single bed looked forlorn on a square of old brown carpet Lucy recognized as having been in the dining room of the last vicarage.

'Wait till you see mine,' Caro warned. 'Rev calls it the cathedral.'

And: She always called him Rev, Lucy thought. Once it had been a joke. Now it struck her as an endearing habit and a familiar landmark in a strange country. On impulse she put an arm round Caroline's plump shoulders.

'It's like school,' she said. 'All it needs is lino and those awful blotchy curtains.'

They laughed, looking round together and trying to imagine it.

'There's lino in the vestry,' Caro said. The everyday discomforts of Rev's life in Middle Linford were very important to her: the brown lino, the howling draughts, the cracked mirror half obscured by worn-out surplices. She felt for him, plagued by such unnecessary ugliness in his surroundings. 'Rev says it'll have to stay even though it's drawing the damp up through the tiles or something. He says you have to live here two generations before they ask you over the threshold. Of the cottages, I mean. And throwing out the lino would be bound to cause offence. It would be *three* generations at least after that.'

They laughed again. In the bare room they stayed close, feeling alone together in the cold, unlovely house just as, perhaps, they were both coming to feel alone in a cold, unlovely adult world.

'It's sure to be sardines for tea,' said Caro, pulling a face. She had forgotten she was nineteen. She might have been one of the twins. And Lucy thought, how odd, sardines again, how she would always associate Rev and Caro with sardines which they both hated but which seemed to form a disproportionate part of their diet.

The house reverberated in quick succession to a gong, slamming doors and running feet. A high, exasperated voice, which did not sound like the vicar's, shouted instructions from very far off.

Suppose I have a baby, thought Lucy.

Her hair has changed, thought Caro. She thought the sun must have made it lighter, the glorious sun that shone too infrequently on Linford to have any effect on her own dull curls.

They looked at each other in the old searching way. They really needed Margot, Margot the strong and happy, then they would be complete again, the invincible trio. But Margot was being finished – finished off, Joyce called it, for the last time she'd seen Margot she had thought her quite finished enough – and would never in her life have to face sardines or fried luncheon meat, never be summoned by a gong down a green-tiled corridor to a kitchen permeated by the reek of boiled greens. Lucy's eyes suddenly filled with tears. Maybe Margot would be a stranger if they met again. As she feared Oliver might be. She did not understand love, its growth, its death. Only in books, she thought, were all obstacles overcome.

'I'm so glad you're here,' declared Caro. 'I wasn't sure . . . I thought you'd changed. But you haven't.'

For a moment they stayed there, still with their arms around each other, before they obeyed the summons of the gong.

# I I

CHRISTOPHER, who had been in Cambridge on business, decided to lunch in his mother's favourite restaurant and was no sooner through the door than he was molested by Nina Scott's boyfriend – molested being how he described it to himself afterwards when he could bring himself to remember.

'It is Chris, isn't it? Toby Porter. I've met you at Lucy's. Are you eating?'

'Ah,' said Christopher helplessly. He hoped he looked non-committal. The small room seemed already overfull. 'I don't think there's a table,' and he turned to make his escape.

'Share mine. I'm all alone,' said Toby.

His brain still engaged with pentium chips and graphical interfaces, Christopher could not immediately produce a convincing reason for refusing. He sat down.

'Together?' asked the waiter.

'No,' said Christopher.

'Oh, have it on me,' said Toby. 'Well, on Nina. She won't mind.'

'I really couldn't . . .'

'Why not? I recommend the squid if you like squid. And how's life treating you?'

'I'm always very busy. I can't take too long.' Christopher looked at his watch as if to reinforce the words.

He had forgotten why his mother liked this place so much except that it had endured where others had come and gone, and the staff knew her and gave her bottles of wine at Christmas and on her birthday. He thought a woman must be pitifully lonely to set store by such things. Now he was trapped here, scanning the huge menu on which there were very few dishes but all copiously described – as if they hope you'll cook your own, perhaps, he thought, having been practically given the recipe. It was not the sort of food he cared about. He would have preferred a plain steak, a few mushrooms and some new potatoes. He would have preferred, too, not to be sitting opposite Toby, with whom he could have nothing in common. Nor did he want it supposed, even by Italian waiters, that they had had a date. He did not relish misinterpretation. He didn't remember Toby in previous encounters having such a tan or such a loud shirt or such a way of draping himself across a table as if he were about to impart the latest and filthiest scandal. Unless it should be imagined he was interviewing a media personality, it would be difficult to pass this off as a business lunch.

'Lucy eats here a lot,' Toby informed him, as if he might not know.

'That was why I came. She's often mentioned it. I was up at a demonstration, thought I'd drop in. Is it always so busy?'

'Always. Great food but too small.' Toby glanced about happily. He spent a lot of Nina's money here.

The first course arrived. Christopher, whose appetite was receding, stared at his for a considerable time while Toby took several large mouthfuls of his own and made appreciative noises. Toby's friendly blue eyes smiled across benevolently. This was a disconcerting intimacy between strangers, Christopher thought. For they were strangers, Nina notwithstanding. He sat further back in his chair as if he hoped somehow to keep himself out of range.

'And what about this house in Greece? Isn't our Lucy a dark horse.'

'Is she?'

'Nina had no idea, she said. No idea Lucy knew any old archeologists, though why she shouldn't, God knows. She has a remarkable circle of friends.'

This last remark – and an odd way of putting it, Christopher thought – brought about a prolonged silence. Toby ate on steadily. The waiter asked if everything was all right. The woman sitting back to back with Christopher complained that her father was on his third wife, to which her companion replied, 'And last, we hope,' with a short laugh.

'D'you know Greece at all?' asked Toby, having finished and looking surprised Christopher had not.

'No.' He felt he was being asked if he knew a certain overture or the new people down the road. 'No,' he repeated, and put down his knife and fork. Then: 'It's only a house,' he said. 'Just a house. I don't see why there should be any fuss.'

'You make it sound so modest. The house.'

'I don't think it's anything special.'

'Not special? Dear me. Try *Famous Homes of* . . . Sure it was of somewhere. Can't remember. Coffee-table book. Divine photos, as Nina would say. It was in there, three or four shots. Makes your mouth water. Marble tiles, gardens, pool, antique statues.'

'Statues?' Christopher had, until this moment, imagined a small, rather spartan building painted white, the sort of place that might be on the cover of a brochure for villa holidays. He watched the arrival of his next course with anxiety, both for its content and for the conversation that might accompany its consumption.

'Magical,' continued Toby affably, apparently still talking

137

of Lucy's house. 'The man had taste. And luck. Luck or a hell of a lot of influence.'

'He was very well known. Still is.' Christopher cut into his meat carefully. It was too pink for his taste. 'I mean, in archeological circles.'

'Famous. The bloody man was famous,' declared Toby.

In his suit and sober tie Christopher felt hot. Outside the pavement was thronged with tourists passing in groups, often straggling away from their gesticulating guide to look in on the packed diners. The sun shone. Others might siesta in such heat but the English, Toby thought, carried on with martyred expressions.

'Notorious,' and Christopher began on his second glass of mineral water. 'Lussom. Liked his drink, I believe.'

'I don't know about that. I only know about the house. Your lucky ma.'

'Well, I don't think it's worth much.' Christopher had spoken before he could stop himself. He felt immediately ashamed of expressing any such opinion, especially to a man like Toby. Indeed, he wasn't sure he even counted him among men. He thought his looks, his little-boy manner, his living off a woman old enough to be his mother, removed him to a shadowy and sexless area of human life.

'Millions,' said Toby emphatically.

'Millions of what?'

'Well, not drachmas. And for pity's sake don't talk exchange rates at me. I don't know anything about them and don't want to. Millions sterling. I liked your "It's just a house". I'll tell Nina about that. She'll be tickled.'

In silence Christopher drank off his wine and in silence noticed Toby's wide brown wrist shown off to advantage by the flat gold links of a bracelet it seemed reasonable to assume Nina had bestowed on him. I never liked Nina, he thought. He had never understood Lucy's devotion. They had always seemed such opposites. He had once heard his father refer to her as a tart.

138

'Oh, I really don't think so,' he said, giving an uneasy laugh. 'Not millions.'

Toby looked at Christopher's gaunt features, his neatly brushed hair, his excellent suit, his expensive, unremarkable neckwear. Everything top-class and dull, he thought. He could see a vague resemblance to Lucy, who was also tall and, for a woman, gaunt. But Christopher, who had been a sensitive boy, had been made diffident and nervous by an unhappy marriage. Where Lucy's energy flowed outwards his was contained and destructive. Only in discussing those pentium chips might he become animated, authoritative. In everything else he was always brought eventually to a crippling pitch of doubt. And he could no more have worn Toby's red silk shirt than he could have flown.

'Not even a million?' Toby asked softly, beginning to be intensely amused.

'Mother would have said.'

'Perhaps she didn't think it was your business.'

And it certainly isn't yours, thought Christopher. 'Oh, I usually help her with her investments. All that. Since Father died. I'd be the first to know anything was worth serious money.' He realized as he spoke that Lucy had not consulted him for a long time. He would have to speak to her about it.

'My God, you don't think you could buy a place like that for much less than a million these days, do you?' Toby asked.

Christopher felt alone and floating in the noisy little restaurant, as if in a dream, rising up and away from Toby's disbelieving, disconcerting gaze. He had never, in all his speculations, thought Paleochora worth more than a few thousand, a few thousand that could be safely put away to pay for Lucy's nursing home when the time came. Numb, he sat through pudding and a coffee, handing his mint and petit four to Toby who so adored chocolate. He could not say what he had eaten. He felt adrift from the world as he knew it. He toiled among the cloud-capped peaks, seeking a foothold before they too were left behind and below.

The bill came. He made no protest when Toby picked it up. He thought it would draw unnecessary attention, would look from across the room like a lovers' tiff. Well, damn Nina, he thought. She can pay after all.

'Good old Nina,' said Toby with affection.

'Yes.' Christopher stirred, passing a hand over his damp brow. 'You must thank her for me.'

'Oh, I shan't tell her.' Toby looked arch. 'You know, she thinks your mother should marry again.'

She would. 'I suppose she has someone in mind,' said Christopher. It came out sourly. It struck him he had no right to be sour when it was Nina who had bought his lunch. 'I'm sorry, I can't stop.' He tapped his watch. 'The car.'

Before he had reached the door he felt an arm over his shoulders. 'Great meal. I hate eating alone.'

Christopher doubted Toby often did so and wondered why, today of all days, he had been so inopportunely unencumbered.

'Give my regards to Nina.'

'I shall.' He would probably not mention the restaurant at all but he would say he had bumped into Chris, and he would describe him unkindly. Nina would be amused.

The heat outside was tremendous. Hotter than at Paleochora? He thought of Lucy briefly, but Christopher's imagination was restricted by what he thought Lucy ought to be, not what she was. In this instance he pictured her swimming rather decorously with the children, a woman whose joints were growing stiff. He decided to ring as soon as he got back to his flat, see how they were all getting on. Then he might hear that it was just an ordinary sort of house after all, just an ordinary house on the coast worth an ordinary and sensible amount of money. He knew Ginny would describe it in loving detail and from that he could extrapolate, form an accurate impression, and lay to rest the irrational fears Toby had roused.

For a moment, on the pavement, he thought Toby might kiss him. He extricated himself clumsily from the embrace. Then he walked away stiffly, trying not to look as if he were hurrying, but even in his car with the windows fully down to let out – and in – the stifling air, he still felt overwhelmed by the spicy blast of Toby's aftershave.

The children spent all day swimming or trying to catch geckos or eating, in that order. In the afternoon, overcome by the remorseless sun, they dozed in hammocks which Yannis the gardener slung between the posts of one of the lower terraces. Later Lucy would go with them to the beach. Or maybe she would row them along the coast to another stretch of sand or to the little secret bay to climb the promontory. They would swim from the boat while she lay back, her hat over her eyes.

Prepared for disappointment, she had done what little she could to arm herself. But Paleochora was as beautiful, as untouched as ever. There were still few tourists, no new hotels, no beach bars. It was not that nothing had changed but that nothing of any importance to her had changed.

We only loved here, she thought. We never quarrelled. Their only quarrel, if it could be called that, had taken place in Athens, in the lobby of a hotel, a too-public place. They had spoken in harsh lowered voices, unnatural and foolish. Oliver had silenced her by saying something as absurd as it was dramatic, something about ruining her life. I can't remember, thought Lucy. I can't remember. She probably hadn't been listening, or by then had been beyond words. But I was drinking tea. It came back to her with shocking clarity: the clink of cup against saucer in her trembling hands, inelegant hotel china, steam rising. Quite ordinary, everyday occupations are frequently interrupted by tragedy, she thought, and are remembered for ever, while all the subsequent anguish and activity blur and dwindle. What on earth could he have said about ruining her life? It was like a line from one of the stories Mrs Treece read every week and recounted over coffee or while sorting the ironing. Her husband apparently never caused such palpitating moments. 'I live my life through fiction,' she had said once to Lucy, drawing on her rubber gloves and gazing at them with distaste for a moment for they, like the Vim, were only too real.

At Paleochora Lucy sensibly put on her hat and went down to the beach. The design of this house had been Oliver's passion, she thought, its building, its completion, its embellishment and improvement. Did she possess him at last, then, possessing this place?

Barefoot in the warm shallows, she took off her hat and let the sun strike her bare head. How he would laugh at such silliness. Possess how? Possess what? he would ask. Surely we only join hands, he would tell her, and walk a small way together pretending we're not still alone.

Then what have I, having Paleochora? she wanted to ask.

My hand in yours, he said.


'Did you know Maurice had a mistress?' Bernadette asked Alan, and they looked at each other.

Alan was alarmed by the word mistress, which sounded archaic, but he was not really interested. He had been busy checking Bernie for signs of emotional disintegration, at the first hint of which he would suddenly remember he was supposed to be giving a lecture.

'No, I didn't know.' It could hardly matter now, he thought.

'A woman who worked at the library or something. He met her once a week.'

'Why not more often?' How dull, he was thinking, how boring, how predictable, how very like his father.

'How could they? There'd have been a scandal.' This

word too seemed from a bygone age. Nowadays it was only found in newspapers, those repositories of anachronism.

'Not in the sixties,' Alan said lightly.

'But he couldn't have wanted Mother to find out.' Bernadette needed to give Maurice full marks for discretion, for sparing Lucy's feelings.

'Of course not. He'd have been terrified she'd leave him. He wouldn't have risked that. She made his life so comfortable.'

'Mother would never have left him.'

Alan was about to retort, 'Wouldn't she?' when the look on Bernadette's face warned him. After a moment he said gently, 'No, of course she wouldn't. She never did, did she, even when we all left home and there might have been nothing to keep her. I often think they were fond of each other though they never gave much sign of it.' He was conscious he was in the process of damping down his sister's emotions as if they were small fires that must be contained at all costs. Like a man automatically selecting a sound bucket for the water, he modulated his voice, smiled as if at some happy memory of his parents' marriage. 'Bernie love,' and he sounded very reasonable and, he hoped, very soothing. 'Bernie, it was all a long time ago.'

They were in Alan's rooms in college, surrounded by the smell of old leather, books, coffee and the sweet peas outside the open window. Bernadette had driven herself to Oxford in something of a daze, had struck the porter as mentally deficient, and now looked disorientated and hot among her brother's orderly possessions.

'Mother knew all about it. Apparently she laughed.' This had made a deep impression.

'Very sensible. It sounds laughable.' 'Besides, you can't possibly know what really went on. And it's none of your business.'

'It was our business *then* if only someone had told us.

143

It wasn't just Mother he was deceiving, it was all of us.'

'But we were nearly grown up, weren't we?' Well, some of us were, thought Alan. He recalled Bernadette in her wild phase that seemed to have broken over him along with puberty so that at times there had almost been too much to cope with – too much undirected emotion. An electrical storm of hormones, he thought. Lucy had seemed permanently exhausted and no wonder, Bernie absent without leave or, when present, aggressively defiant. Always extremes: from deeply religious to deeply irreligious to chaos, then to all these years of trying to climb back on to that rock of absolute faith, struggling, slipping, growing more irrationally determined every time she knew herself falling . . .

Alan counted the notes in his wallet.

'Let's go for a drink.'

Bernadette's arrival had knocked out his plan for the evening, but he felt no resentment. She had often been the cause of last-minute cancellations, panicky phone calls. It goes on and on, he had thought, finding her outside his door, but the thought simply rose and fell away again. He had long ago given up feeling exasperated.

They walked through the college followed by the scent of the sweet peas. It occurred to him that she hadn't mentioned religion yet or the latest offering from Father Brace. She looked better than usual in a simple black sundress that showed too much of her ample, heavy breasts to be clerical. Thank God, he thought, and then smiled to himself at the irony. He would hate her to know how unimportant he found her involvement with this God, this endless tussle of hope and doubt. She would think she herself was unimportant to him.

'Do we have to go out?' As they emerged into the street she hesitated, swaying, as if buffeted by a current.

'Yes, we do.'

He had always found the best way to deal with her was to ignore the inevitable protest and carry on, for she invariably followed. What was no use at all was stopping to argue the point, as Lucy had found, and poor David, and Chloë, and anxious, harassed little Father Brace who secretly would far rather have punted her romantically up the Cam than wrestled for her soul.

'You look nice,' Alan said as they walked along. He wondered if she was falling in love. It could account for a sudden blossoming of hair and skin.

'I had to wear this.' She sounded disparaging, brushing her fingers over the straining black cotton at her breast. 'It was so hot in the car. And ninety miles. I nearly melted.'

They had reached his favourite pub and chose a table outside, crammed into a corner under a great unpruned rambler. Here and there a few flowers still bloomed, blowsy and sweet, and petals dropped into his beer glass. He slung his jacket over the back of his chair and groped for his cigarettes, lighting one and dropping the lighter on the table-top.

'You still smoke,' and she sounded surprised, as if she hadn't seen him for years and years or had forgotten. 'That was Daddy's lighter.' She remembered as she spoke that she had given up calling Maurice Daddy. Old habits, she thought. 'We can do anything if we only try,' was what Father Brace told her frequently with his touching optimism. Bernadette was not so sure.

She picked up the lighter but then, as if it were too heavy for her, returned it immediately. The memory it brought back was of Maurice dead in the hospital bed, smelling of antiseptic and drugs and vomit. They had long ago forbidden him the small cigars he loved. Only the lighter remained, like the last pathetic keepsake of a love affair, pushed behind the water carafe on the locker behind the small bunch of flowers, the letters Lucy had read out to him and the cards wishing him better soon.

'I don't know where Chloë is.' Bernadette opened her eyes and found Alan looking at her oddly.

'Are you all right? Oh, Chloë's fine. Anyway, she doesn't need permission to be out and about. She's all grown up, Bernie.'

'But I usually know where she is.'

'Poor kid. I hope Mother didn't know where I was a lot of the time when I was nineteen.' It had been a time when he had gone about his own affairs with the heartless singlemindedness of the young. He had scarcely given a passing thought to Bernie, coping alone with a three-year-old in a poky flat with no garden. Mother'll look after her, was what he said to himself. 'Gone to pieces, poor girl,' said Mrs Treece. 'And what can you expect?' She saw life as a series of dark tunnels from which one emerged for short periods of air and rest and, if one was lucky, ordinary happiness like weddings and births and a win on the horses. Bernadette had entered a particularly long subterranean stretch when David had been killed and it couldn't be expected she would see light ahead for some considerable time. 'It's not fair on Chloë, though, if Bernie's going to weep and gnash her teeth for the foreseeable future,' the young and callous Alan had pointed out.

'Poor Chloë,' he said now, remembering.

'She hasn't been here, has she? She hasn't rung? She always liked you best.'

'Did she? I never knew. I suppose I made a fuss of her. She was such a solemn, anxious little thing. No, Bernie, I haven't spoken to her for months.'

She looked doubtful. She was primed for deception now, for Maurice had deceived her, living his secret life, and Lucy, by keeping silent.

'You'd let me know straight away if you did?'

'You know I would.'

As they got up to go he put an arm round her. She felt solid and warm. He wished suddenly that he could provide someone less abstract than God, less complicated than the Church, for her to love.

'Are you staying the night?'

'May I?'

He thought it would be tiresome to sleep on the sofa but he was mellow now, ready to make the sacrifice. He had, in any case, always been tender with her once he had got over his egotistical stage. He liked women, and had recognized her early on as one of those most easily bruised. He sometimes tried to shield her, to encourage her faltering steps in adulthood. And: She's forty, he thought. Poor Bernie.

On the way back to college he made her laugh. She had a nice laugh, strong and unaffected. But how often do we hear it, he asked himself.

'I do wish I knew where Chloë was,' she was saying, walking along with her hand through his arm.

'She'll turn up. I can't imagine Chloë up to mischief.'

'Everyone says that: "She'll turn up," they say, as if she's just popped out to post a letter. There's the degree, her whole future . . . I don't think anyone's bothered.'

'Bernie, we're all bothered about Chloë,' said Alan.


Chloë's metal watch strap set off the security buzzer and there was the indignity of a search.

When the plane took off and turned south – or what she supposed was south – she felt liberated, as if she were at last on her way to fulfil her destiny. She found herself smiling at strangers, but distractedly, for her mind was not on them but on herself.

She did not even listen to the captain's disjointed remarks on altitude or the weather. She gazed out in delight at the damp clouds through which they climbed and climbed. Like Ginny, she took pleasure in the ritual of flight, the boiled sweets, the drinks trolley, the plastic trays of insipid food. After every interruption she looked at her watch. The hours were ticking by and in a while they would begin to come down from the heavenly blue, buffeted through more cloud, lower and lower until that sudden bump as the wheels touched land and they were there.

She had never felt so happy.


'Hallo, Mother,' said Christopher with some relief. He had gone sadly to pieces with Evangelia who for some reason had thought he was a journalist.

'I wasn't expecting you,' said Lucy. 'Are you well?'

'Never better.' He sounded falsely hearty. 'How are *you*? Settled in? What about the children?'

She put them on. Adam was defensive, Ginny expansive. As he had hoped, she gave him a detailed inventory of her bedroom. 'And it has a marble bathroom,' she ended, having kept the best till last.

'Splendid.'

'And the pool is gorgeous. Cool.'

He was unsure if she meant the temperature of the water or not. He was suddenly conscious of the distances between them. He asked carefully, 'And how's your Gran?'

'Amazing,' breathed Ginny. She said am-aze-ing.

'Cheerful?'

'Ever so. She swims. And we all drink wine. And we laugh a lot with Evangelia.'

'Who?'

'The housekeeper. She's teaching us Greek.'

Handed back to Lucy, Christopher said peevishly, 'And I suppose the weather's fantastic?'

'Too hot, darling.'

'It was eighty-five here today. The office was unbearable.'

'Then I hope Marianne's finished that wretched book and is down the garden in the hammock.'

'Marianne?' Christopher thought that Turk, apparently like much else in his mother's life, was a subject best left alone.

'Have you heard from Bernie?'

'Oh, several times. She's in a state as usual.'

148

'I expect Father Brace will sort her out,' said Lucy comfortingly.

'No. It's Chloë. She's missing or something. At least, Bernie doesn't know where she is.'

'Bernie used to do that to me. D'you remember? Minutes have never passed so slowly. But she came back, staggeringly unrepentant, and even asked me why I'd been worried. I could have strangled her quite cheerfully and after I'd actually prayed – prayed! – for her to walk through the door.'

Christopher felt he had never caused such anguish and should be given more credit for it. His had been a blameless youth. He couldn't imagine he had ever caused Lucy a moment's anxiety, had certainly never brought her to her knees before a God whose existence she doubted. Bernie had been impossible, of course, until she married. He said as much and then added that Alan too had been troublesome, like a tom cat, out every night after conquests. Had Lucy prayed for *him*?

'Mother, you're not listening,' he accused, hearing whispering and a distant, thready music.

'I am, dear.'

'Mother.'

'I'm giving instructions to Ginny.' There was more whispering. The music faded away.

'This house . . .' He paused. 'I've seen some pictures of it in a book. It's rather special, isn't it?'

'It used to be quite famous. While Oliver was famous.'

'Bit of a playboy, wasn't he? Renowned for his parties.'

'And his scholarship.'

'Drink. Women.'

'Oh, both of those.'

'But this house.' It was as if Toby's voice spoke in his ear. 'I hadn't realized it was so out of the ordinary.'

'Oliver had it built before the war when he was still a young man. He loved this coast. His first work was here. The Greeks made difficulties but he won them round. He

149

lived here all his life until the last eighteen months. He knew he was going to die. He leased the house then and went from hospital to clinic to nursing home. Moira Hannaford was with him. She'd been with him for several years but they didn't marry. He never married. Anyway, she dragged him all over the place hoping for a remission but it wasn't any good. It was never going to be any good. He knew that.'

'But why you?' Christopher was moved to ask again. 'Why leave the house to you?'

'Probably a whim. He had no family, you know.'

'He had Moira whatshername,' said Christopher, irritated.

'I believe she had most of his money.'

It was all very unsatisfactory. As a last fling he said, 'Well, you'd better make the most of it while you can, I suppose. Has Laura rung? I thought she'd be bound to worry about the children.'

'Once or twice. I think Ginny put her mind at rest.'

'I ought to go and see her.'

'Yes, you ought.'

'Well, I'll say goodbye for now. I'll ring Friday. You'll be there Friday, won't you?' It was a command, not a question.

'I might be,' said Lucy.

# 12

THEY felt sorry for Rev, and Sunday church became a crusade.

'He tries so hard,' said Caroline, inspecting her fingers for frostbite on their return. 'And there are never more than seven people there. I count every week.'

'Seven and us,' corrected Lucy.

'Oh, we don't really count. We're really only there for moral support.'

'I expect Rev hopes you're there because you believe in God.'

'Well, I don't.'

In spite of this drawback Lucy thought that Caroline would make a good vicar's wife, much better than Joyce who forgot and mismanaged and muddled through. It was Caro who always remembered names and family circumstances, who asked the old ladies about their unspeakable ailments and who spoke cheerfully to the cantankerous sexton. It seemed to come easily to her, this ability to give people time. In the services she sang strongly, oblivious to the imperfect notes all round. She wanted her father to believe he had a congregation of fifty, a hundred. If she prayed at all to the God she didn't believe in it was always to bring down on Rev the blessing of success.

Life at the parsonage, however, was unredeemably chaotic.

'The boiler's burst,' Caroline announced one morning, returning with chilled bare feet from an excursion downstairs.

'What does that mean?' Lucy struggled awake, not keen to put her head out into the frosted air.

'No hot water. No baths.'

The baths were huge and white and had small notices pinned over them: 'Four inches of water only.'

'I can do without baths,' said Lucy.

'So can I. Oh, move over. I'm frozen.'

Caroline was wearing a pair of her father's old pyjamas under her nightdress. From her head she plucked a red woolly hat.

'Your feet!' cried Lucy, retreating.

It was an elderly double bed with a hollow in the middle. It creaked and whimpered alarmingly.

'Can you imagine anyone making love in this?' Caro asked.

I'm not expecting a baby, Oliver doesn't love me, I shall never see him again, I want to die, thought Lucy.

'Mother's trying to ring Mr Cooke to come and mend it.'

'Mend what?'

'The boiler.'

'We could always go to the Fox and Hounds for a bath.'

'Pay, you mean? It would look awful. We'd have to troop in like a family of paupers and it would be all round the village before we could pull the plug out. And Rev would feel horribly ashamed.' Caroline always considered the vicar before everything, even her own cleanliness.

Nevertheless they lay for a moment imagining a whole bathful – up to the overflow – of hot, hot water. Then Caro laughed, and laughing, rolled helplessly into the hollow. She found Lucy warm but painfully thin, bones protruding even through two vests, pyjamas and a knitted waistcoat donated by one of the twins.

'I'll miss you when you go,' she said.

'I don't seem to be going. Father hasn't written.'

'Perhaps you'll stay for Christmas. That would be nice.'

'Father probably hopes so. He's used to other people taking his problems off his hands. He only cares about how ancient Greeks wore their hair combs.'

Caroline snorted. She burrowed deeper among the thin pillows. 'You're old enough to do what you like. Why not get a job?'

'Doing what?'

'Anything. But then . . . what about Greece?'

'You'd love it, Caro. So beautiful. Unspoilt. I could get a job there.'

'Could you?' Perhaps anything was possible after all. Caroline's head moved from the pillows to Lucy's shoulder. 'No exploding boilers,' she mumbled. Lucy thought she was laughing but then she felt the tears penetrating all the layers and dampening her flesh.

Neither of us is happy, she thought.

She cradled Caroline's head with a new tenderness. The hair she stroked was thick and coarse. She wished she could carry Caro away to Paleochora and show her paradise, but that would involve showing her Oliver.

'Caro, suppose I told you . . .' But she could not tell.

'No, don't. Whatever it is hasn't made you happy, has it? Just tell me about Greece again. Make me forget cold baths and cold churches and cold beds.'

Her head was still tucked into Lucy's shoulder. As Lucy spoke, lovingly, enthusiastically, she relaxed and relaxed, breathing evenly like a child on the edge of sleep, relinquishing the burden of her family.


On the third day, Mr Cooke having failed in his endeavours, they coerced the twins into the enamel hip bath in the kitchen, ladling hot water from the stove.

'I'm really very sorry,' Lucy said to Joyce. 'We've tried to be careful.'

Joyce clutched the teapot she was carrying hard against her chest. Horror bloomed and faded in her eyes. 'It can't be helped.' She trod through water to the table. She was entertaining the Jumble Sale Committee in the drawing room and more tea was imperative, more tea to ease the prolonged silences, the old rivalries. Through a fug of steam she saw Henry and Stephen, in bathing trunks, capering across the tiles screeching, wielding sponges. 'It can't be helped,' she repeated.

Lucy went for another bath towel from the upstairs cupboard and coming down the great bare staircase saw the late post on the doormat: 'Miss Lucy Cavendish' and in a hand she knew. Her heart contracted. She felt unable to breathe.

Dropping the towel, she went down on her knees on the freezing flagstones and reached out her hand for the letter. It felt promisingly solid, but when she opened it she found a not very successful photograph of Paleochora taken from the beach and so few lines of writing on the single sheet of paper that she could have wept.

'I hope wherever the old man sent you is bearable,' he had put. All the sentences were short, dashed off, as if he wrote under pressure. He hoped she was all right. All right? What is 'all right', wondered Lucy. Perhaps he worried she might be pregnant. But it seemed, in that case, a rather offhand inquiry and late in the day. Altogether it was an impersonal, anonymous communication. He hadn't even signed it. She blinked her eyes on tears.

'And all this bother about offal . . .' cried a high-pitched female voice, and the drawing-room door opened. It was the Jumble Sale Committee, unsatisfactorily entertained by the weak tea and Marie biscuits, thoughts already turning to the domestic chores of the evening and away from shrunken woollens and defective mincers and whether or not to take shoes, there were so many diseases and deformities among local feet.

Lucy swept up the towel but was too late. She was forced to stand and be greeted or look impossibly rude. For a minute she, like Joyce, thought they would never go but would stand about in the hall indefinitely, children's teas and husbands' suppers left to get themselves.

'Sometimes I think I can't bear it,' Joyce exclaimed, shutting the door on them at last. 'And if anyone mentions bunions or verrucas to me again tonight I shall scream.'

Harold wrote and suggested she spend Christmas at the vicarage if the Horringers would have her. He was not in a position to offer much interesting seasonal entertainment after all. He was writing a series of articles and preparing his Athens lectures. The weather was cold, Sofia had unidentifiable pains, Evdoxia a sore throat.

'Oh!' cried Lucy and tore the letter in two.

When she told Joyce, producing the mutilated evidence, Joyce said calmly, 'Don't worry. He was always like that.' She thought it would be nice for Caro to have Lucy there at Christmas. She turned the bacon in the pan, leaning her hip into the stove.

'I'm so sorry,' said Lucy, hating Harold for always being 'like that'.

'But we'd love to have you. Andrew was only saying yesterday how bravely you and Caro sing in church.'

'It's Caro. She knows all the tunes.'

'She has a lot to do at Christmas. We all go demented. And there'll be a respectable congregation for once.'

'It seems mean to only come at Christmas and Easter and weddings and funerals.'

'Oh, I don't know. I'd only go to those if I weren't a vicar's wife. People like a bit of colour and familiar old songs. They like the theatre of it. And those are big events. People make an effort for them.'

She handed Lucy the knife with which she had been

tormenting the fry-up. Her footsteps rang through the vast cold larders. Returning she said, 'Sardines again,' and put two tins and a loaf on the table for the twins' tea, staring at them gloomily. She had tried, with Caroline, to pickle and preserve and salt down as a good country housewife should, but ambition and ability were poles apart, the shelves only held sticky pots of unidentifiable and oily substances, often breeding interesting moulds.

'I ought to get a job,' Lucy said tentatively.

'Is that what you want? Well, I suppose it is, really. You'd better start thinking seriously, then.'

'I could do a course.'

'Harold won't approve. If I were you I'd fix it up and just get on with it. He'd surely give you enough to pay rent on a room somewhere till you were earning?'

They both thought about it for a moment but with misgivings. Then the crash of the outer door heralded the vicar, his hair on end, his cheeks puce, his overcoat flapping open, two buttons missing.

'A chapter of accidents,' he announced cheerfully. 'My chain came off. Then I lost these struggling with that gate to Glebe Farm. And the wind. More like a hurricane going across the common.'

'Darling, Lucy wants a job.'

'Immediately?'

'As soon as we can think of something. Harold's ducked out of Christmas.'

'Well, we thought he might.'

How humiliating, thought Lucy. They've talked about it. They were prepared. Although she was fond of them and reason suggested they must, out of her hearing, discuss tactics and probabilities, even money – for she had to be fed – she felt wounded. She was not wanted anywhere, she thought. She was simply a nuisance. Harold and Edith had made her a nuisance by packing her off to people who were only too glad to have her until they understood how long she was to stay. Once or twice excuses had been made. Perhaps another time, they said. So in the end Margot and Caro had, in a sense, adopted her. They both came from families that were as capable of absorbing stray people as stray cats. But I'm beyond all that now, she thought. I needn't be a nuisance any more. I can be independent.

'Funds,' said Rev ominously. 'The problem is funds.'

'Harold has masses of money,' said Joyce, who only assumed he had because he was so mean.

'That doesn't necessarily mean he'll finance Lucy through a year's training or whatever.'

'I could be a nurse,' suggested Lucy.

'I should proceed with caution if I were you,' said Rev, alarmed.

'Harold was always unreliable. Edith used to tell me so in every letter,' said Joyce, looking fondly at her husband in his rumpled black and bicycle clips. He met her glance. They both knew Edith had been equally unreliable and had always hoped they had done something in the way of damage limitation.

'There you are, then,' Rev said to Lucy. 'No such thing as ideal parents. Either they cling on and suffocate you or they push you out before you want to go. It's not sardines again, is it? And where's Caro? She said she'd go down to see old Mrs Dawes about holly. I can't make that woman hear. She sees me coming and takes out her deaf aid.'

'Caro's gone down to the farm for milk.'

'Then who's the bacon for?' He leaned forward, looking hopeful.

'For me. I haven't had any lunch yet,' said Joyce.

In the middle of 'It Came Upon the Midnight Clear' Lucy felt the tears running down her cheeks. She stooped awkwardly over her book, too tall for concealment, but the flow continued, her nose blocked, she ceased to sing.

Caro was separated from her by the twins. She could do

157

nothing but look anxious. The twins themselves were busy extracting the tobacco from a cigarette they had found between the kneelers. Later they would try it in the old pipe they had hidden in the vestry.

Lucy extricated her handkerchief and blew her nose. The music swept on. Caro's strong voice covered her distress. She was singing for both of them, both of them and the twins and poor dear Rev and Joyce who never sang but only hummed and all the feeble and half-hearted in the congregation. Although she sang bravely, with her head up, her eyes apparently glazed with rapture, Lucy knew she noticed everything: Miss Ealing at the organ, old Bill hand-pumping valiantly beside her, the torn hem of Rev's surplice, the patches of mould on the walls, the woodworm in the pews, the smell of mice, damp books, cheap perfume, carbolic soap, mothballs, wax candles, cows. This was Rev's first Christmas here. Everything must go well. It would set the tone for years to come.

As the singing finished Lucy blew her nose again. She saw the vicar step forward to usher Mr Blower to the lectern. It was Mrs Blower who had won in the dispute of the jumble-sale shoes and who had justified her stand by selling every pair bar one, so hideous even she could throw them away without a murmur.

'And it came to pass . . .' began the deep country voice, trained on bullocks and apple-stealing children.

Oliver, cried the voice in Lucy's head. Oliver.

Harold conveniently forgot Lucy until well into the new year when a letter from the vicarage found him in Athens on the point of delivering his lectures. Lucy wrote that she had arranged a place for herself on a secretarial course in Cambridge starting in May. She could not stay with the Horringers for nothing until then. She must either come back to Greece or be sent enough money to rent a room.

The tone was unexpectedly peremptory, Harold

thought, but then he had never known the humiliation of being an object of charity.

'What am I going to do?' he asked Evdoxia.

The Horringers kissed her goodbye with genuine regret, they would have kept her for ever if necessary. Rev told her she had cheered up the house so much he had almost come to terms with its hideousness. Caroline, who had promised not to cry, wept furiously into the collar of Lucy's winter coat.

It was all too much to bear, Lucy thought.

She had joked with the twins all morning until the moment of departure. They were robustly unsentimental. Goodbyes as yet meant nothing to them. But when she stood on the platform of the tiny station, her one suitcase at her feet, the family round her, she felt only desolation.

A bell rang and down the track a signal fell. Distinctly on the still air they heard the panting of the branch train as it struggled with the mild gradient beyond the signal box.

I shan't cry, thought Lucy. I'm going back to Greece.

But the tears stung her eyes. She could not look at Caro's stricken face. When the train came it was nearly empty and there was no one else to get on. It seemed to have barely stopped before it pulled away again. Lucy huddled miserably in the corner of a carriage and the Horringers in a tight knot on the very edge of the platform, waving pointlessly.

There was no one to meet her in Athens. Harold had muddled the times or had not been reminded by Evdoxia. At the British School they told her the Professor was in Corinth, but a small man in heavy spectacles hurrying by with a large cardboard box said on the contrary the Professor was visiting friends in Kalamata.

Lucy took a taxi to the Fieldings' house.

As she ran up the steps a man ran lightly down.

'Oliver,' said Lucy.

He stopped, turned. She was filled with the old delight, the inevitable inner turmoil, and a sense of shock that he hadn't recognized her. He took off his hat.

'Lucy?'

So this was how such things ended, she thought. A coldness settled in her, every other sensation draining away. He did not even take her hand. If anything he looked, having got over surprise, irritated that he might have to deal with her, perhaps make conversation about the weather, about England, about Harold's forgetfulness.

'I can't find Father,' she told him.

'And you've only just arrived? That sounds like Harold. I didn't know you were expected. He never mentions you to me when we meet.'

'I don't suppose he does.' She glanced at her watch. 'I landed an hour and a half ago.' It might have been a year. She felt unable to cope with so much disappointment.

'Have you tried . . .'

'I've tried everywhere. Mrs Fielding was a last resort.'

'Bunny's in hospital. Woman trouble. Fielding's in Cairo, or so I've just been told by a neighbour. Have you eaten?'

'I'm not very hungry.'

'Then we'll have a drink while I try to find Harold for you.'

They walked side by side along the narrow street. He did not offer her his arm when they crossed in front of the traffic. For her part she pretended not to care and kept her hands pushed down into her pockets.

All those tears, she thought. How quickly one fell out of love. It seemed hardly worth the trouble.

He took her to a large, impersonal hotel where the drinks were expensive and the staff attentive. Her coat was whisked away by the cloakroom attendant. The Powder Room was pink with gilt mirrors. It could have been London or Rome or Paris. She wondered if he had brought her here because it was the sort of place a wealthy middle-aged man might take his niece for a lemonade. When he led her to the lounge no one even looked up. No one is speculating, she thought. We're respectable people in a respectable place. He left her with a tray of tea while he went to phone Evdoxia.

'She's coming,' he told her, returning almost at once. 'She was at the flat with her feet up. It was a bit of a shock.' He smiled and repeated in Greek what Evdoxia had said: 'Damn Harold. He told me Thursday. Oh, the poor child. Is she very upset?'

'Well, I'm not,' said Lucy. The teapot seemed immensely heavy. She was afraid it would fall. 'I'm used to it. But where *is* Father?'

'Back at the site. He'll be here tomorrow.'

'Then where do I stay?'

'With Evdoxia in the flat. Harold rented a small place near the English church, not too far from the Fieldings. If I'd been sure Evdoxia would be there I'd have taken you straight away.'

Lucy wondered if Evdoxia's presence in this small flat needed any explanation, but perhaps she was being over-sensitive or naive. She kept silent, looking down at her hands.

'You've changed,' said Oliver. He leaned back to summon the boy for another brandy.

'It's been four months.' She must respond to his indifference with indifference, she thought. 'I've had chilblains, a permanently red nose and a surfeit of church. And I've never stopped feeling hungry.'

'I thought you were looking thin.'

'Spam and sardines.'

A woman in a green hat asked if she could appropriate their ashtray. Oliver handed it to her with his charming smile.

'Dear God! Spam and sardines!'

Lucy looked up. I hardly know him, she thought. She

had once supposed love brought insight in its train as a rocket scatters stars. Now she knew that love, far from shedding light, only showed up the darkness. Such darkness. He seemed amused. Did he think she wanted to make a joke out of the spam and sardines? Was he hoping to banter away the last minutes before Evdoxia arrived, easing the awkwardness with some childish humour? Suddenly she heard her own voice, rushed and desperate and not pitched low enough for such a public place, saying: 'My friend Caro would expect to be married before she let a man make love to her. But then she's a vicar's daughter. I'm not.'

'Have they filled you with guilt, then?' And in a low, angry voice: 'Did you tell this Caro all about me?'

'She's my best friend.' She and Margot. Women are more constant, thought Lucy.

'If Harold ever came to hear . . .'

'What could he do?'

'Something ridiculous. Hurt you terribly. Leave all his money to . . . I don't know. Be a worse parent than he is already.'

'He was never really any kind of parent. I don't need him any more.'

'You only think you don't. He's all you've got. And you'd hate to quarrel.'

'Why should you care?' She had picked up her cup in order to give her hands something to do, in order to show the people sitting nearby, the people staring, that there was nothing wrong. Nothing. 'I was just a few days' fun. I don't mind. Why should I mind? I knew what I was doing. But please don't pretend you care about me.' Her voice, unnaturally suppressed, cracked and rose. Across the room the woman in the green hat knocked ash into the ashtray and smiled at the dark, attractive man who had handed it to her, as if she could tell he was having some silly little trouble and was prepared to offer adult consolation.

'Lucy, behave. Don't make a scene in public.'

'Is that what I'm doing? I'm sorry. I didn't realize. But I can't be the first.' She saw this was a fact. She was glad to cause even a tremor of embarrassment. So there had been other scenes, uglier, more prolonged, and that was why he would not suffer hers though she was just a girl and on the verge of tears. 'I don't expect I'll see you again,' she said, going on doggedly. 'I hoped . . .'

'For Christ's sake. I behaved badly. I told you at the time. We're lucky there were no other consequences than this,' and he made a gesture with his hand as if to indicate their sitting apart like this, mutually angry.

'Yes, it is, isn't it? What a bother it would have been.'

'Lucy . . .' He was truly angry now. His face had darkened. She had known he could be formidable. Instead of shrinking she sat more upright and lifted her head as if ready to ward off blows. Her soft hair, faded by her long winter at the vicarage, fell back and revealed her thin young face. He looked at her and away. His voice was unsteady. 'I'd never have married you. You know *that*. But d'you know why? Because I wouldn't ruin your life. You could have begged on your knees but I wouldn't have done it.'

The teacup trembled in her hands. She felt exhausted. All these words, she thought. They were just sound, painful sound. She closed her eyes.

When she opened them Evdoxia, in a pink suit, was hurrying across to them. When she got near she threw her arms wide as if she would scoop Lucy up.

'My dear. My dear. How could Harold have been so silly?'

Her glance at Oliver was swift, but Lucy noticed it. They shared some secret, she thought. Or was Evdoxia, who was young and well-built and fun, another of the women in Oliver's life?

'I must get my coat. And my hat,' she said.

'You must be so tired.' And Evdoxia took her arm in a motherly way, steering her between chairs to the door.

'Goodbye, Lucy,' said Oliver.

# 13

'IT took hours,' said Chloë, gratefully finishing the second helping of salad Evangelia had put in front of her along with bread and wine. 'And I'm bruised all over.'

'Oh, country buses!' exclaimed Evangelia, ardently sympathetic.

Lucy said nothing. She hadn't got over the shock of finding her grand-daughter on the doorstep, her black clothes dusty, her hair a tangled mass.

'This place is *miles* from Athens,' said Chloë.

'You could have told that from a map,' Lucy pointed out.

'I looked at a map. Perhaps I mistook the scale.'

Adam and Ginny, having inspected Chloë from a distance, had returned to the pool where they had devised some new game that involved much diving and uninhibited shrieking.

'Anyone would think they were still babies,' Chloë remarked. 'All that row.'

'Oh, they have fun. And they never fight.'

Cries like gulls scrapping seemed to refute this but were followed by the sound of prolonged splashing and then laughter. Evangelia went out with the dirty plates and

Chloë sat back, lifting her face to the sun filtering through the vines.

'I thought I'd never find you, Gran.'

'Why not tell me you were coming? Why not tell your mother?'

'I don't know.' Chloë's eyes flew open. Her look was almost passionately reproachful. Must there always be a reason, the look demanded. 'Bernadette goes on so about Rick,' she said. 'On and on. You'd think we were living fifty years ago. You know. When nice girls didn't even hold hands till they were engaged.'

'That's rather an exaggeration.'

'But she doesn't trust me.'

It's other people mothers don't trust, thought Lucy. And she found she was not prepared to listen to a long tale of Bernie's shortcomings. To avoid it she sat forward in her chair, deciding that she would get up and walk down to the beach.

'I don't really like him much any more,' Chloë said just as she started to rise. At once Lucy subsided. There had been such a note of bewilderment. 'I don't know why. I don't know . . .' It was shocking not to know when it had happened, this growing apart, this disillusion. Had he always had those habits she now noticed and so disliked? He must have done. Then had she been blind or had she suffered them willingly, for love? For love's sake, Chloë thought. Is that what one does in love?

'Have you told Bernadette?' asked Lucy gently.

'About Rick? She wouldn't listen. She never listens. Well, only to Father Brace, and she even grumbles about him, she says he can't really know much about life living in the presbytery with that mad Irishwoman to cook for him and Father Whatnot for company.'

'He hears confessions,' said Lucy feebly. She thought of him, a small, kindly, anxious man if she remembered, composing himself each week for frightful revelations, made party to the worst of other people's lives. Or not.

What had Maurice confessed to on those rare occasions? To arguing with Bernie, unreasonably, over homework? To envy? To not going to Mass? By the time it was Blaine's every Thursday he had practically given up going to church and only grumbled about it, as a man might grumble about a less than perfect wife who had left him.

'He must find Bernadette tough going,' said Chloë. 'She probably turns the confessional into a sort of psychoanalysis session.'

'I wonder if she remembers all the sleepless nights she gave me,' said Lucy.

'I can't imagine . . . It would have been a sin to stay out late.'

'She gave up God for the duration.'

'Bernadette?' Chloë sounded more than astonished. Outraged?

There was the slap of wet feet running on the tiles. Adam dashed round the great stone dolphin that was all the ornament that remained on this upper terrace.

'Gran. Gran, please come. I think Ginny's dead.'


Ginny lay unconscious in bed and Evangelia brought Lucy a brandy.

'Everything will be all right,' she said.

'So the doctor tells me.'

'Don't you believe him?'

Ginny had looked so white, bluish shadows under her closed eyes. Her breathing had seemed shallow.

'We're so isolated here,' Lucy said. It had never mattered before. But the burden of other people's children was ten times that of one's own, she thought.

'Soon she'll wake and be herself again.' Evangelia saw she must assume the role of optimist. She sensed Lucy's loss of strength. It's this house, Lucy could have said. I'm just a girl in this house, no strength, no experience, no wisdom.

She crept to the bedside and away again. The little

pointed face looked so like Chris, Chris as a very small boy, always shy and pale, hanging back because Maurice, who had strong views on the duties of firstborn children, always expected him to come forward. And I wasn't much good as a buffer, Lucy thought. I never smoothed his path. I simply made Maurice more irritated, more unreasonable, and he took that out too on poor Chris. Things always went from bad to worse.

A great tenderness moved her. She remembered Chris as a toddler, hot and heavy on her lap, remembered the endless repetition of that one special story, the animal noises, the ritual counting, the end where they always laughed, rocking back and forth together.

In the early evening Ginny woke.

'Did I hit my head?'

'Very hard.'

'It was a game.'

Lucy smoothed back her hair. 'Yes, darling. Adam said you slipped.'

'Did I?'

In the morning the doctor called again.

'She must be quiet and still today,' he told Lucy.

'But she is all right?'

'Why not?' And he puffed his cheeks at her foolishness, hurrying away to some more interesting case where recovery was uncertain.

'What a funny little man,' said Chloë, who had put on a summer dress which exposed her fragile shoulders and delicate neck. 'There are some books in one of the bedroom cupboards, Gran. They might do for Ginny.'

Later, taking in lemonade, Lucy found Chloë and Ginny asleep, Chloë sunk forward on the bed, her hair spread over the page she had been reading aloud.

'Everything is all right, isn't it?' Adam felt out of things, had been forced to hang about on the terraces in a state of anxiety. He had been reckless and belligerent. In avoiding him Ginny had fallen and hit her head on the side of the pool. 'She might have died,' he said to Lucy. He had been repeating this silently for hours.

'The doctor says she's fine.'

This was no reassurance. It was Lucy's own opinions he depended on. 'Have you rung Mother?'

'No.'

'Are you going to?' She would ring straight away if she was worried, he thought.

'Perhaps tomorrow,' said Lucy. 'I don't want to upset her for nothing.'

They both pondered for a moment on Laura's frequent upsets and how they were to be avoided at all costs.

'Then I'll go to the beach,' Adam said.

He wondered if it would be boring swimming without Ginny. Though she could be irritating she was usually good company, and allowed him an escape back into childhood without loss of face. She might have died, he thought again. He pulled off the shirt he wore, on Lucy's strict instructions, to guard his pale English skin from the dangerous sun. Then he took a run at the water, galloping in till he fell flat, crowing and spluttering.

It didn't look as if Lucy was going to make anything of the accident. He had wondered if they would be sent home. It had been his greatest fear after the fear that Ginny would die. He swam easily and when he reached the rocks marking the outer limit of the little bay he turned and swam easily back. Then he floated, eyes closed. He could see red, the red of his own blood, he thought. It was somehow comforting. A great peace came over him and beneath it an odd sensation of excitement.

If only Mini could swim with him while Ginny was in bed, Mini with her thick black hair and her small pointed breasts. She always knew when he was looking and bent down or reached up so there was more to look at, delighted with herself and, apparently, with him.

He floated, smiling as he thought of her.

★

Lucy rang Laura twice but she was out. Dutifully she tried Bernadette.

'You mean she's there? In Greece?'

'It was a spur of the moment thing,' said Lucy.

'But where did she find the money?' Bernadette was thinking of her own youth, pitifully underfunded.

'She's given up Rick and doesn't like college much. I think she just needs time alone, time to sort herself out.' I sound like an answer on the Problem Page, thought Lucy.

'Only she's not alone. She's with you.' There was an edgy resentment in Bernie's voice.

'Sun, sea and free lodging,' replied Lucy brightly, trying, as she always had done without noticeable success, to lift Bernadette's mood.

'Mother, did Maurice really have an affair with a woman at the library?'

Lucy held the receiver away from her and looked at it.

'Mother?'

'I've never heard you call him Maurice before.'

'Did you hear me?'

'You asked if he had an affair.'

'Well, did he?'

'Yes. Is it important?'

'But I never knew,' said Bernadette.

'I never told anyone,' said Lucy.

'Other people knew.'

Other people were more nosy and less self-absorbed than you, Lucy thought, and then felt mean. 'Darling, it was very ordinary, even . . . silly. They had lunch every week and sometimes afterwards they'd go to her flat. Now I'd have gone straight to the flat and lunched on love and sandwiches, wouldn't you? To the best of my knowledge,' which in view of Nina's vindictive and salacious interest was considerable, 'that was all there was to it. I only hope she gave him whatever it was he needed.'

'How can you say that? It was hateful of him. I'm surprised you . . .'

'It was all such a long time ago.'

'But . . .'

'He must have been lonely. There was so much I never shared with him.' Jokes, she thought, good novels, passion, domestic triumphs, Mrs Treece's varicose veins, Turk's greatest reviews. 'Anyway, it's history. Forget it.'

'But he shouted at me,' Bernadette said. 'He shouted. I was late home. I think you were at a funeral or something, staying the night somewhere. He called me a little whore. And all the time he was just a bloody hypocrite.'

Caro's funeral, thought Lucy: rain, sour, brown, wet leaves underfoot, Rev suddenly so old.

'Darling, don't take it to heart so. He was angry. We all say stupid things when we're angry.' It's the fate of mothers, she thought, to talk in clichés all their lives. 'He hated you to be out late. He worried.'

'I've never forgotten how he shouted. And I actually felt ashamed. I actually thought I'd have to try to be more like the daughter he wanted, I'd come home early, I'd work hard, I'd go to Girton and do modern languages . . . And all the time he was carrying on . . .'

That was one of Mrs Treece's favourite phrases, thought Lucy: carrying on. No doubt she had reported to Mr Treece that Dr Flecker was carrying on with another woman, for there wasn't much she didn't know after all those years in the house. She liked to think of herself as part of the family, as necessary to its well-being as the kitchen she inhabited. Being an avid reader of advice columns, she was always ready for problems, for they had always all been dealt with by Mary Something or Betty Somebody Else in the magazines she kept under the sink. When she learned that Maurice was unfaithful she mentally composed a desperately sad letter from Lucy and mentally answered it in the persona of Margery Bottomley of *Woman's Life*, counselling fortitude and patience. 'I don't know what the world is coming to,' she said when she got home. Her legs ached and she had begun to have hot flushes. 'And that poor Miss Horringer dying and Mrs F like a wraith,' she would say once a week until Caro died and Lucy, in a daze, packed an overnight bag for Dorset.

As the vicarage was sheltering relations, Lucy had booked herself into the Fox and Hounds. There had been a thin candlewick bedspread, an electric fire with a frayed flex and a crudely coloured picture of the young Victoria. She had gone to bed but had not been able to sleep. She had cried for Caro, for Rev bereft, for the twins – grown men but confused, like babies – and for the old people who had loved her and the Sunday school children and the village women who had dusted and scrubbed and done the flowers at her direction.

Back in Cambridge, still shivering – from the experience, she thought afterwards, not the cold – she had found Mrs Treece reading her horoscope: a good week for Capricorn. 'I don't know about that,' said Mrs Treece. She had hoovered upstairs as a mark of sympathy for Caro, and even done the baths while turning over in her mind Margery Bottomley's probable reply to the heroine of the romantic story of the week whose emotional tangles were quite horrific. 'Bit of a set-to last night,' she told Lucy. 'Dr F and young Bernie. Hammer and tongs.'

But Lucy was drained. She sat at the kitchen table with a cup of black coffee, and if there was an atmosphere she did not notice it, it was nothing to the atmosphere she had endured at the graveside. I don't want to know, she thought. I can't take any more.

'Librans can expect difficulties with loved ones,' said Mrs Treece ominously to Turk.

'Well, that's nothing new,' said Turk.


They went shopping in Pylos and bought olives and wine and cheese and some sandals for Chloë. Ginny held Lucy's arm. They walked slowly, keeping to the shade.

'Should we stop for a drink?' asked Lucy.

'But what about the others?'

'They'll come back. It'll teach them to wander off.' They're young and full of life, thought Lucy, I can't make them stop. It's the old who stop, and that's for refuge, not refreshment. I can't cope with the memories.

'Chloë's beautiful,' said Ginny as they settled at a table.

'She's like her mother. But taller.' Bernadette had missed beauty because her face had always been shadowed by anxiety or sulkiness. She had been so touchy, fearing slights, and always eager for Maurice's approbation. Such devotion, thought Lucy. And he would have chosen the one night I was away to tell her what he really thought of her behaviour. It was me he'd grumbled at before. And I'd made excuses, I'd shielded her as best I could.

'Only two weeks left,' said Ginny mournfully. She gazed about her as if already taking leave. The straw hat that sheltered her tender head was misshapen where she kept bending up the brim.

'Don't you miss your friends?' asked Lucy.

'No.' Every holiday she was bundled away with girls who were certainly not friends, never could be friends. The only one in whom she could confide lived in Tiverton. 'But I never get to go *there*,' said Ginny. So she was snatched from one event to the next, immersed in relentless activity: sailing, riding, tennis, even go-carting. 'The children never have a moment to spare,' Laura would tell people, sounding self-congratulatory.

'How's the headache?'

'Oh, better. Gone,' said Ginny.

'Here they come at last,' and Lucy looked across the street to where a tall, slender girl with a plait of dark hair was stepping into the sunlight. Behind her the boy followed at a distance. They looked like sleepwalkers.

Dear Chloë, thought Ginny with an upsurge of affection. She could confide in Chloë now, Chloë who had read to her, talked to her, forgone sun and swimming for her sake.

Chloë's understanding and sympathy were unstinting. Hadn't she wrestled with parent problems all her life? 'Too much of one and none of the other,' she had said lightly, as if to indicate how little it really mattered. Ginny, however, had recognized the tone.

'You'd think they'd hurry just a little,' said Lucy, though what was there to hurry for? It was pleasant in the leafy shade with the life of the town passing in front of her.

Adam's thinking of Mini, Ginny would have told her if she'd had the courage. Or did Gran know, she wondered. Recalling Mini's small, firm body, the brown arms, the solid legs, her sweaty, spicy smell, she was astonished at Adam's lapse of taste. What could he see in Mini? She frowned into her lemonade. How strange people were, she thought, even people one had known for ever. For ever. And she gave Adam a sharp, bleak look.

'Can't we go home and swim?' was all he said.

The hot weather in England had broken with thunderstorms. Grey drizzle had followed and a depressingly chill wind. Now there were umbrellas down King's Parade and the tourists were huddled in disconsolate groups, only looking forward to hot baths and any kind of food. Turk cycled slowly, her basket filled with grapefruit, filleted sole and three bottles of rather pricy white wine. She was enveloped in an old riding mac, the vintage variety, putty-coloured and devastatingly weighty, teamed with a plastic sou'-wester that had once been Chloë's, and Lucy's waterproof gardening clogs.

At the terrace she bumped the bicycle down the basement steps and shoved it amongst the rubbish. The basement, once the original kitchen, then children's playroom, contained the detritus of years, as if by some strange process unwanted articles had fallen through the floors above to rest there. Here leaned other bicycles, two very small, with a sledge, plastic bags of outgrown clothes, pogo sticks, skates, boxes of seed potatoes shrivelled to marbles, the trunk known as the Dressing-up Chest, a stainless-steel sink, half a ping-pong table and the croquet hoops they hadn't used for years.

Turk squeezed through to the door. The stairs to the hall were steep. Halfway up she stopped to change her shopping to the other hand and knew she was not alone in the house. The hair at her nape prickled. She stood with her hand on the wall, braced, scarcely breathing. Like a wary animal's her ears grew keener. She could distinguish the faintest creak of floorboards, low, muffled voices.

By the front door was the umbrella stand full of Maurice's collected and inherited walking sticks, some with usefully large knobs. Turk took six swift strides, seized the heaviest, and burst through the drawing-room door with teeth bared. Afterwards Christopher said, trying to make a joke of it, 'You looked like an illustration from Rider Haggard,' but at the time he simply retreated from Lucy's writing desk to the window, confused.

'You!' cried Turk.

'Who did you think?' Christopher's colour returned. He stood up straighter. 'We used my key,' he added, glancing across to Laura on the sofa.

'You could have rung first.' Turk removed the sou'-wester. 'How was I to know who it was? Lucy never said you'd be popping in unannounced.'

'You know I have a key.'

'I expect you all have. It would be just like Loo never to think of getting them back when you left home. Still, I'd like to know what you're doing here, creeping about.'

'Creeping about?' Christopher took refuge in indignation.

'We were making sure everything was all right,' said Laura.

'Of course it's all right. What did you think?'

They looked guilty, Turk thought. They looked as if they'd been caught 'at it' as Mrs Treece had put it. The cats next door had often been 'at it' on the basement steps, necessitating pails of water thrown inaccurately, eyes averted. But it seemed unlikely that Chris and Laura had been suddenly reunited in extempore sex on Lucy's drawing-room floor. So what had they really come for?

'I'd love a coffee,' Laura declared bravely into the silence.

'Well, you know where the kitchen is.'

The riding mac had become irksome. Turk needed to take it off and light a cigarette. Besides, the sole ought to be put in the fridge. She retreated to her own part of the house and found herself incandescent with a fury she hadn't felt in years. Why the hell should they arrive like this, creeping about – they had certainly been creeping, and talking in hushed voices. What were they after?

In a while she heard noises in the kitchen and hoped they had failed to find the coffee. Did they know it was in the tin marked 'Salt'? She flicked through her latest pile of manuscript, scowled at the word processor, caressed the keys of the elderly typewriter, and then heard her name being called. She smiled to herself.

'We can't find the coffee,' said Laura. She had never lifted a finger in this kitchen, it had been overfull of managing women already, she had felt squeezed out: Lucy, Turk, Mrs Treece, sometimes Bernadette.

'Here.' Turk brought out the tin and opened it.

Christopher said, 'Everything in this house is past its prime.' He sniffed at the stuff suspiciously. He had disinterred the old Cona from beneath the sink and was boiling water in that, refusing to use the Italian gadget he hated which made coffee that was too strong, too bitter and too much of the past.

'It's a nice house,' Turk said. Was she casting bread on the waters? 'Homely.' He would notice the crack in the Cona shortly, she thought, and then would grow agitated, peering at it frequently, dreading disintegration.

'Shabby, you mean.'

'I've always thought it was lovely,' put in Laura, who had been fiddling with the sugar spoon. She looked strained and unhappy. 'Think of the proportions of the rooms. Beautiful.'

'Loo would never be bothered to tart it up,' said Turk.

'No. But someone else . . .' Christopher stopped. He had spotted the break in the Cona. 'This thing's going to leak.'

'I don't know why you used it. What someone else?'

'Why hasn't Mother thrown it away?'

Turk prayed that the Cona would split and the hot coffee burn Christopher's hovering fingers. 'What someone else?'

'Well, it's getting run down. It's a burden. I'd like to see her settled somewhere more convenient.'

'She wouldn't like that.'

'I don't see why not. Though there might be other solutions.'

'Solutions?'

Christopher was busy pouring. He gave the impression of being quite happy now he had made it clear he knew best. In contrast Laura appeared to have shrunk and looked pale and nervous. Apart from her hair and thin, tense hands, she was hardly different from the girl Turk had first seen at this table on the night Christopher had brought her home.

'Coffee, Marianne?' Christopher held the Cona to the light and squinted at the crack. 'This really ought to go. Why won't Mother ever throw things out? She needs to get organized,' he said as his mind returned to the main theme. 'She needs to think about the future.'

Turk found Laura looking at her. Don't, don't, don't, said her eyes.

'I expect that's what she's doing at Paleochora,' she said calmly and with a smile. The smile took effort. But then she was not aware of ever having felt sorry for Laura before. The effort was rewarded. Those wide blue eyes now expressed gratitude, shining slightly. Oh God, not tears.

'Does it mean anything? Paleochora?' asked Christopher.

'Old something,' said Laura boldly.

Old loves, old happiness, old what you like, thought Turk. Another life, before you, before me. Lucy's own.

'More coffee?' And she held out her cup.


Christopher had rung Laura because, after all, money was the only thing they had never quarrelled about. He had been doing some research since his lunch with Toby and now it was time to explore the options. They're Lucy's options, not ours,' Laura said to his surprise when he picked her up.

'They involve all of us,' he told her.

She had been anxious about Turk, and even when it became obvious Turk was out Laura felt obliged to lower her voice. They went round silently after a while, Christopher ceasing his litany of repairs needed. There were so many repairs.

'You're being finicky,' accused Laura. 'It only needs paint really, new wallpaper.' She felt uneasy, a trespasser, and wished herself somewhere else.

'It needs a new roof.'

Downstairs she sat on the edge of Lucy's sofa and he stood at Lucy's desk and gazed at the picture of Maurice with a baffled expression, as if he had never seen him before or remembered him as someone quite different. There was a pause and then he said, 'The best thing might be for you and the children to live here. Mother could modernize the flat and live in that.' He began to sound cheerful. He could already see it taking place. 'I thought . . .'

'But Turk lives in the flat.'

'And doesn't the bitch know when she's on to a good thing. Years she's sponged off Mother. Years.'

Laura glanced unhappily at the door. 'Lucy . . .' She thought she had better not say that Lucy loved her, that Marianne loved Lucy. She had hardly thought what to say when Christopher continued coldly, 'She hardly pays any rent, you know. And the whole house smells of her cigarettes.' Cigarettes, pipes – Maurice had smoked a pipe – reminded him of childhood. But we're grown-up now, healthy and sensible I hope, he might have said.

'Turk and Lucy are very close,' said Laura bravely.

'Well, if it's not the flat it'll have to be a decent modern bungalow. She'd have more time to do what she wanted. That ought to be an attraction.'

Laura was sure Lucy had never been stopped from doing what she wanted by lack of time. She had certainly never bothered with housework beyond wiping the basins and making the beds. Even in the days when Mrs Treece skimped everything, though the house was full and baths had tidemarks like the wrack of industrial pollution, Lucy closed her eyes and the doors to it all and brewed coffee and worried about Bernie or Alan's friends or Chris's brainless sylphs.

'Do you remember Mrs Treece's varicose veins?' Laura asked, having gone so far down tracks into the past that she had been overcome by a strange nostalgia.

'. . . and if she had to leave the flat or the bungalow and go into a nursing home there'd be enough for that. And the rest in trust for the grandchildren.'

'Mrs Treece,' insisted Laura. She could see her now, stocky and brutal-looking in a pinafore covered in robins. She had had a son called Arthur who had ended up in borstal. 'And good riddance,' she had said. 'I never got my sleep when he was at home. Police knocking on the door any hour of the night. He was always going to come to a sticky end.' She had told Laura this one afternoon when her legs had been more than usually painful, and she was grateful for any sympathy, however tentatively offered. She thought Laura a fey creature and, meeting her as a stranger in a bus queue, would have diagnosed tubercu-losis. Still, she was a Virgo. 'And so was my sister, poor thing – we buried her when she was seventeen,' said Mrs Treece. In no time she had turned to her magazine and Stars for the Week, and from there it was a short step to marriage, pregnancy, breech births, Arthur, Mr Treece's unreasonable attitude when the boy showed an interest in art, and so on and so forth to the moment borstal loomed and Mrs Treece felt an unexpected motherly pang. The stars could not have been in Arthur's favour. Or if they had been he had failed to take advantage. Who could say?

'What on earth are you talking about?' asked Christo-pher. 'I couldn't stand that woman. She called me "Chris-dearie", all one word.'

I wish I'd never come, thought Laura. A paralysing sense of guilt was overtaking her. At first she had thought this visit could do no harm. Surely Lucy would not mind? Also, it gave her a chance to talk to Chris directly instead of through solicitors, something he had so far avoided. Now she saw the impossibility of talking about anything but the house, either this one or the other in Greece. He seemed obsessed with both, and with Lucy's imminent collapse into senility. When he had rung to ask if she'd care to spend the afternoon with him in Cambridge, Laura had agreed in grateful surprise. She was over hysteria. There were practical difficulties they could easily sort out if . . . if he hadn't brought me here, she thought. And then, feeling sudden fright: I wish Lucy was here.

'It's not long before Lucy comes back,' she remarked, for her thoughts had moved on a step.

Christopher had just been saying how Lucy needed to re-route her life into well-marked financial motorways instead of wandering aimlessly down by-roads, muddling through. He gave Laura a sharp look. He had never thought she paid enough attention. 'We can't let Mother fritter all her capital away. She'd give it to some homeless girl begging at a street corner before she'd invest it, I sometimes think.'

'I suppose that *is* a kind of investment.'

'Are you all right?'

'I'm not sure. I don't think we should be here.' Her voice dropped lower and lower.

'Don't be so ridiculous,' he told her, and put out a hand to straighten the picture of Maurice which, he thought, he really couldn't bear.

And then Turk burst in.

Nina made Turk answer the bell by the simple expedient of keeping her finger on it until she came.

'Marianne dear, I've lost Lucy's number.'

'Is that all?'

'I know I could have rung you but I thought no, I'll just pop in. Toby and I have been to the races.' Nina was dressed without regard for the weather in a lemon-coloured silk suit and a wide-brimmed cream hat.

'Ascot?' asked Turk.

'Really, Marianne, do be sensible. I never go further afield than Newmarket. Toby hates horses, hates crowds and is terribly unlucky. My only pleasure is dressing up and having a couple of drinks.'

In the kitchen Turk wrote out Paleochora's number on a piece of torn-up typing paper.

'Yes, well . . .' murmured Nina, taking it. She smoothed the ragged edges and then folded it up and tucked it inside her glove. 'And have you seen any of the family?'

'Why?'

'Oh, a general pricking of the thumbs.' Nina tottered about the room reading notices and shopping lists. The short skirt of her suit showed off her plump calves.

'Isn't Toby waiting?'

'It won't hurt him. He's been insufferable. I'll never go with him again. I'll get George Prendergast to take me. You know he'd send his love. Toby, I mean. He adores you. Lucy seems to have a dental appointment tomorrow. Shouldn't she have cancelled?'

'I'm going instead. One lot of teeth is much like another, I expect.' Turk wondered if Nina were hanging about for a drink just to keep Toby fretting a little longer.

'Edward Mordant, Osteopath.' Nina read from the card. 'He sounds quite sinister. I didn't know either of you went in for osteopaths. Oh, Lucy was going to lend me a book. I can't remember what. Fish cookery or something. I was going to lend it to Trish.'

'It's around. I've seen it recently,' said Turk. She thought that Trish, Nina's eldest daughter, could hardly be badly off for cookery books.

The drawing room was chilly. There was the swish of traffic passing in the wet outside. Nina paused to stare at the photo of Maurice on the desk, a picture that did him more than justice, she thought, by not having caught his habitual expression of dissatisfaction. In it he looked bland and decent, eyes front, regular features subtly lit. It showed the man Lucy thought she had married: dependable, honourable, uncomplicated.

'Did he ever look like that?' Nina asked. She altered the angle. It looked as if someone had half-turned him to the wall.

'It's how Loo wants to remember him.'

'Is it? I'm surprised she wants to remember him at all.'

'This is it.' Turk produced a slim old hardback from the shelves.

'Poor Toby,' sighed Nina, glancing out of the window. She was not very interested in the book.

'Bugger poor Toby,' said Turk. 'He's doing very nicely.'

'He gets bored easily. He doesn't stick at things.' Nina was not making a complaint. These are simply the facts, said her tone.

'He sticks to you,' Turk said. 'Six years. That's something, isn't it?'

'Is it that long? I never count. I really must go.' She flicked through the pages of the cookery book but there were no illustrations to divert her. 'How old-fashioned!' she exclaimed. 'Trish will adore it. Antique recipes seem all the rage, like antiques generally. Did you say you'd seen Chris?'

'No, I didn't say anything,' said Turk.

'But you have. So have I. And so has Toby. And I bumped into Bernie yesterday in Sidney Street – she needs to diet if you ask me – and I smell a conspiracy. I thought I'd warn Lucy. This house of hers in Greece is worth a fortune and . . . well, I won't say it.'

'Oh, Loo's tough,' declared Turk. 'They won't bully her.'

'All the same, I'll get my pennyworth in. Lucy would expect it. I've always been vigilant. I don't like to see her done down.'

From outside came the blare of a car horn.

'Toby's getting impatient,' said Turk.

# 14

IT was Bonny Fielding who gave the party Lucy was never to forget.

'How delightful you look,' were her first words when they arrived, Harold steering Lucy by the shoulders. She could mean anyone, thought Lucy. She isn't even looking at me. There was no obvious sign of the woman trouble that had laid her low. Did all women have such troubles and overcome them so easily?

'Glad to see you've escaped the rectory,' said David Fielding, appearing with a glass of wine for her.

'Vicarage.'

'Is there a difference? Yes, of course.' He looked about gloomily. 'Well, I can't tell you Harold missed you. I suppose that's obvious.'

'I didn't expect him to.'

'Not in the circumstances.' He gave a laugh which sounded embarrassed, although why there was cause for embarrassment was a mystery. 'You look charming,' he continued, but she felt he was making an effort, steering hard away from rocks. 'So Trollopian life wasn't so bad after all.'

'It was nice to feel part of a family,' she told him.

'I'm sure it was. Good practice perhaps too.' He gave her a direct, amused look that was intended, she was sure, to mean something significant.

All around people stood crushed in groups, smoking and drinking. The noise was tremendous. Lucy, in her plain dress and with her hair caught back in a slide, felt clumsy and schoolgirlish. Why did Father make me come, she wondered.

'Lucy. How are you? Fielding.'

'Hallo,' Lucy said calmly. She took a mouthful of wine so as to be seen to be occupied.

'I thought you'd be here somewhere,' said Oliver, but he was looking across the room at Bonny, or perhaps at Harold, there were so many people between.

I must get used to this, thought Lucy.

A week ago when she had visited the British School with Evdoxia he had passed them, had said good morning. 'He is not good-looking but he has charm,' Evdoxia had remarked thoughtfully, gazing after him. He had hurried away through a distant door without looking back.

'There's someone waving at you, I think,' Lucy told him now. Her glass was empty, the wine not having proved a long-lasting refuge nor having had the desired effect. She felt entirely sober and, if anything, saw with greater clarity than before.

'Lucy.' His hand gripped her elbow as if he was afraid she might step away. But still he didn't look at her. He looked in Harold's direction, Harold and Bonny and Evdoxia and some woman in a red dress. There was a lot of silly laughter. Other people were looking the same way, stirred by momentary curiosity.

'What's the matter?' asked Lucy. Why are you standing so close, holding my arm, not speaking, she wanted to say. Let me go, let me go . . .

And then Bonny was waving, calling for quiet. The chatter round them faltered, picked up, began to die away again. Oliver said into Lucy's ear, 'Keep smiling. Look as if you knew.'

'Knew what?'

Bonny was saying something about friendship, about marriage. Her voice was shrill because she had raised it to be heard above the hubbub and now was excited and self-conscious and couldn't bring it down to a normal volume. They would all be glad to know, she said, that Harold and Evdoxia ... Her bright, tinkling tone went on and on until it was overwhelmed by the first of a flurry of congratulations which she accepted as if she herself were the bride-to-be. She was all smiles, happy to be the hostess with such news to announce in the middle of a successful party.

'Married?' cried Lucy. 'Father and Evdoxia?'

'Hush. Smile. I guessed you didn't know. I warned Bonny but she didn't believe me. Why the hell didn't you see it, you little fool? They've been living together in the flat all winter.'

'But they have separate rooms.'

'Don't be absurd.'

She had pushed away suspicion although Harold and Evdoxia had appeared domestically cosy. More than once she had felt an intruder. But Harold was grateful to anyone who saved him from dull meetings or demanding visitors, and from the beginning Evdoxia had made herself indispensable, keeping his life orderly, just how he liked it. So I never imagined *that*, thought Lucy. She had shied from imagining anything. And they had been careful, for she had never even seen them touch. Now Evdoxia was to be her stepmother. Why didn't he tell me, she wondered. How dare he not tell me? Why keep it a secret? Why secret from *me*?

'Why didn't he tell me?' she asked Oliver in a low, low voice, leaning on him a little for he still stood so close. She was glad of his hand now, of his fingers biting hard into the tender flesh above her elbow. He was lending her his strength until hers came back. He knew how she felt. After weeks of avoiding her he had sought her out only for this.

'I think he's ashamed in a way. She's not much older than you.'

She had not thought much about Evdoxia's age. Twenty-five? Thirty? She couldn't tell. And tonight happiness made her quite childlike, her rounded pretty face all smiles. She was stooping here, then there, accepting kisses and good wishes. Soon, working across the room, she might come to Lucy.

'Bonny was sure you knew. How could you share the flat with them and not know? Everyone's been talking about it. Poor old Harold. People think it's a bit of a joke.'

'How could she?' Lucy asked. All that young, energetic beauty thrown away on a dry, humourless old man, she thought. She wished Oliver's hand would encircle her thin arm for ever. Oh, don't leave me, she wanted to cry. Don't leave me now.

Instead she said, 'I feel so silly.'

'Of course they all think Harold told you first, before anyone.'

'I still feel silly.'

'Why not feel angry at being treated so shabbily?'

She had had no wine, she realized, to toast the bride and groom. She was surprised they hadn't married before she came back since breaking the news to her seemed so problematical. How many clues had she missed these last weeks?

'I thought it was odd how he insisted I come tonight,' she said. 'I didn't want to but he made a fuss.' Then, after a pause: 'It isn't a year since Mother died.' Edith, who had seemed far away, came closer suddenly as if demanding notice.

'That was never much of a marriage,' said Oliver.

'No. No, it wasn't.' She had tried not to understand that too, had kept up the fiction of a work-obsessed father and an invalid mother united in spirit but kept apart by circumstance.

'Poor Lucy. Such disillusion.'

'But why Evdoxia? She likes clothes and food and dancing. Father hates dancing. And what can they talk about?
She's not really interested in his work, only because he's
important, he sometimes has his picture in papers and
magazines. She'd be just as happy organizing meetings for
the chairman of . . . of a chemical company. Typing letters
to other chemical companies. Or for Mr Fielding, ordering
tractors.'

'There's sex.'

'They could have that without being married,' said
Lucy, and felt the hand on her arm tighten a little and
then fall away.

'Dear Lucy!' cried Evdoxia, intoxicated with wine and
general euphoria. Her arms reached out. Lucy avoided
them adroitly, put her cheek against Evdoxia's, kissed air,
said, 'I do hope you'll be happy,' and extricated herself.

'Lucy, my dear.' Harold, still shaking hands with a
small bald man, screwed his head round. He was coming
as fast as he could, his look said.

Lucy smiled vaguely. I have no kisses left, she thought.
She stepped back and back, delicately, retreating.

'Take me away,' she said to Oliver.

He fetched her coat, spoke to someone. To say what?
Tell Bonny I had to rush: urgent meeting, phone call,
dinner at the Embassy. Some people had only just arrived,
screaming over the heads of others how they'd been held
up, how could Bonny forgive them? In the confusion
Lucy slipped out, clutching the coat round her shoulders,
hurrying down the stairs to the street and the blessedly
cool evening.

They walked. Somewhere in the maze of steep alleyways
Oliver spoke for the first time.

'Don't take it so much to heart. What does it matter?'

'I just wish he'd told me.'

'He spent years forgetting you existed. He can't get into
the habit of fatherhood now, it's beyond him.' Oliver

walked with his coat blowing open, his head up as if he was scenting spring in the hills.

'Do you think there'd be a job for me at the British School? I could rent a room, couldn't I?' She looked up at the old buildings as if they might open up like dolls' houses and reveal just the place.

'Harold wouldn't like it.'

'Could he stop me?'

'He could certainly make sure there was nothing for you in Athens. He'd rather you were packed off safely with an English husband.'

Lucy stood still. She thought of Evdoxia, small, plump, so very Greek. A flame of anger shot up and died away. 'He has what *he* wants,' she said. 'Why can't he just listen for once to what I want?'

Oliver came back and took her arm. 'You look cold.'

Say: Stay with me, she prayed. How neatly it would solve the crisis. Paleochora, perhaps children ... She would learn to look away when Oliver enjoyed other women. She would make a life's work of constancy, like Penelope, so that affection and admiration would always draw him back even when passion failed.

'Lucy? You're shivering. We'll go for a coffee.'

Later, walking back through deserted streets, back to Harold's worried looks and Evdoxia's prettily raised eyebrows, Oliver said, 'I'll write to you.'

Is that all, she wanted to cry.

In the shadow of the buildings he had suddenly pulled her close. She felt the dizzying fall, the desire ... what a silly word, she thought afterwards, and ugly too. Desire. Desire. If he had made to take her there she would have acquiesced.

'All your life I'll write to you. Promise you'll reply?'

'Letters,' she said. Her heart steadied to its usual beat. 'Just letters.' She felt so weak she buried her face in his coat.

'Promise.'

'I love you,' she whispered.

He detached her gently as he might a kitten or a child. When he spoke his voice was quite normal as if instead of 'I love you' she had spoken of the weather or food or electrical engineering.

'Dear Lucy, you wouldn't love me long if I took you home and pretended to be domesticated. We'd come to quarrelling and then to hating. Everything would go in the wreck. And I don't want to lose everything.'

'But it doesn't have to be like that,' she said.

'It does. It always has been.'

'If you love me . . .'

He smiled, putting her away from him.

'It's because I love you that I'm going to write the letters.'

Lucy went home to England and took her typing course in Cambridge, met Nina and through Nina found herself a job. Harold smoothed her way, writing to old colleagues, perhaps in the hope she would find romance over drinks in the Fellows' Garden.

In Greece Evdoxia gave birth to a son.

So when Maurice met Lucy and, temporarily besotted, offered her marriage, she accepted because she was bored and confused and she knew it was what Harold had always wanted. Besides, there was no one else and at twenty one is inclined to consider opportunities lost as gone for ever. If she had thought for a moment that she was subconsciously trying to compete with a six-month-old baby for Harold's attention she would have drawn back, horrified. In the event she appeared cheerful, caught up in wedding plans like paper in a strong breeze. She could not stop to think at all. She would rather not think.

Harold and Evdoxia came to the wedding and the Fieldings sent silver teaspoons and a charming note.

Oliver sent a letter.

'Be happy, damn you,' he wrote, which was just like

him and, Lucy thought, rather childish. 'You're still so wretchedly young. Be happy while you can.'

'I am happy,' she wrote back, still on her honeymoon in the cottage on the Welsh borders. She wrote while Maurice slept, sprawled on his back, breathing noisily. She wrote by the window open to the sultry July night and the moonlight spilled across the page, across her hand, across the small dark strokes of ink.

'I *am* happy,' and she underlined the word, then again and again.

He'll know at once it's a lie, she thought, and screwed up the page and put it in her pocket, going out quietly and down the stairs, down to the front door, out across the lawn. Here was the river, small and swift, flickering over the stones. The moon seemed caught in the branches of a thorn by the bank. Lucy sat down with her bare feet in the watermint and thought soberly at last of her life to come.

Then she launched the crumpled sheet of paper on the water and watched it out of sight.

# 15

NINA'S call to Paleochora was interrupted by Toby's arrival with a bottle of champagne and a punnet of strawberries.

'Toby's got a new job,' Nina informed Lucy.

'Again?'

'He can't fail to make his fortune with this, he says. And it's just what he's always wanted.'

Lucy did not ask what it was. Experience had taught her that Toby's wants were various and changeable, like light on water.

'Darling, have you heard from Chris?'

'Why?' Lucy was struck by Nina's tone. Something is coming, she thought.

'I think he has plans for you. And the house.'

'Nina, it's *my* house. Besides, why should Chris be bothered?'

'Because he likes things parcelled up neatly and put away.'

'Even his own mother?'

'Especially his own mother,' said Nina with a perspicacity she seldom showed.

'And what else?' There was more, Lucy divined.

Otherwise she would already be hearing about Toby's new job which, like all the others, couldn't possibly fail.

'I ran into Bernadette in Sidney Street. Well, she ran into me. She was always clumsy, wasn't she? And that big bust, and the hair, and the way she strides out ... quite extraordinary how people don't change. She said Chloë was with you, seemed put out, and said of course you'd have to get rid of the place in Greece, it would be irresponsible to do anything else. So I said look who was calling other people irresponsible and it was none of her business anyway.'

'That was tough talking. In Sidney Street too. You must have caused a jam.'

'I always fight your corner. You know that.'

'Yes, I do. It's not that I don't appreciate it. Did she look unhappy?'

'No worse than usual. Perhaps it's that job of hers, the dark side of human nature day in day out, all those court cases. And then only those gloomy priests for weekends.'

'Not the whole weekend.'

'But priests!'

'Well, you could always lend her Toby,' said Lucy.

This made Nina laugh, which in turn made Toby ask what was going on. He had got over the rigours of Newmarket and was full of plans for making his fortune without lifting much more than a finger.

'But how are *you*?' demanded Nina, for the line had crackled and she was afraid Lucy was slipping away. 'I mean, how *are* you?'

'Fine.' I can hardly say: Disorientated, floating, not myself, thought Lucy.

'Good,' said Nina, but she had heard the note of alarm. She doesn't like to be asked, she decided. 'Good. And Toby sends his love.' Toby was making impatient gestures in the hope she would ring off so that he could open the champagne and celebrate his new career in the yacht charter business.

'We all miss you,' ended Nina, a little wistfully, for she foresaw several evenings of alcoholic enthusiasm before Toby settled, and she would far rather have been packing for Greece. She also knew that it would all end, metaphorically, in tears, for whatever shining virtues Toby possessed, the ability to make something of these slightly questionable jobs was not one of them.

'Nina, do go and have a drink and congratulate Toby and stop wondering what I'm doing just because you can't see me.'

'But I know what you're doing. You're sitting with a book in a huge chair full of cushions on a terrace overlooking the sea. No, don't say anything. I'm going for my champagne. Toby's having apoplexy. Really, you'd think he paid the phone bill. You know, I sometimes get quite exhausted with celebrating. It won't be long before we're raising our glasses to something quite different. Poor lamb,' said Nina. 'But he does take it all very seriously while it lasts.'

Alan said, 'I suppose I seem old to you.'

'Mature,' the girl replied.

They were crossing Magdalen Bridge. She was striding along at a great rate, a raking, big-breasted girl. Formidable, thought Alan. In her company he did not so much feel mature as withered. He could hardly keep up.

She worked as a hotel receptionist. It was a dead-end job, she told him. She felt exploited. 'I wish you were one of my students,' he told her. She would adorn the most deathly tutorial, he thought.

'I'm glad I'm not. Too much hard work.'

She crossed the road abruptly at a sudden break in the traffic and he was forced to follow, dodging bicycles.

'Have you time for a coffee?'

'No.' She swung on, Amazonian, relentless. He strained to stay with her, shoulder to shoulder. He felt the damp springing under the rim of his panama, between his shoulder-blades. Then: 'What do you lot do all summer without students?' she flung over her shoulder. 'Play croquet?'

'Oh, there's plenty to do.' He knew she wasn't interested. 'What about dinner?'

She paused. They were almost at Carfax, so quickly had they progressed. His heart was disturbed. When he looked down he thought he saw his shirt fluttering. 'Dinner?' he repeated. He had no breath for any added enticement.

The girl's young, strong, serious face turned anxiously to him for a moment. Then she looked away. 'I'm going swimming.'

'With Sue?' He thought benignly of the squat, cheerful girl who shared her house.

'No. Alone. It's my night for it.'

'I'm losing my touch,' he told Lucy on the phone that evening. 'I'm growing old, Ma.'

'Stood up, darling?'

'For the ecstasy of ten lengths in dilute chlorine. How're the kids?'

'No trouble.'

'Kids are always trouble. Look at Bernie. And hasn't Laura been on the phone every other minute reminding them to wear clean pants and brush their teeth?'

'No.'

'No?'

'I had to ring her to let her know about Ginny. The silly girl slipped by the pool and knocked herself out. Anyhow, Laura was just subdued. Concerned, yes, but she took it very quietly.'

'No panic? No theatrical scenes? You know, she squeezes those children so tight there's no breath left in them.'

'When we're unhappy we behave badly.'

There was a silence. 'Is chasing young girls behaving badly?'

'It has a lot of potential for being undignified.'

'I wouldn't argue with that.'

'Unless you're in love. There's no dignity in being in love. It reduces us to idiots.'

'Yes, Mother,' said Alan.

'I sometimes worry,' Lucy added, as if they had been talking about this all along, 'that Bernie might imagine herself in love with Father Brace.'

'She always had a penchant for clergymen. Remember when we spent that holiday in Sussex? Aunt Polly's curate? And wasn't David's uncle a deacon?'

'Father Brace isn't a curate or a deacon,' Lucy pointed out. 'He's a Roman Catholic priest.'

'And he's going bald, isn't he? Or is that someone else?' asked Alan.

Bernadette lit a candle for Lucy and one for Chloë. In the vast draughty cavern of the church they seemed to burn feebly and erratically, surrounded by the stubs of yesterday's offerings. She sat and watched them for a while but no prayers rose in her to accompany them, no hopes, no identifiable wishes. They were simply two flames representing the most important people in her life. After a while, feeling the chill of the tiles striking up through her feet, she stood up and dropped the required amount in the box marked 'Small 10p. Large 20p'.

Going down the aisle between the yellow varnished chairs she thought how ugly everything was, and how oppressive. At the 'shop' where a pile of *Catholic Heralds* would be enticingly displayed on Sunday two women were counting service sheets. Soon Father Brace would appear, his perpetual frown deepened by domestic worries – another brush with his unsympathetic housekeeper – and would be inveigled into taking a cup of coffee from the thermos sure to be waiting behind the holy cards and parish newsletters. How sad, thought Bernadette, as if seeing it all with new eyes. But she supposed someone had to keep the service sheets in order and that Father Brace was better for the coffee and the kindly attention of the female workforce. Strangely, Bernadette seemed to see Laura in the shadows. As the women had become involved in the church, in Father Brace, because they had little else, so Laura had applied herself to the role of perfect wife, mother and housekeeper. For a moment Bernadette understood loneliness. Poor Laura, she thought. And how much better if she had been left in the end for another woman, to have been able to fight, futilely but hot-bloodedly, over the old, well-trodden ground.

Father Brace had emerged through the curtained doorway that was the priests' private entrance. Even at this distance it was obvious he had spilt his breakfast egg down his front. The women noticed and smiled. They would wipe it off later, tidy him up. At the last moment he saw Bernadette and started forward. He had never seen her in the church this early. She had been a rare visitor any day but Sunday recently. He cleared his throat to speak but she had already gone into the porch, not even glancing in his direction though he was sure she had seen him.

I ought to be a nun, she was thinking.

She had always wanted to be a nun. She had felt, even during the hour she was married, that she could have achieved great things in a habit. It would, at the very least, have lent her the authority and sense of purpose that she craved. Now for the most part nuns had thrown off their habits and struggled along with everyone else, generally undistinguished, certainly indistinguishable. Maurice would approve of that. For it had been Maurice who mocked the religious life. 'Poor pious Bernadette. You'll soon grow out of it,' he had said.

Bernadette had reached the water stoup, dipped in her fingers. She crossed herself in the old hurried way. A structured life, she thought, infused with spiritual awareness, perhaps some teaching, care of the dying. For a second she remained stationary in the dimness, her hand

196

still touching her breast. She realized that she had only returned by an uncomfortable and lengthy diversion to the very place where she had started.

Chloë wouldn't mind a mother in a convent, she thought, and then: I'm sorry, Maurice, I've grown into it again.

She pushed open the outer door and stepped from the holy gloom into the windy sunshine. Father Brace, hurrying after her, saw her pedalling away strongly through the traffic lights, the picture of resolution.

Lucy said, 'Come out for a few days. I want you to see the house. Then we might be able to fly home together.'

'For Christ's sake,' said Turk. 'I'm busy.'

'Just come, Marianne.'

'And leave everything?'

'What everything? You've finished the book.'

'Reviews. That piece for Jill Morrison.'

'You could do them here.'

'Like hell.' And there was a click and silence.

At first when Laura called she thought there was no one at home. Certainly no one answered the door. She went cautiously down the basement steps and did not know whether to be anxious or relieved to find herself inside among the bicycles and musty paraphernalia of family life. After the sunshine the basement was very dark. There was a smell of rust and old rubber. She half hoped the door to the house stairs would be locked after all but it opened quite easily as if newly oiled.

In the hall she grew irresolute. She stood listening. I'm trespassing again, she thought. Twice in one week. It was only after a long time, the silence pressing in on her, that she understood what was different.

This house was usually full of noise: Lucy's pleasant strong voice, tea cups rattling, gin bottles, Mrs Treece going on about mumps just to put the wind up Alan, feet running, the monotonous clack clack of the typewriter interrupted by muffled obscenities. 'I like your mother,' she had once said to Christopher, and then had tried too hard to make Lucy like her, a task whose success was still in doubt. Like someone straining blindly after objects on a top shelf, she had blundered for years for Lucy's approval. But all she could be sure of was that today she would say, 'I love your mother,' and that Christopher would be embarrassed.

She sat down on the mock Jacobean settle next to the umbrella stand. The settle had begun life as a stage prop and Lucy had bought it from a junk shop for ten and six when she and Maurice had hardly been married a fortnight. It was hideously and cumbersomely ornate, deceptive too – Nina avoided it since she had tried it once and found her short plump legs dangling like a child's. She had only sat there to recover after out-arguing Maurice on Lucy's behalf. 'That frightful woman!' Maurice had said later to his librarian in Blaine's, but his thoughts crowded uncomfortably about Nina's heaving bosom. 'The old goat,' said Nina to her husband of the moment. 'As if I didn't know what he was thinking.' She had sunk on to the settle in exhausted triumph but the settle had betrayed her. She had looked silly. Of course Lucy was the only one who sat on it usually, and 'Lucy has legs like a giraffe,' said Nina.

Laura too sat uneasily. She was tormented by the quiet, by doubt. She was trying to imagine Lucy in the flat, in any flat, in sheltered housing, in a Home. She's not even old yet, she thought.

The kitchen was empty but there were signs of recent occupation. The back door to the garden was open, a pair of canvas shoes kicked off anyhow on the mat. Laura went out and saw Turk down by the hammock with another woman, a young woman who leaned up against one of the trees, laughing. As she crossed the lawn towards them she felt a sudden fright, for they both looked at her, she thought, as if she were somehow ridiculous and pathetic.

Turk made no introductions. This was usual but always had the potential for later awkwardness. The young woman had red hair and a white skin. How lovely she is, thought Laura, and surprised herself for she rarely noticed other people except as an audience, dim faces beyond her footlights. Casting back, she felt she had known Turk in love before. Men or women, they had been passions of the moment and then gone. Not that I noticed much, Laura decided. She had always been a little afraid of Turk. Perhaps, like Mrs Treece, she had seen her as a sort of pagan spirit.

'I came to talk to you about yesterday,' she said boldly.

'Oh, that.' Turk had never been gracious.

'I thought . . .'

The young woman stepped forward. 'What about a drink? It's so hot again. Marianne, why not put up the umbrella?'

Laura found herself being walked back to the kitchen. 'There's lemonade, home-made. Is there ice?' she was asked. Obediently she opened the fridge.

Outside Turk had lodged the ancient canvas sunshade over the table on the terrace. The three of them sat in silence, looking away down Lucy's border to the fruit trees and the hammock, the drunken trellis hiding the vegetables.

'I'd hate Lucy to leave this house,' Laura said suddenly, for the words, like yeast, frothed up uncontrollably. 'Unless she wanted to, of course.'

'Lucy'll do what she wants.' Turk spoke quite gently. She was looking oddly at Laura as if she recognized this new vulnerability.

'I couldn't sleep last night. I got up in the end and just sat thinking.'

'That's why you look so anaemic. Did you have any breakfast?'

Laura shook her head. 'Only tea. An old packet of

something, gone musty. I'm out of everything. I haven't been shopping properly for weeks.' She nearly added: I must pull myself together, it's about time, but was afraid Turk would agree too heartily and the red-haired girl would find it amusing.

'Then you'd better stay to lunch. Finny's leaving.' As if commanded the girl rose, smiled kindly at Laura, did not look at Turk, and departed.

'Chris really believes he's doing everything for the best,' Laura said. She shifted a little in her chair. It had been new in the sixties, an indefensible extravagance of Lucy's. Now sagging and unravelling, it offered limited support.

'So do most people who cause havoc. His main problem is total lack of a sense of humour.'

'Perhaps I don't have one either,' Laura suggested. She could not remember when she had last laughed at anything.

'I seem to think you did, way back. I don't remember. You were such a mouse.'

Laura drained her lemonade like a child taking medicine. Its tartness constricted her throat.

'It's to do with this house,' she said at last. 'This house in Greece. Chris was like a little boy yesterday, a little boy who knows he's going to get a bicycle for Christmas. He hardly told me anything but every time I looked at him I could see him mentally rubbing his hands in glee. Does that sound daft? I suppose it does. Marianne, what *is* going on? Am I the last to know something?'

'I don't think so. Perhaps Chris has just found out exactly what this house in Greece might be worth.'

'A lot?'

'A tidy sum, as they say.'

Back in the kitchen Turk produced a Camembert. It was ripe and high.

'Lunch,' she said. 'Bread and cheese.'

'After the divorce . . .' Laura began. She was looking round the kitchen and smiling. Her eyes came to rest on

200

Lucy's coffee-maker. After the divorce, she thought, she and Lucy would forge a new relationship.

'There's still going to be a divorce, then?'

'What did you expect?'

'God knows. I thought yesterday you'd had a reconciliation. To begin with. It seemed unlikely the more I thought about it.'

Laura, piling tomatoes in a glass dish, paused and saw how unlikely it was with a strange relief she had never expected to feel. Her inability to stage-manage this tremendous drama, her failure to influence Adam or even Ginny, these last few weeks entirely alone – not even seeing friends, she had been a hermit – had wrought unexpected changes. Last night was not the only one she had sat up with cups of tea at two or three, watching the sky pale and bloom. For the first time in twenty years there had not been Lucy to run to or the children to keep her going. 'Oh, she kept going for the sake of the children,' Mrs Treece had often said about women bereft or beaten or otherwise overtaken by disaster. No mother, no husband, no children . . . it was harder to keep going for oneself, Laura had thought. She felt at a total loss as she had when her parents had died. Something had gone for ever and there would be a strange twilight state to be endured before she grew used to the fact.

She was somehow separated from everyday life.

'I get along at half-speed these days,' she said, for Turk was looking at her strangely, she thought, perhaps wondering why she was taking so long with the tomatoes. 'I'm in a dream.'

'That's shock.'

'Shock?'

'Chris leaving.'

'Oh,' and Laura, trying to sound as if it would be childish to care about it, said, 'Oh, it was always only a matter of time. We've only been semi-attached for years.'

She had done some modelling in her twenties. Chris

had been proud but protective, it was such an alien world. Though all the jobs had been bread-and-butter there had eventually come the chance of a television advertisement, toothpaste or floor cleaner or gravy browning. Laura had turned it down. She was pregnant with Ginny. 'Ill-timed,' said Lucy, but she knew it would not necessarily have mattered. Pregnancy was a convenient excuse, saving face all round. When Laura failed to cope so well with this second baby, Christopher tactlessly said it was a good thing she had nothing else on her plate, the doctor said it was all hormones, she'd get over it, and Lucy thought: I can't interfere, I'll only make things worse. By this time anyway Laura could scarcely have modelled for anything but a harassed mother. It was a year before she looked well or took any trouble over her appearance.

'It's still a shock,' said Turk. She was licking Camembert off her fingers after cutting out a small piece to see what it was like.

'Yes.' Laura had forgotten what they were talking about.

Unlike Christopher Alan had long ago lost or returned his key. When no one responded to his frustrated jabs at the bell he stood looking at the railed-off green in front of the houses beyond which traffic pounded along the busy road. His shoulders sagged. He felt weary. He was not sure why he had wanted to come. Standing there, he suddenly remembered dashing up to these steps on his bicycle, bumping it down to the basement, haring to the kitchen for tea and flapjack, rock cakes, Chelsea buns, whatever Mrs Treece had left in the larder. The thought of it depressed him further, but reminded him of the other way in.

Even from the hall he could hear the female voices in the kitchen. One, husky and forthright, was Turk's. Out here there was only an air of deadness, as if with Lucy away the front of the house was never used. Also everything seemed unfamiliar, as dearly loved possessions often seem when about to go under the auctioneer's hammer. He found himself looking at a water-colour of Byron's Pool which Maurice had bought and which had always hung by the settle as if he had hardly seen it before. It was not really very good, he thought.

'I could hear you laughing in the street,' he declared, exaggerating to cover his surprise. Turk and Laura were roaring over the wreck of a perfect Camembert, a wine bottle between them.

'The prodigal! You're in time for the last glass,' said Turk.

'Why on earth you always call me that I don't know,' he replied lightly. They both knew it was because Lucy would forgive him anything.

'Sit down. Help yourself.'

'I will.' But for the moment he walked here and there, touching things, re-acclimatizing himself. He thought Turk looked a lot younger than she was, but middle-aged women were always surprising him these days. Don't start looking back, he warned himself. But he looked, saw again his young self staggering in late – Maurice would have something to say about it in the morning – and making a tipsy lunge, bumping noses as he angled for her mouth. He would never forget her response, the kiss she gave him. Seventeen, in those days hardly fledged, he had been brought to a pitch scarcely reached with any of the girls he punted manfully every weekend under the all-concealing willows. She had disengaged herself adroitly, had turned her back as if to say: Well, that was what you wanted and now you'd had it. He had been left incandescent, embarrassed, speechless. But she had not meant to be cruel.

'Hallo, Lolly.' Alan bent to drop a kiss on Laura's silky head. She smiled up at him, a wide, uninhibited smile.

'I don't know how I'll drive home.'

'You'll be fine after a coffee.' Turk rose to rout out the coffee-maker.

'I came to ask your advice,' said Alan.

'How desperate you must be. Shove over that spoon, will you?'

'I'm taking a sabbatical. I'm going to travel. And I want to write a book about it. You know people who might be interested in that sort of thing.'

'I might.'

'I've thought about it for years. If . . .'

'Why now, then?'

'Oh, I just finally got around to it, I suppose. I've been in Oxford sixteen years. Too long. I'm on the way to being like Father, forty years plugging away at the same problems.' He became aware of Laura's glazed expression. 'Lolly, are you all right?'

'Leave her alone,' said Turk. 'Get the cups, why don't you?'

He took the Spode for himself. He felt he was owed this small thing at least. He had often felt disregarded when he lived at home, always the last and least. 'The favourite,' Mrs Treece had always told him, smacking his eager dimpled hands from cake tins, new crusts, jam pots. She meant Lucy's favourite, and it hadn't always stood him in good stead. Maurice had thought him insolent and untidy, noisy, lazy . . . There hadn't been a vestige of affection between them. Though Alan didn't know it, two revelations had coincided with his birth: one was that Lucy had known from the moment he was put into her arms that here at last was a child she was going to like and understand; the other was that Maurice, for various obscure reasons, actually doubted this was his baby at all. When Lucy learned of his suspicions shock kept her silent. Instead of the blazing denials he had expected, Maurice encountered only hostile withdrawal. 'If you think so badly of me, what's the point of my saying anything?' she asked. The baby, as if to torment him further, simply grew more and more like Lucy.

So Alan was the favourite but no one showed him any

favouritism. For years Lucy killed herself in the struggle to be impartial. 'Which is easy for food and drink and pound notes and visits to the circus,' she told Nina with a sigh, 'but more tricky with emotions.' Christopher was apparently indifferent to attention, Bernie resentful. It was a relief to be with Alan, to go for long walks on the Fen, to play Poohsticks, to explore the fishier backwaters of the river. Later, growing up, he would sometimes recount his exploits for her. He could always make her laugh. What he left out she never probed after, she respected his secrets. And I respect hers, he thought. Still, he was disappointed to learn he was Maurice's after all. He had never felt anything for this man who so plainly disliked him. Learning of Maurice's long-ago accusations, he had felt a leap of hope. 'I'm sorry, darling,' Lucy had said. 'I've been so boringly virtuous.' Always? Or until when? He had seen her flirt gently with old friends. He thought he knew her too well to believe she had never been tempted.

Favourite, but once the rest were broken the last Spode cup had rarely come his way. He looked into it now as if he might find a message there. Mrs Treece would have read the coffee grounds, he thought, as she read the tea leaves and palms and every trivial omen, half-excited, half-guilty. Her Ted had never approved, not since the day she had predicted his brother's death and it had come off, like some clever – but in this case irreversible – sleight of hand.

'You look tired,' said Laura suddenly. She was still flushed, a little unsteady.

'Remember Mrs Treece?'

'Oh, Christ! That woman!' Turk exclaimed.

'Incredible aprons. Bad legs,' said Laura affectionately.

'What on earth made you think of her?' And Turk looked at him with disapproval.

'I don't know.' But he did, for he turned the cup in his hands and caught a glimpse of pattern, of a crow or a dog or a crown. Mrs Treece would have known what it meant. 'Now look at that . . .' she would have said, speculating with relish on all possible meanings, love, death or money.

'Loo said all she ever did was brush the dirt under the sofa,' said Turk. 'I don't remember.'

Mrs Treece had never approved of her. 'Wanton, if ever there was,' she told Ted Treece right at the beginning. When Turk's first book was published she affected never to have picked it up, but she pointed it out to friends in the library. Once she purloined Turk's cup and read her tea leaves, finding disappointingly only riches and confusion, nothing unlikely or dangerous. Still, she could watch Turk's coming and going with a jaundiced eye, although since the flat had its own front door she rarely saw visitors and had to make up a great deal of what she told Ted over his tea. Once she thought she heard sounds of love-making in the afternoon, over the drone of the afternoon play and through two heavy doors. The problem pages might frequently encourage sex by daylight but Mrs Treece called it indecent. 'And in a house with children,' she said out loud, thinking about it in the solitude of her own little back scullery.

Alan, who had been in that scullery the day of her funeral to fetch the flowers Lucy had left there overnight in a bucket of water, recalled vaguely only that Mrs Treece had once called Turk 'bohemian', disparagingly or admiringly he could not be sure. For his part he had hardly noticed Turk until he reached the age where sex began causing him problems, every morning an anxious look-out for spots, evenings a humiliating pursuit of what he was seldom allowed to have. He had counted her old but she was only thirty, and beautiful. He saw her one night emerging from a noisy party in the flat to replenish her own store with Lucy's gin. She had been all warmth and life, laughing at him hovering in the shadows. Sexually stirred, he had waited a moment in the drift of her perfume before going slowly upstairs to finish his homework. It was a few days after that that he had kissed her.

And what would Mrs Treece have said about that?

'I must go,' said Laura, standing up and leaning on the table. 'I feel so tired.' And she yawned and her eyes closed.

'Go and sleep it off in the hammock,' said Turk. 'You don't have to hurry home, do you?'

'No, but I really ought to go.'

'Then I'll drive you,' said Alan.

They went out together. On the steps Alan put his arm round her shoulders and she leaned her head against him. He was afraid she had fallen asleep. He thought he had never known her so relaxed. Or so drained? He had always found her slightly childish, hyperactive, obsessive. Now, looking down at the curve of her jaw over which wisps of fair hair lay, soft as a baby's, he felt amused and as protective as a father. In the car her eyes closed properly. He did not even try to make conversation, even to ask what she and Turk had been laughing about, such enervating, cathartic laughter. When he had opened the door and they had looked up, Laura had brushed away tears.

'Are we there?' she asked as he pulled up.

'We are.'

She leaned over and kissed his cheek, a little clumsily, her eyes still not properly open.

'You were always sweet,' she said.

He had not intended to sleep with her. Nothing had been further from his mind, at the back of which small voices whispered that such a union was probably incestuous. Now where had that idea come from? All the same, his goodnight kiss was extended and redefined and he found himself eventually in the spare bedroom – which being Laura she kept in perfect order, bed made up, even flowers – undoing the buttons of her shirt.

'I'm taking advantage, Lolly,' he said, but she said

207

nothing, only looking at him expectantly as if sure this new experience would be pleasant. He felt very tender towards her and rather curious, for he seemed to have known nothing about her after all, and still didn't, though he had undone all the buttons and removed every other obstruction and her eyes were wide open, staring into his. He found her innocent and delightful, she could scarcely have progressed from the young Lolly of long ago. He remembered her modelling outfits in a London department store where he had gone with Lucy to see her, not at all interested but lured by the promise of lobster for lunch. He could not remember how she had looked, but another time, on the catwalk of a lesser fashion house, she had floated by in something electric blue, her hair swept up and studded with paste diamonds. She could have been Titania. Even now, he thought, her neck looked too fragile for the weight of her head.

He found it touching that she made love as if for the first time. She was so thin he was afraid she would bruise easily, or even break. Only the slight crease between her fine brows and the softness of her breasts showed that any time had passed since he had kissed her cheek on her wedding day.

It was this day he remembered when he woke at dawn, wondering where he was. He reached for her and drew her close and she slept on, breathing evenly, while he remembered Lucy's nervous anxiety and Chris's nervous exaltation and Bernie dwarfing the bride in every photograph and Mrs Treece in a new powder-blue suit keeping well back because, after all, she wasn't family. He could see everyone gathered to watch the happy couple leave at last, could see himself coming out almost too late, having gone from Laura's bedroom where he had found her in her slip plucking the artificial flowers from her hair to the dining room where he had indulged in the left-over champagne. No doubt he was obviously tipsy. Maurice had edged round the crowd immediately, furious.

'How dare you behave like this.'

'Like what?'

'Don't be insolent. You can hardly stand. I expect a son of mine to have some sense by the age of fifteen.'

'But I'm not a son of yours, am I?'

Maurice's face, at first white and then startlingly red, had haunted Alan from that moment to this. He had often wondered if his father had really believed him privy to some dark secret of Lucy's. No doubt, when all the guests had gone and his parents were alone, there had been a row of some kind. It might only have been half-hearted – he hoped so – for Lucy had been exhausted and Maurice had had indigestion. They had done their best for Laura seeing she had no one else, but the day had taken its toll.

The wish to disown Maurice had always stayed with him, Alan thought. But lying there, listening to the first birds twittering in the rose on the wall beneath the bedroom window, Maurice faded and grew ghostly. It was Laura he recalled most clearly, sitting there in front of the glass hurrying to take the flowers out of her hair. Daringly, he had put his hands on her bare shoulders and leaned forward. She had turned her face so that he could kiss her cheek. Her frailty surprised him. He thought she was lovely and hardly real.

The birds sounded as though they were squabbling. He wondered how, when she woke, Laura would treat him and how, later in the day, they would part. There seemed no certainties, only conjecture. He kissed the top of her head tenderly and began to plan his travel book.

Lucy and the children had visited Harold's site and had even stood on the wide curving steps that had caused him so much gratification. They had also been to see the more famous site a few miles further on and learnt a great deal about Linear B and Blegen, King Nestor's black bulls and the shortest way home to Ithaca.

'But it's so hot,' cried Ginny who only wanted to swim.

It was unbearably hot and there were other tourists equally dehydrated and weary. In such circumstances one stone looks very like another.

'I shall sit down,' said Adam. He looked about for shade.

'How feeble you all are,' said Chloë. Today the dark plait was pinned up in a business-like way and she had paced on indefatigably for hours, sometimes casting pitying and exasperated glances over her shoulder. They had straggled in her wake, less and less enthusiastic as she drew further away. She was always in the distance, in a store room, by a hearth, pausing to read the guide. Once Lucy thought she paced out a measurement. How Harold would have approved, she thought.

'I can't go on,' said Ginny. She sat on a low piece of wall and shuffled her toes in the dust.

'I'll tell Chloë it's time to go,' said Lucy. Her feet were swollen and her back ached. They had stayed far too long. She could not even see Adam any more, he had taken himself off into the shade and scent of the cypresses and might even be asleep. When he wasn't swimming or eating he slept, just like Alan used to, she thought, as if growing up were such an exhausting business.

'Darling, it's nearly time for lunch. We'll come back another day,' she said, finding Chloë frowning down at some mysterious indentation in the ground. Beads of sweat had trickled from her forehead down her nose and now and then she dashed a hand at them automatically, too preoccupied with the stones to know what she was doing.

'Is Ginny all right? She hasn't a headache again?' Chloë asked, but her look back over the site was vague. She was not thinking of Ginny.

'No. No, she's fine. But it's getting hotter and Evangelia will have lunch ready and I thought we ought to make a start. The car will be like an oven.'

'I suppose it will.' Chloë looked around as if saying a reluctant farewell. She closed the guide and tucked it under her arm. She would certainly come back. There was no doubt of it.

'A drink would be nice,' she admitted as they retraced Lucy's steps. Ginny was not where she had left her but had gone to join Adam in the shade. 'But the shade's as hot as the sun almost,' Adam complained. 'You ought to go round places like this by moonlight to be comfortable.' He thought he sounded very calm and reasonable considering the rage he felt at having to spend another morning in a heap of ruins, jollied along – as he decided he had been – by a trio of females. He had hoped to be left at Paleochora where Mini would be doing the washing or preparing the salad. Everything she did was delightful to him. And how could there be anything delightful in ruins or having one's shirt stuck to one's back or one's grandmother wandering about without saying anything except one or two disjointed remarks about sunstroke? Was this a sign of senility? Mentally he tried out a string of words his best friend at school used regularly after every miserable maths lesson. He would shock Gran, he thought, if he said them aloud. Perhaps then she would come out of this daze or dream or whatever it was and start taking notice again.

'Oh, God,' he said under his breath as they reached the car. It was, as Lucy had predicted, an oven.

'Onward,' said Lucy, though not with any untoward show of enthusiasm. 'Remember you're a Cavendish.'

'But I'm not,' protested Adam.

'Is that what Great-grandfather used to say?' asked Ginny.

'Frequently.'

Silly old bastard, thought Adam. He had been disconcerted twice in the last few days at finding Harold's photograph in museums. Once he had seemed august and distant, as remote, perhaps as mythical, as any great man of history. To find him acknowledged, even quoted, his face staring down above a cabinet of his finds, brought him nearer only as a dinosaur bone brings the dinosaur nearer. And Lucy seemed unmoved. She had even stood on his staircase without blinking, telling the story of its discovery on a perfectly normal voice. Even she failed to conjure him up as real flesh and blood, and if she couldn't, who had seen the first step exposed to the sun, then who could?

Chloë, who had been silent, her arm dangling out of the open window, suddenly asked, 'The Prof's site isn't complete, is it?' They had taken to calling Harold the Prof to cover any embarrassment.

'Not complete?' Lucy had been thinking, it was clear, of other things. Evangelia? Lunch? It was very late. 'No, I suppose it isn't. They were always going to extend it to the east. I forget why. An even earlier city or something. Anyway, they never did.'

'Then I think *I* shall,' said Chloë.

# 16

HAROLD died suddenly and without fuss while eating a picnic on Samos where Evdoxia had taken him on holiday. His heart had been troubling him but no one had told Lucy. After she married she saw him so infrequently it was like the old days, the days of school and Tours and the parsonage. Brief letters spoke only of his work and the boy Nikos. 'Why didn't you tell me he was ill?' Lucy wrote to Evdoxia, and received a scrappy, evasive reply.

Everything, except a small sum in trust for the grandchildren, went to Evdoxia and Nikos. Lucy was sent her mother's rings. There was a lengthy obituary in *The Times*, a radio tribute, some pieces in magazines, and at last a serious and honest assessment by Oliver Lussom, who had taken over Harold's site. 'He lived for Greece and his work,' Oliver wrote to Lucy. 'Whatever happened – or perhaps didn't happen – between you, you should be proud of him.'

Evdoxia did not keep in touch. She went back with the child to Thessaloniki, her home town, and married again quite soon. Lucy's Christmas cards were never acknowledged, no replies were ever sent to her letters. Then someone at the British School wrote to tell her Evdoxia had died in a car accident, had left three daughters. There was no mention of Nikos. 'Where is he? What's he doing now?' Lucy asked, but there was no one to tell her and she had no address.

'Why bother?' asked Maurice.

'He's my brother,' said Lucy.

'It's not as if you've ever met.'

'That's the whole point.'

I used to wonder once, she thought, how people searching for long-lost relatives and friends could ever have mislaid them in the first place. Now I know how easy it is, it can happen without one noticing, like grass growing. She knew that if she really tried she might find him, but a year passed, and then two, and then too many.

'Well, he obviously doesn't want to meet *you*,' said Maurice.

At a god-daughter's wedding Lucy sat in the hard pew thinking about the cold beef and salad Mrs Treece would have left out for supper, about Alan's report – of the usual could-do-better variety, not yet shown to Maurice – and about Turk's trip to America. The congregation made a sudden hasty movement to kneel, self-conscious in wedding finery, and a hush fell. Maurice intoned the responses in a loud voice but rocked slightly on his knees as if anxious for his trousers with their perfect crease. Lucy was silent, her hands clasped loosely. As always at such times her mind went blank. Then slowly, like shadows gathering, people glided into view behind her closed eyelids: Chris, Bernie, Turk, Edith even. Bless them for me, God, if you're listening, she thought.

And bless Nikos.

She opened her eyes. The name had simply come, following the others naturally as if she knew him well, saw him often. But it's years, she thought. I haven't bothered about him in years.

'Are you asleep?' asked Maurice as she rose unsteadily for a hymn. For a moment he thought she looked faint but told himself he had imagined it. She shook her head anyway and sang steadily and sweetly – as a reproof, he wondered. Her attention was not on the service anyway. When it was over he lost her in the crowd leaving the church, and going back, irritated, he found her in the Lady chapel by the blaze of candles looking for all the world as if she had just lit one.

'Are you coming?'

'Do you ever light candles for people?' she asked.

'No.'

He hurried her outside. Maurice was always hurrying at weddings, she thought, hoping they would be over long before they generally were. 'How godawful,' he would say at the reception, or 'How they do go on,' during the speeches, and he would look at his watch every five minutes after the bride had gone to change and murmur, 'They'll be late,' several times until she came down.

This time: 'I hope to God we can get away early,' he said as they came out through the church gate into the road. Confetti stuck to his shoes.

Nikos, where are you, thought Lucy.

Lucy went down to stay at the parsonage because Caroline was ill. 'And there's not much time,' wrote Rev. It was spring but seemed as if it would never be warm. Remembering the chill, the gothic gloom, Lucy packed sweaters and cardigans and her old tweed suit, but she knew that when she was there she would be cold with the knowledge that this would be a last visit. She had resolved to be brave, but when she got out at the station and saw Rev waiting by the old car, resolve failed her and she wept into his overcoat.

'They give her six months,' he said calmly. He had said it often by now, his voice no longer trembled.

'The doctors are divided,' said Caro. 'One says one thing, another another. They're only agreed on the outcome.' She was so wasted that Lucy hardly recognized her.

And then, the next day or the next, the sun shone. The spring has come, thought Lucy. Now in the clear mild evenings she could walk arm in arm with Caro, talking. Sometimes they looked at pictures of themselves as children, or of Margot, enclosed with letters over the years, Margot in expensive suits, with dogs and men with guns, in chic late fifties hats, at some château with her sophisticated children. She had married a diplomat. 'And lives like a diplomat's wife,' laughed Lucy. Her letters still came. 'We shall meet before long,' she had written. 'But we never shall,' said Caro.

She tired so easily that they had to sit every few minutes. When Lucy held her she held only long bones in soft dry skin. Rev prays to God, Lucy thought, and if God is there He'll surely answer, but what about me? She felt as if she were dying of helplessness as surely as Caro of cancer.

'You and Margot were my family,' she said. She was sitting on the garden seat with an arm round Caro's shoulders. 'I wanted my children to grow up as close and loving. I thought of you writing Rev's sermons and Margot dancing with her mother at the grape harvest dance . . . but I don't know. Only Alan ever makes me feel I'm getting anything right.'

'Rubbish.'

'Bernie's impossible. And Chris goes out with girls who look like mice and hardly speak.'

'You can't blame yourself for that. I went out with a farmer once, who turned up in plus fours to take me to a village bash. Mother nearly died. Loo, promise me something. Promise you'll find Nikos.'

At their feet the photographs of Margot were scattered among daisies, Margot young and smiling, Margot being married. Lucy thought: She was so full of life, so . . . so *vital*. We need her now as we needed her at school, to give us courage, to make a cold world bearable.

'What on earth made you think of Nikos?'

'Families. Thinking of families. Promise.'

'I promise,' said Lucy.

On the phone Caro said, 'I don't want to see you. You understand, don't you?' She meant she did not want Lucy to see her.

'I could easily come down again.'

'Not easily. And you mustn't.'

We're saying goodbye, thought Lucy.

'Lucy, you promised to find Nikos. Your father would have wanted it.'

'He wasn't much of a father.'

'Well, not like Rev.'

'No, not at all like Rev.'

There was a silence. 'I've such a headache tonight,' said Caro, who had never complained before and whose voice was suddenly small and distant.

It was Turk who prised the receiver from Lucy's fingers and wiped her face and put her to bed in the flat, sitting by her while the grief ebbed and flowed, holding her until she slept.

Lucy failed to keep her promise for some time. Nikos was elusive. Perhaps he's dead too, she thought, and for a while, because of Bernie, because of Maurice and his librarian, because of life's rich tapestry as Mrs Treece would say, relating a suicide or crime of passion over the potato peelings – because of all this, she forgot him.

Then Oliver wrote at the time of Chris's wedding and of course she described it to him as she could describe it to no one else: all the maternal pangs, she thought with a smile. All the misgivings. 'I know weddings are supposed to be happy,' she wrote, 'but how they cost us in emotion. I keep telling myself they'll be all right. I told myself all morning in and out of the hairdresser's, florist, the half-hour with Maurice and a double brandy, and then up the aisle and all through the service and the reception and right through the night until I got up to make some tea at four. There were birds singing already and it seemed so pointless to be weighed down with such dread. I can't help them to a long and loving marriage, can I?' She enclosed a wedding photo in which Chris looked unnaturally stern and Laura as tragic as Ophelia.

'I suppose you get something out of this lark,' Oliver wrote back. 'Out of being a parent.' He had never married. He had no children. 'And thank God for that,' he told her. 'There seem few enough compensations for all the fuss and worry.' His letter this time ran to several pages. He is trying to make me laugh, thought Lucy. Instead, she smiled and the smile lasted until she reached the very end, the usual dashed-off 'Oliver' and the postscript. He had put: 'By the way, I've found Nikos.'

He was in an English boarding school teaching classics, which seemed absurd, and Lucy rang at once and established some kind of shaky communication which culminated in a train journey to Peterborough and then a taxi drive. There seemed endless fields of stubble and the gold light was dusty. When they passed a single field still uncut the taxi driver said suddenly, 'Here today and gone tomorrow. They don't hang about, do they? Up and down, up and down, a couple of hours and that's it, harvest in for another year.' He turned up the school drive rather cautiously. 'I don't hold with private education really,' he said. He would come back for her at six, he agreed.

So I have to stay till then, she thought, even if Nikos doesn't want me. He had sounded aloof and faint on the phone, disembodied. She hoped, though it seemed unlikely, that it was simply something to do with the line. Ringing the school bell, she felt like her ten-year-old self brought to a party she didn't want to attend, clutching her present under her coat, hoping no one would come so that she could go home. Then the door opened and a dark, good-looking version of Harold appeared, shyly holding out a hand, not smiling.

'Come in please, Mrs Flecker.'

They got over Mrs Flecker. They got over Evdoxia, the letters not answered or returned. He had not known, he said. His mother had never mentioned them. And he had been at school, at college, in Thessaloniki, New York, Reading, and now here, such an unlikely place to come. He was sorry he had never been in touch himself but he had been told Lucy cared nothing for him, for Harold even, for Greece.

'It isn't true,' said Lucy, but she could see they were skirting bogs only to fall among rocks.

'Well, I'm going home at the end of these holidays,' he said. 'I shouldn't be here now but there were two boys who needed coaching for Oxford entrance and they let me keep my room until the new man comes. I'm going to a school in Athens.' He looked at her warily. He had Harold's trick of putting his head back and to one side when expecting adverse comment. His eyes, though, Lucy thought, were wholly Evdoxia's, huge and dark.

The tea was strong, the cake dry. The housekeeper had made it. The food grew unpalatable, Nikos said, when the boys were not there, though when they were he grew tired of stew and dumplings and luncheon meat with pickled beetroot. He was unfalteringly polite, as if his bedtime reading was a book of manners. But he doesn't really look at me, thought Lucy. He isn't curious. I might be the parent of one of his boys, to be entertained and reassured, sent away smiling. Damn him. Damn him. Why can't he look at me?

When they parted he said, 'If you ever come to Athens again . . . ' The sentence hung unfinished. He offered nothing.

'One day I'll come,' she heard herself assure him.

'Here is your taxi. On the dot,' he said, and stood up immediately. In case I should linger, Lucy thought.

Before she went, though, he wrote down the name of the Athens school and its address. He did not give her a telephone number, anywhere she could always reach him. She took it as a warning not to go beyond the tea and cake, especially not to evoke Harold who had contributed both to their genes and to this unnecessary estrangement. Nikos was delighted to meet her for an hour and a half on a summer afternoon but he was shortly going home to be a Greek amongst Greeks once again.

'Only his name's Cavendish,' snorted Maurice when she told him.

'He doesn't call himself that in Greece. He uses Rodopoulos. It was his stepfather's name.'

To Turk she said, 'I kept my promise but nothing came of it. Caro never thought of that, that he wouldn't care to know me.'

'After thirty years how can you expect to meet and fall on each other's necks?' asked Turk reasonably. 'He'll keep in touch. See if he doesn't.'

'Perhaps.' She felt defeated.

'Poor thing, she's tired out,' said Mrs Treece when Lucy had gone up to have a bath. 'Such a way to go just for a cup of tea.' She sat down heavily on a kitchen chair to ease her troublesome legs and her heart, which she was sure beat in a new and unnatural rhythm these days. 'You'd think he could have managed lunch. Her own brother.'

'I expect the housekeeper objected. And the school's miles from anywhere. No pubs. You know.'

'I'm sure the horoscope said financial and personal success this week. But perhaps it meant something else. There was that five pound note on Tuesday, the one she found behind the tea caddy. Then I thought: She'll have a jolly time with him on Friday, bound to, and that's the whole thing come out right.'

At this point Turk escaped before she could be called on to give her opinion of horoscopes.

★

Oliver wrote: 'I'm in London on the sixth. Meet me. We can have dinner. Anything you like.'

After all these years, thought Lucy.

She went to the locked drawer in her desk where she kept the old brown envelope. Inside were pieces of her past, but snatched at random as if from a shipwreck: letters from Caro, a picture of Margot in a bikini, Edith's rings, never worn. There was the announcement from *The Times* of Nikos's birth, Harold's obituary, a valentine, Bernadette's baby teeth. From among all these Lucy pulled a small photo taken from a boat of a foreign coast, parched and steep. With difficulty one could make out a house set into the hillside above one of many beaches. There was a figure on the sand, standing waving. It was a black and white photo and failed to convey any true sense of season.

For a long time Lucy stood looking at Oliver and at Paleochora. She had rowed herself out rather too far and had not kept the camera steady. She remembered how disappointed she had been, how she had thought: It will have to do. She had shown it to Caro quite happily, for it revealed nothing, the man could have been a gardener, fisherman, tourist. Now he was old and had invited her out to dinner. It was November. They would wear coats and scarves and the taxi would grind through fog. And we won't know what to say, she thought, for we have said so much in the letters. We have been closer in the letters than we ever were in that lost summer.

'I can't come,' she wrote.

He replied, 'Darling, how wise you are.'

# 17

WHEN Lucy had tried, in the early days of her marriage, to explain something important to Maurice, he had frequently missed the point. More and more, she thought, he resembled Harold, single-minded and self-absorbed. As with Harold, she felt she got nowhere with him. She felt he had become – perhaps had always been – an obstacle around which she must direct the tides of life.

His will held no surprises. Although she had the right to stay on in the house, she had barely enough to run it. She let Chris sell some shares and reorganize her building society accounts and bully her bank so that he felt in charge, doing his duty. She thought it was the least she could allow him after seeing his quite genuine grief at the funeral – a fanatical stare he had always used as a small boy trying not to cry – and hoped that fussing with her money would be a safety valve. 'But not very safe for me,' she said to Turk, for it was not long before he was badgering her to sell something else, to move accounts again, to pay all the bills by direct debit. 'Now what am I to do?' Lucy cried, besieged. But she must have done it, for little by little he ceased to interfere.

'But what *did* you do?' asked Nina.

'I distracted him.'

It was an old game. She had played it for years with Maurice, diverting his attention from exam failures, Bernie's boyfriends, Alan's pub-crawling. Though not always successful, she had grown cunning enough. And if all else failed she could lapse into abstraction, sometimes to the point where Chris feared senility.

'Do all women deceive someone?' she asked Turk.

Mrs Treece had deceived Ted, who was more of a child than a husband now, she confided to Lucy. Since he retired he sat snug at home with his newspaper while she cycled to the terrace in all weathers and then back again in time to get him lunch. 'Which he could perfectly well get himself,' said Lucy. For years Mrs Treece had done ten till four but now it was mornings only and no cooking. Often, seeing the state of the larder, she would make a cake or some chelseas, but always at twelve-thirty her lips would set, she would take off her apron with cross, jerky movements, and put on her coat and headscarf with a sigh. 'If you'd rather not come at all you know I'd understand,' said Lucy sympathetically, misinterpreting this behaviour. To her astonishment Mrs Treece's eyes filled with tears and she had to make a to-do about losing something, searching her handbag and her pockets until the dangerous moment was past. 'I told him I *had* to come,' she confessed. 'I said you couldn't manage without.'

Until she died she continued to do mornings. Scones and cakes, seed, Battenburg, Bible, continued to appear, cooling on wire racks in the larder. Afterwards the kitchen seemed unnaturally quiet, as if waiting for the slap of her over-stretched slippers and the rattle of the cups as she read the family fortunes for the week. Even Turk, whom she had loved to hate, felt surprised not to find the little piles of magazines under the sink, every one folded to the problem page or the horoscopes.

'Just the two of us left,' she said to Lucy. 'Tottering along until we join Maurice and Mrs T in the heavenly choir. The ladies of Llangollen translated to Cambridge, digging their vegetables, mismanaging their money, throwing out a bay window.'

'We can't have the bay window,' retorted Lucy. 'The house is listed.'

She was sitting on the upper terrace in the early morning light, lying back in one of the uncomfortable, institutional chairs, her bare feet on another. She had always liked to sit like this. Maurice had often found the indentations of her heels in every cushion in the house.

'Oh, Gran,' Ginny had sighed. It was as bad as leaving for school. Packing induced a feeling of suspension, of being adrift between worlds.

'Can't we stay another week?' Adam had asked, but lightly, not wanting to sound like a pleading child. And he wouldn't like to think Lucy suspected his motives. Mini had allowed him to kiss her and next time – he was sure there would be one – he would be more prepared and more experienced.

'No, darlings. We have to go,' said Lucy.

'But we'll come back? Otherwise why learn all this Greek?' demanded Ginny.

'Of course you'll be back,' cried Evangelia.

'Tomorrow I'm going to spend the morning on the terrace. I've letters to write,' Lucy told them, and here she was, hours before breakfast, her feet up on the chair, watching the sky take on the colours of the day, writing nothing. She sat absolutely still thinking how, providing she did not look at her hands, she could imagine she was nineteen again.

Later Chloë came out in her nightdress and sat at her feet, her head leaning on Lucy's knee.

'I wish I could swim naked,' she said, pulling apart one of Evangelia's rolls but not eating, taken up by another sensation: the cool of sea-water on her skin.

'But why not?'

'Not allowed.' Chloë popped a piece of bread in her mouth as if that was an end of the matter. 'Well . . . and there's Adam.'

'There's no policeman for miles. And anyway, Evangelia's taking the children to the village. Lots of goodbyes to say. Why not swim, then?'

Chloë brushed crumbs from her lap. In her mind she had already finished her swim and was dressed and preparing to tackle the problems of the day.

'Gran, I'm going to change direction.' She leaned back so that Lucy could stroke her loose hair. 'I'm going to give up the English degree. I'll have to start again.'

'If it's what you want.'

'Of course, Bernadette won't like it.'

'You must do it anyway. She really only wants you to be happy.'

'*She* isn't happy. Poor thing,' and Chloë, safe and warm and with Lucy's familiar hand smoothing her brow, thought sadly of her mother pedalling furiously to Mass and as furiously home, neither warm, safe nor lovingly caressed. 'She gets so involved. All those earnest discussions with Father Brace – and *he* always seems harassed and muddled – and then filling every weekend with titivating the church and helping that dreadful Mrs Brinkley sell rosaries and statues of St Christopher. It's such a struggle. And . . . false. She doesn't really believe . . . I mean . . . there's so much paraphernalia I'm surprised she can find God underneath it all. She'd be happier on an island by herself, then she'd be able to hear if He spoke to her. He can't get through for the racket.'

The fine lawn of her nightdress had slipped to expose the frail collar-bone. This tender mood could not last, Lucy thought. There must, inevitably, be battles. Still, it was the first sign of sympathy the child had ever shown for Bernie and like the first bud might herald a more general blossoming. And Alan might be enlisted to help, she decided, for Alan was fond of them both.

'Gran, what are you going to do with this place? You haven't said. And you've been miles away. All the time we've been here you've hardly talked, not really talked, like you used to in the kitchen. D'you remember? When Bernadette was at Mass and Marianne was out and you always said, "Thank Heaven Mrs T has Sundays off," and we'd have toast and coffee and talk and talk.'

'How funny you should remember that,' said Lucy, who had forgotten. 'But then how many times had it happened? Two? Three?'

'And now this house. Oliver Lussom. I'd like to know about him. I don't mean his work, his books . . . you knew him. You spoke to him. I suppose,' for this, she thought, must be what had shocked the family, 'you loved him.'

'Yes,' said Lucy. 'I suppose I always loved him.'

'And when did he tell you he was leaving you Paleochora?'

'Years and years ago. I don't think I ever took it seriously until just before he died.'

'And why did he?'

Lucy covered the pale, fragile bones, smoothed the dark hair. Motherly gestures, she thought. In Edith they would have seemed an affectation, too seldom used to be credible. Now why should she think of Edith?

'Gran?' Chloë tipped back her head, hoping for revelation.

'I wanted to marry him once. I wanted to live in this house, have his children. I was your age. He was much older. I think he was ashamed of encouraging me, he had to keep making sure I understood he wasn't about to become chaste or sober for my sake. It was all just . . . a few weeks one summer. One of those unaccountable, wild, brief attractions. All over in a moment.'

'A moment?' Chloë repeated, and then: 'Oh look, there's Adam going for a swim before breakfast,' as a figure charged across the lower terrace and vanished down the beach path. 'You were right. I'll wait till Evangelia's taken

226

them off. What a lump he is, always mooning after that girl. If he knew how his thoughts show up in his face.'

From indoors came the clink of cups, the scrape of a chair drawn back, Ginny calling out to Evangelia.

'He must have loved you,' Chloë insisted. 'He left you this perfect place.'

'We only wrote to each other. I never saw him again. Well . . . I saw him on television, in the newspapers. I know what he looked like as an old man. But we only met on paper.'

'How strange.' For a moment it struck Chloë as perverse and totally unsatisfactory.

'I don't know. Was it?'

'Though perhaps . . .' She would grapple with this mystery, expose its moving parts. 'I suppose you could end up knowing him better than anyone. And he left you the most precious thing he had, didn't he? That woman he was living with, she only got his money. Money wasn't important to him, was it? So anyone could have that. But Paleochora was special and he gave it to you.'

'How romantic you make it sound,' said Lucy. She was twisting a strand of dark hair round and round her finger. Life could be viewed from such angles, she thought. Did Father Brace see Bernie's confusion as a noble quest for true faith? Or did he simply admire her figure and her unfailing reliability for menial jobs, dashing about the parish on her bicycle? She smiled. Could she see her relationship with Oliver through Chloë's eyes?

Had she then achieved what she had desired? She hadn't married him but yes, perhaps she had shared as much as, even more than, many of his other women. She had not borne his children but he had shared hers from birth to teenage dramas to ill-starred weddings. He had laughed at her, given half-mocking advice, counselled patience or action. 'Parenthood by proxy is the best,' he had once told her. 'No recriminations. They don't even know I exist.' On Maurice they rarely exchanged views. Lucy felt she had chosen badly, for all the wrong reasons, and that reproaches would have been justified. But if anything, by occasionally showing Maurice to her in a slightly different light, Oliver had sustained what little affection she had left in her marriage.

And Paleochora?

It was like horoscopes then, Lucy thought. For them to come true there must be a certain mental adjustment. Like the week Mrs Treece had been assured money would be significant and so prayed for a Premium Bond, but all that happened was a mistake with the milkman's change. One might feel understandably disappointed and yet there had been no cheating. It had been in Lucy's stars that Paleochora would be significant but without any indication when, or in what way. And the young Lucy could no more imagine being a grandmother than she could imagine, in those few weeks, a life in which Oliver would never again appear in person.

'It might be handy later,' Chloë was saying. Her eyes were closed. Behind them she was watching herself making steady progress from student to world authority. 'This house. I mean . . . the Prof was right, Gran. I'm sure he was right. Why did they ever stop digging?'

'Money, probably. And Oliver was never convinced, I know that.'

'I suppose he and the Prof were rivals.'

'Well, they fought their own corners. My father was considered one of the pioneers of modern archeology – as it was then – but Oliver was recognizably a modern archeologist. He had never known his tutors throw artefacts away simply because they weren't from the right period, Iron Age for instance when the dig was for Roman remains. Keeping meticulous records was second nature to him. All the things the Prof had argued for and fought over as a young man were taken for granted after the war. But I suppose . . . he'd spent so many years arguing and fighting that he had grown permanently touchy and belligerent. He and Oliver agreed on so much and yet there were often squabbles. There was one over dating some part of the site and another over extending it.'

'How silly,' said Chloë. She could grow disillusioned, she thought, with this adult stupidity.

'The truth is they didn't like each other,' admitted Lucy.

Evangelia appeared. She carried a tray.

'Breakfast. No, do not move. Chloë will fetch another cushion.'

'You spoil me,' said Lucy.

'But I was told to.'

'By whom?'

'By Mr Oliver. Who else?' exclaimed Evangelia.


Ginny was sitting on the front steps. She had retreated here to be as far away as possible from everyone else before she lapsed into tears and sulks. The rough drive, winding away, guarded by its oil jars, only reminded her of the journey she must make in the morning when she would be hustled from this paradise to the commotion of a big city, an airport, a plane taking off. I shall probably be sick, she thought with satisfaction. In London Laura would be waiting. Ginny saw Laura as a tiny figure in the distance waving fondly. It was not how Laura generally behaved but there she was, in Ginny's imagination, pushing out of the crowds, weeping with maternal relief. Well, she *ought* to be glad to see us, thought her daughter. She rubbed her brown neck as if she could already feel the scratchy school shirts, the throttling tie. Autumn term: hockey on raw foggy mornings, dull wintry food, the smell of wet cloakrooms.

A car was approaching slowly and cautiously. It wasn't a taxi, she thought, and there was only one person in it. She waited, not standing up until it had drawn to a halt in the shade below and the man had emerged, glancing about.

'Did you want Mrs Flecker?' She was putting Evangelia's teaching to good use, she thought. But then, what if he replied in an accent she could not understand?

'Lucy Flecker? Yes. Yes, I do.' He stood on the bottom step looking up. 'But who are you?'

'I'm Virginia Flecker.'

There was grey in his hair though he was so dark. Then he's old, Ginny thought, obscurely disappointed. As old as Aunt Bernie. As Daddy.

He climbed the steps, reaching out to shake her hand solemnly. He looked hot in his suit. 'Where is Mrs Flecker?' he asked. But in the cool of the house he seemed to forget his hurry, stopping by the table where Chloë had put down a pile of Harold's books. He picked up one, then another, glancing at the titles and inscriptions.

'You shouldn't move people's bookmarks,' Ginny admonished in English.

'No, you're quite right.'

'Oh.' Now he scarcely sounded Greek, she thought. 'Chloë left those out. She's my cousin. She's not a Flecker, she's a Morrish. Chloë Morrish. She's going to give up English and start archeology. She wants to tread in the Prof's footsteps.'

'The Prof?'

'My great-grandfather. Chloë's great-grandfather too. Professor Harold Cavendish.' She spoke boldly but shook back her hair suddenly, a nervous gesture. She had been told never to boast. 'Have you heard of him?'

'Heard of him? But he was my father.'

'Nikos!' cried Lucy from the doorway.

'Has somebody come?' Adam asked. Evangelia was keeping Mini in the kitchen, so he was suffering the agony of frustration alone by the pool. He knew he couldn't face visitors.

'A man.'

'What about going to the beach?'

'I've already said goodbye to the beach.'

'Well, say goodbye again.'

She winced at his tone but was resolute. It was only because of Mini he was unsympathetic, she told herself. 'No, I can't.'

'Suit yourself.' He began to walk away.

Before, Ginny thought, he would have known instinctively how she felt, would have appreciated such painful rituals could not be repeated, that visiting the beach again would make her cry.

'I think he's Gran's brother,' she told him. A parting shot? A Parthian shot perhaps, whatever that might be.

'But Gran doesn't have a brother.'

'I know.'

'Or perhaps . . .' Adam dug his hands in his pockets, hunched up, remembering. Hadn't Laura said something once? But what? 'What did Gran say to him?'

'She called him Nikos. And they kissed each other.'

In Athens Nikos and Nikos's wife Anna and two of Nikos's grown-up children waved them goodbye. So I have Greek relations, thought Ginny, awed at this turn of events.

'Fancy turning up at the last minute,' said Chloë to Lucy as they struggled into the plane.

'Someone at the British School told him I was at Paleochora. He said he just thought . . . hold these for me, will you? Where's Ginny? Adam, do help Ginny. Well, *I* think it was curiosity. Or perhaps it was just time.'

He had told Lucy that he had thought of writing to her but had felt that there was no point. 'What does she care?' Evdoxia would have said. Now it would be a while before he could take his proper place as . . . as what? wondered Lucy. Brother? Friend? Or simply Harold's son?

'There. That's the last of Greece,' said Adam as the plane banked and climbed. He felt a lump, a real physical lump, in the pit of his stomach.

231

'I can't hear you.' Ginny had her hands over her ears. Her eyes were shut. If she opened them, she thought, he'd see she wanted to cry and he'd be beastly; he'd been beastly all morning and even leaving true love didn't give anyone an excuse for such beastliness. And Mini wasn't his true love; she didn't love him in the least, she just liked to see him looking, down her front or up her skirt . . .

'Darling, have a barley sugar,' said Lucy, leaning over.

'No, thanks. I'll be sick.'

Adam was looking out at a wet fog of cloud. He felt powerless, shut in a tin cigar and hurtling through the sky. At Paleochora Mini would be doing something routine and domestic. Would she stop to look at the sea or at the arc of blue above it? Would she think of him?

Love could not be endured for any length of time, he thought. He could understand now why people were said to die of it. He felt he was doing so and nobody, nobody at all, was noticing.

# 18

IT was not so much a family conference, Bernadette thought afterwards, as a fiasco, the more so somehow because it took place so early in the morning.

'What a night!' said Christopher. 'Though I suppose downing tools at peak times is inevitable. To cause the most inconvenience.'

'I don't know that anybody downed tools,' said Lucy.

'But you were diverted to Manchester.'

'We were diverted back.'

'Six hours later, Mother.'

They were in the kitchen at the terrace and it was five in the morning. As always at such an hour and in the aftermath of minor crisis the electric light seemed too harsh, everyday objects tawdry. Turk, in a dressing-gown with rents – as if, Christopher thought, she could afford nothing better – slopped about making coffee and tea. Like an old slattern, he decided.

'It was sweet of you to wait,' Lucy told him.

'I could hardly do anything else.'

Bernadette, who had been waiting for them since seven the evening before, placed the Spode cup in front of her mother. 'You must need that,' she said.

I need my bed or a bottle of champagne, Lucy thought, gazing down at the tea. She seemed to have done nothing but drink tea for ten hours, in plastic cups and paper cups and thick china cups still decorated at the rim with old lipstick.

'Are the children all right?' she asked.

'Ginny and Chloë have gone to bed,' said Turk.

As if to signal his individuality Adam came in as she spoke. He looked fresh and self-possessed. Sensing the atmosphere he kept a tactful silence. He had been upstairs to clean his teeth but had decided that going to bed at five in the morning was out of the question. Besides, he was hungry.

'Do some toast if you like,' Lucy told him.

'Your mother should be here soon,' Christopher said. He pushed back his cuff to consult his watch. 'She and your Aunt Bernie arranged a welcome home dinner but I rang last night to put her off.' He had spent an hour on the phone at Heathrow darting messages about the country.

Adam said nothing. He placed two wedges of bread on the grill rack. The gas popped alarmingly as always and a dreadful reek arose from the uncleaned pan.

'Poor Chris,' said Lucy. 'What a trying time you've had.'

Poor us, thought Adam. *He* just had to sit and wait. We were the ones carted off, no food, no getting off, half-baked explanations. And Ginny was sick. Well, she would be. Can't blame her really. Not expecting to land and take off again. He cast a surreptitious glance at his grandmother. She ought to be worn out at her age. But she looked dreamy rather than tired, as vague and smiling, as placid, as *removed*, as she had been in Greece.

'You all look well, I must say,' remarked Bernadette. She too had been studying Lucy.

'Even after all that nonsense.' Christopher was not going to let it drop. 'And I thought strikes were a thing of the past.'

'I'm sure it wasn't a strike. They said it might have been a bomb,' Lucy intervened. They had said nothing of the kind, only vague phrases about security.

'What bomb?' Christopher was dismissive, as if for once he saw through her trick.

'It wasn't only our flight that was diverted.'

'It seemed to be.' Crowds had come and gone, he remembered, come and gone. All night. All bloody night. Only this flight from Athens had skewed off mysteriously. He had feared hijack. His impassioned enquiries had received evasive answers.

'And how was Greece?' Bernadette was still trying to lift the gloom.

'Hot,' said Adam, turning his toast.

'Beautiful,' said Lucy.

'And the house?' Christopher rose, thinking he heard a car.

'Perfect.'

'Well, I'm glad you had a good time,' and he went out to let Laura in, for Laura it must certainly be.

'Oh God,' murmured Lucy, closing her eyes for a moment. 'I didn't expect a family gathering.' She had hoped to be met by Turk in the Dyane.

'It was to be a family dinner,' Bernadette reminded her.

'Lucy!' cried Laura, running in like a girl – to dissociate herself from Christopher who was following? She stooped impulsively for a kiss and then offered a cheek to Adam. Amazed, he pecked it dutifully. She seemed too affectionate, too alive to be his mother.

'Well . . .' began Christopher.

'I think I must go to bed,' said Lucy. Soon there would be no point, she thought. 'Lolly, I'm sorry to leave just as you arrive.'

'Never mind. You need your sleep,' Christopher told her, helping her from the chair as if she was an old, old woman. 'Poor old girl,' and she felt a light kiss on her hair.

When they reached the foot of the stairs he said: 'Give me a ring in the next few days. I know just the people to handle the sale.'

'Sale?' She turned on the first step, her eyes on a level with his.

'The house in Greece.'

'But I'm not selling.'

Behind them the kitchen had been pitched into stillness. Through the open door came the reek of burnt toast and gas and nothing else, not a breath, not the scrape of a chair.

'Not selling?' Christopher looked horrified and then disbelieving.

'No.'

'But Mother . . .'

'Oliver gave it to me because he knew I loved it. He gave it to me to live in, to enjoy with my family . . .'

'I don't want to know what went on between you and Lussom. All I can see is this great expensive millstone . . . *Live* in?'

'I thought you'd be pleased. I'll be out of here so you and Bernie and Alan can make some sensible decisions about what to do with it. Wasn't that what you wanted? Look, I must go up. Or there'll be hardly any point in bothering.'

'Mother, how can you?'

'How can I what?'

'Live in Greece.'

She smiled at him gently as she used to when he was a very small boy making a nuisance of himself. Then she carried on up the stairs resolutely, leaving him speechless.

Long after they thought she had gone to bed she sat on the ottoman by the window looking at the road through the trees. From below in the house came the ceaseless murmur of argument and speculation, the sudden closing of doors, feet hurrying on the hall boards. The day had brightened though there was to be no sun. A small breeze moved shrubs and branches uneasily. Beyong the railings Father Brace was hurrying, skirts flying, his babyish face a pale blur of concentration. Had Father Donovan, his superior, thrust some parish business at him before breakfast then? Lucy gazed down on him kindly. She thought that however hard he tried he would never please Father Donovan or Monsignor Buckley or his belligerent housekeeper or even his flock, who were tired of jumble sales and papal exhortations and too many extra collections.

There was a creaking on the landing. 'Lucy?' said Laura softly. Lucy waited for the door to open but it did not. In a moment the footsteps receded.

They'll all get used to it in time, she thought. I've had to get used to all the changes they've wrought in my life.

There was another tap. The door opened silently.

'Hello, Gran,' said Chloë. 'They told me you were asleep.' She carried a small tray which she set by the bed. 'I've brought you lemonade and some cake.'

'Breakfast?'

'Of sorts. I couldn't find much in the larder, only tomatoes and fruit and something marinating. Oh, and bottles and bottles of wine. I daren't ask Marianne – she looks as if she'd like to murder everyone. And they're all talking as if they're wound up: yap, yap, yap.' She curled on the bed and took an experimental bite of Lucy's cake.

'I hope you were kind to your mother,' Lucy said.

'I tried to be. She looks better somehow. Healthier. She ought to lose weight though.'

'Don't nag her about it. Remember how you hate her nagging you.'

'Anyway, what's going on? When I asked all I got was the children-don't-need-to-know treatment. Has something happened?'

'I told your Uncle Chris I was going to live in Greece.'

'Oh, is that all?' laughed Chloë. 'I thought somebody was ill.'

★

Nina felt she was not an encouraging sight in the morning and refused to emerge until she had 'put herself together' as she phrased it, a process which generally took some considerable time. So that it was Toby, a piece of toast in his hand and his feet bare, who opened the door to Christopher.

'I'm sorry to call so early,' said Christopher with that unfailing politeness which could have been engaging if it had ever sounded sincere.

'Well, come in.' Toby tried not to look taken aback. 'D'you want Nina? She's in the bath. Or retouching her eyebrows. God knows. Sit down. Have some breakfast.'

'I've had mine.'

'Well, whatever. Coffee?' Toby poured at once, pretending not to see Christopher's impatient shake of the head. Nina had once told him he must always keep guests occupied.

'My mother got back from Greece this morning,' Christopher announced in an ominous tone. Toby felt he was required to find the news significant but couldn't for the life of him see why.

'Did she? Good.'

'I suppose you've heard from her while she's been away?' Christopher did not touch the coffee, nor the milk and sugar Toby thoughtfully arranged in front of him.

'We might have. I'm not one for correspondence. It's Nina you should ask.'

'Darling, how marvellous, visitors for breakfast,' cried Nina, having heard voices and chosen the moment of entrance. She saw that Toby was looking disconcerted, Christopher grim. So that's all chance of a pleasant mouthful of muesli up the spout, she thought.

'Chris dear. You've never called on me before. How lovely,' and she reached over to peck his cheek. 'It's not Lucy, is it? There hasn't been an accident?'

'Of course not. The plane was delayed, nothing more. But I wanted to know if you'd put her up to this nonsense.'

'What nonsense?' Nina had been flourishing about the table resetting cutlery and cups and marmalade pots. Now she paused, looking up.

'Going to live in Greece.'

'So she's decided. What fun for her.'

Christopher was growing tired of all these childish exclamations of delight. Shock and anger were receding a little and he recognized the possibility of making himself ridiculous.

'You knew about these plans. You egged her on,' he accused.

'Egged her on? What an odd expression that is. I've done nothing of the kind. If anything I warned her against it. Such a responsibility. I had a letter from her, yes, but she said nothing about the house or staying in Greece.'

'Selling Paleochora could guarantee her a happy old age.'

'And everyone else,' murmured Toby.

'Don't,' hissed Nina, flicking his shoulder. 'Well, if Lucy's decided she's decided and that's that. And a home in the sun is what she deserves, poor love. She never went anywhere with Maurice. He was always going to take her to Naples or Nice or somewhere but never did. What an old bore he was. You know, I can't think why you've come here at the crack of dawn looking like a walking tragedy. If it's a happy old age you want for your mother what's wrong with a happy old age abroad?'

'It's hardly dawn. It's nine thirty,' protested Christopher.

'And to walk in accusing me . . .'

Toby looked up from his third slice of toast. 'She'll sell up in Cambridge then?'

'The Cambridge house belongs to us. To her children,' said Christopher coldly.

'Darling, eat up,' commanded Nina, standing at Toby's elbow. 'I can get by easily with the vocabulary I used when the children were toddling,' she had once told Lucy wistfully. But like a toddler, he was sometimes irrepressible.

'I don't see what the problem is,' he said. 'You wanted her to move, didn't you? Well, she's moving. Or are you afraid you'll end up with old Marianne as a sitting tenant? *That* would put off prospective purchasers. But she'll go with Lucy . . .'

'And that's another thing,' exclaimed Christopher before he could stop himself.

'Darling, you can't possibly believe your mother's gay?' cried Nina.

'I don't know what she is,' said Christopher.

Alan was not going to drive from Oxford to Cambridge simply to congratulate Lucy on a sensible decision. He rang her up.

'It's a big house. Paleochora.'

'Easily filled. Friends. All of you. And I might ask old Professor Thing if a spare room in Greece would be any use to Arch. and Anth.'

'Professor who?'

'The one like a walrus. Been there for ever. Maurice used to do an impersonation of him at dinner parties.'

'Hasn't he retired?'

'I'm afraid not. Or in this case, thankfully no. He always had a soft spot for me and Paleochora needs to work a little for its living.'

'You sound cheerful, anyway.' It occurred to him she was as excited by the prospect of change as he was. Just lately he had found he could not even walk up the High without feeling he was doing so for the first time; everything came fresh and touched by enchantment. He found too that he went about smiling at nothing like a man in love.

'I suppose Chris hasn't rung you?' Lucy asked.

'Early this morning. Sounding off. He wants me to persuade you to behave sensibly. Oh, and there was something about sheltered housing and investments. I didn't listen.'

'Bless you,' said Lucy.

Turk spent a morning on the river, rowing herself steadily through the throng of undisciplined punts. Only here and there was an expert, poling along effortlessly. For the most part the water was crammed with tourists muddling about, turning circles helplessly until straightened by a collision or bumped away ignominiously into the bank. The rowing boat passed them without slackening and several times the oars cracked against a trailing pole. It became a test of skill and nerve. Turk concentrated furiously, her teeth clamped over her bottom lip.

'Asking for trouble, shoving through that lot,' said the boatman when she returned, displaying bruises on both arms. 'You should've gone the other way.'

The other way was Byron's Pool where Maurice, giddily romantic for perhaps the only time in his life, had proposed to Lucy over a picnic basket. Turk grunted at the thought of it and walked off to get something to eat.

She was the last person to look back, to shun places because of their associations. She lived entirely, she would have said, in the present. Until Lucy went to Greece. For left alone she had found herself subject to disturbing flashbacks. Restless during the day, at night she had worrying dreams peopled by the long-dead: her parents, her older brother, even Maurice. Others whom she had never met – Edith, Harold, Oliver, Rev – appeared faceless though she seemed to know them. Shaken, she would get up and make coffee, sitting in the kitchen to drink it. But even the kitchen, so long a safe retreat, gave her no comfort. In the early hours it seemed cold and shabby. Once she had put Lucy's gardening coat over her dressing-gown but was still not warmed. The heart has gone out of the house, she thought.

Now, rubbing her bruises as she ate her lunchtime

sandwich in the café, she pondered the nature of her friendship with Lucy. But what conclusions could be reached, she wondered. She had pursued a magnificently egotistical course through life, loving and generous purely as it suited her or until she lost interest. Only to Lucy had she remained true.

'Friendship is golden,' she remarked to the boy behind the sandwich counter as she paid. Now where did that come from? He smiled uneasily, handing her her change, as well he might. Out in the street she paused to light a cigarette. Of course it was Mrs Treece, reading Stella Whipple or Angela Dodsworth – they had all had these most unlikely names – replying to a letter which had probably begun, with a kind of dull inevitability: 'Dear Angela, my husband says he has fallen in love with my best friend . . .'

Lucy is the rock to which I cling, thought Turk, but the rock is moving. She had come back in a roundabout way by now to the Silver Street bridge where there was room to lean her elbows while she smoked. Tourists went by, gazing about in the bewildered way tourists do as if they feel obliged to miss nothing. They looked weary and hot. There was thunder in the air. Poor sods, thought Turk. And then: I've hated the thought of that house from the beginning. That bloody house. Because I knew, I knew . . . and now, do I go or not?

Below someone lost a punt pole in the water, yelping as it slid away through his fingers while the woman in the bows affected to look unconcerned.

'Having sex in a punt is hell, you know,' Turk remarked to a man who had paused to watch the fun. He hurried away at once, astonished.

Lucy would never have misbehaved in a punt, would she? But she misbehaved in Greece once with a man old enough to be her father. And then something that should have lasted all of a week and been put down to experience turned into a lifetime of letters, into an extraordinary and enduring relationship. A paper relationship, not subject to the shocks of married life, not calling for sacrifice or compromise or the hurting of innocent parties.

Turk drew on the cigarette, considering.

Paleochora, visible, tangible . . . habitable. Behind the words on the page, the years of pages, had been real people, real places, real desires. Ah, come on, Loo. Oliver Lussom left you the most precious thing he had. He meant you to live there. You knew that. All along. And I was afraid because it meant nothing would ever be the same.

Constancy and change. Turk leaned her hips into the stone parapet to let more tourists by. Constancy and Change. She imagined two statues side by side, the one still and serene, carrying flowers perhaps, the other in movement, drapery gustily disturbed, possibly with a pair of scissors to symbolize the cutting of ties, family or amorous. Lucy and I, she thought. But now Constancy had thrown down her flowers and was running away, not so much with abandonment as with steady purpose, with determination.

Turk laughed aloud. She tossed the cigarette into the water, watching a moment to see it fall between the disorderly punts.

Bernadette avoided Father Brace for fear of being driven to tedious explanations. One minute she was to leave the Church, the next she was to embrace it more thoroughly in the shape of a nunnery. And she had had no moment of revelation, had not heard God's voice in the darkness, yet there seemed no rational process involved either. She had simply arrived at a decision.

So when she went to Mass she joined Father Donovan's queue, feeling like a traitor. She sat at the back and left quickly, ducking out into the sunshine, saying hallo to people with an accompanying glance at her watch to stress her hurry. Then she pedalled away furiously, head down, shoulders hunched, as if she thought Father Brace might track her like a bloodhound.

'Will you grow resigned to having a nun in the family?' she asked Lucy, panting into the kitchen.

'I shall rejoice, I think.' It's been such a long time coming, Lucy thought.

'Laura congratulated me. Isn't that odd?'

'I don't see why.'

'But *Laura*. I didn't think she'd give a toss one way or the other.' There was a reflective pause. 'Once I was slim like Chloë, remember?'

'Almost like Chloë.'

'She's got her teeth into this archeology.'

'You haven't quarrelled?'

'No.' Bernadette sounded surprised. 'Perhaps we've given up quarrelling.'

'A truce, I expect.' Lucy was stuffing a vase inelegantly full of flowers and miscellaneous greenery.

'Mother . . . ' The tone was heavy and exasperated. 'Oh, nothing. That spotted stuff brings me up in a rash. Once I hid in the bush and came in with itchy legs. Mrs Treece said it was fleas.' She had been very young, she remembered, thirteen or so, and had been experimenting with wearing her hair up. Maurice had objected and she had sulked among the shrubs for hours. Then the frightening spots, itching, Mrs Treece going for calamine, Lucy cross because it seemed an avoidable crisis, unlike many. Bernadette sighed, seeing herself seated on the kitchen table, her legs streaked and blotched with oily pink. But her thoughts, as they were apt to do these days, suddenly leapt forward to the future. The child vanished. In her place was Sister Bernadette. She waited with interest to see what she was doing but the figure was busy only in an obscure way, moving back and forth.

'I hope you'll be happy,' said Lucy as if she saw her too and with a mother's pangs.

★

244

'What's that curious smell?'

'The marinade. Your surprise dinner. It's rabbit. I'll cook it tonight.'

There was sun, a late-summer heaviness. Lucy, calmed by the peace and warmth, sat with her feet up, awkwardly slicing tomatoes.

Turk piled a tray with glasses. 'Do you want me at Paleochora?'

'Of course. I thought you'd never ask.'

'I thought *you* wouldn't.' And Turk leaned forward, lifting her palms. 'Look. I gave myself blisters making the decision.'

Chloë lay in the hammock, her eyes closed. Caught frowning, her mouth pursed up, her hair loose, she looked remarkably like Bernadette. On the grass under the tree sat Laura and Ginny and at a distance, in the sun, Adam sprawled on his stomach, digging at the grass stems, pulling faces with boredom.

It isn't a harmonious arrangement, thought Lucy, coming over the grass with the drink. And there was Chris, mulish and disaffected, and Alan, charming, affable, scarcely adult . . . Motherhood is a bloody business, she decided.

What had Oliver said? 'Go off and make a proper life for yourself . . . Don't hang about here waiting for permission, or blessing . . .'

She smiled, remembering him, and thinking she smiled at them her family smiled back.

# READ MORE IN PENGUIN

In every corner of the world, on every subject under the sun, Penguin represents quality and variety – the very best in publishing today.

For complete information about books available from Penguin – including Puffins, Penguin Classics and Arkana – and how to order them, write to us at the appropriate address below. Please note that for copyright reasons the selection of books varies from country to country.

**In the United Kingdom**: Please write to *Dept. EP, Penguin Books Ltd, Bath Road, Harmondsworth, West Drayton, Middlesex UB7 0DA*

**In the United States**: Please write to *Consumer Sales, Penguin USA, P.O. Box 999, Dept. 17109, Bergenfield, New Jersey 07621-0120.* VISA and MasterCard holders call 1-800-253-6476 to order Penguin titles

**In Canada**: Please write to *Penguin Books Canada Ltd, 10 Alcorn Avenue, Suite 300, Toronto, Ontario M4V 3B2*

**In Australia**: Please write to *Penguin Books Australia Ltd, P.O. Box 257, Ringwood, Victoria 3134*

**In New Zealand**: Please write to *Penguin Books (NZ) Ltd, Private Bag 102902, North Shore Mail Centre, Auckland 10*

**In India**: Please write to *Penguin Books India Pvt Ltd, 706 Eros Apartments, 56 Nehru Place, New Delhi 110 019*

**In the Netherlands**: Please write to *Penguin Books Netherlands bv, Postbus 3507, NL-1001 AH Amsterdam*

**In Germany**: Please write to *Penguin Books Deutschland GmbH, Metzlerstrasse 26, 60594 Frankfurt am Main*

**In Spain**: Please write to *Penguin Books S. A., Bravo Murillo 19, 1° B, 28015 Madrid*

**In Italy**: Please write to *Penguin Italia s.r.l., Via Felice Casati 20, I–20124 Milano*

**In France**: Please write to *Penguin France S. A., 17 rue Lejeune, F–31000 Toulouse*

**In Japan**: Please write to *Penguin Books Japan, Ishikiribashi Building, 2–5–4, Suido, Bunkyo-ku, Tokyo 112*

**In South Africa**: Please write to *Longman Penguin Southern Africa (Pty) Ltd, Private Bag X08, Bertsham 2013*

# BY THE SAME AUTHOR

**Meeting Lily**

Major Baghot dying in Nan's best bed was not only inconvenient, but a watershed. After that, things turned themselves upside down in the Villa Giulia, a small hotel in Italy run for English guests. The major's widow is surprisingly merry, insists on taking long walks in the hot sun and refuses to go home to England; Doctor Fortuno appears to have fallen in love with a pretty guest; Graziella has almost certainly fallen in love with a local priest and Nan, widowed and struggling to keep the hotel on its feet, feels disappointed and unsettled.

But then there is Italy, the sun and – as Father Emilio points out – the prospect of marrying again.

'She captures beautifully the sights, smells and aura of dusty rural Italy in this subtle and contemplative novel, in which romance, bereavement and people's failure to talk to one another are explored with wit and originality' – *The Times*